A Byron Preiss Book

Bad
Behavior

EDITED BY

Mary Higgins Clark

WITH STORIES BY

Thomas Adcock

Paul Bishop

Samuel Blas

Lawrence Block

Christianna Brand

Ann Carol

Liza Cody

Stuart Dybek

Carol Ellis

Winifred Holtby

P. D. James

M. E. Kerr

M. D. Lake

John H. MaGowan

Joyce Carol Oates

Sara Paretsky

Mauricio-José Schwarz

Barbara Steiner

Hernando Téllez

Eric Weiner

Eric Wright

THE

INTERNATIONAL

ASSOCIATION OF

CRIME WRITERS

PRESENTS

Bad
Behavior

Gulliver Books

Harcourt Brace & Company

SAN DIEGO   NEW YORK   LONDON

Library of Congress Cataloging-in-Publication Data
The International Association of Crime Writers presents Bad behavior/
edited and with an introduction by Mary Higgins Clark.—1st ed.
p.   cm.
"Gulliver books."
Summary: Collection of twenty-two mystery stories both new and pre-
viously published by Thomas Adcock, Winifred Holtby, Joyce Carol
Oates, Sara Paretsky, Barbara Steiner, Eric Weiner, and others.
ISBN 0-15-200179-4—ISBN 0-15-200178-6 (pbk).
1. Short stories. 2. Horror tales. [1. Detective and mystery stories. 2.
Short stories. 3. Mystery and detective stories. 4. Horror stories.] I.
Clark, Mary Higgins. II. International Association of Crime Writers.
III. Title: Bad behavior.
PZ5.I58   1995
[Fic]—dc20   94-43344

The text was set in Weiss.
Designed by Jessica Shatan

Printed in the United States of America

First edition

A B   C   D   E
A B   C   D   E   (pbk.)

CONTENTS

INTRODUCTION

Mary Higgins Clark

WHEN I WAS LITTLE, THE MOST THRILLING WORDS IN THE LANGUAGE were "once upon a time." When I heard those words, I snuggled up and waited, eager to be transported to castles with magic gardens, or deep, dark caves where wicked giants dwelled.

As I grew up, I traded fairy tales for mystery stories and spent blissful, totally absorbed hours shivering over telltale hearts, foot-steps in the dark, and piercing screams resounding through empty houses. The more I read, the more discerning I became. Soon I realized that certain characters stayed with me long after I had finished reading their stories. I began to see that some suspense writers are quite simply in a class by themselves—their plots are unique, the scenes they conjure up are always vivid and alive. They made me sense the danger, urge the detective to work more quickly, beg the intended victim to take greater care. That is the essence of storytelling—to so vividly involve the reader (or lis-tener) in the story that he or she virtually is there, not as a spectator but as a participant in the ongoing adventure.

In my first writing class, I was given the most valuable advice that a young writer could receive. The professor said, "Take a situation that intrigues you and ask yourself two questions: *Suppose?* and *What if?* Then turn the situation into fiction."

I've been following that advice for more years than I care to count. But when I turned to suspense writing, I added another question: *Why?* I believe that no matter what the action in a suspense story, the *why* has to be satisfied. Four people may have strong reasons to commit a crime, but usually only one will go over the edge and actually do the deed. *Why* was his or her motivation stronger?

I've always believed that reading a suspense story can be compared to taking a ride on a roller coaster: Your heart begins to pound when you buy the ticket. You are terrified as the car starts to chug-chug up the first steep climb. Your breath quickens as you anticipate the first steep drop, the hairpin turns. Delicious fright. And then, when the brake trips, the car slows, and you arrive safely back at the starting point, didn't you always feel a sense of release?

When you read a good suspense story, I think you experience something similar: You begin with a sense of apprehension. You are involved from the get-go. You are the protagonist. You know more than the detective. You fear for the victim. You share the emotions of fright, discovery, panic. If it's a particularly good story, you start to hear noises in your own house—the staircase creaking, the wind outside, the furnace settling. And when the story concludes, you feel a catharsis of released emotion.

Sometimes a story builds slowly, not unlike a fire that begins in the basement and then stealthily spreads through the walls and ceilings of the house until that terrible moment when it bursts into a no-exit inferno. Some of the stories in this collection are like that—full of slowly building anger, the seeming ability to ignore, cover up, pretend, and then the eruption. A reader interested in such stories might begin with Lawrence Block's "Like a Bug on a Windshield."

Many stories included here explore the psyche, always fertile territory for the suspense writer. Samuel Blas's "Revenge," P. D. James's "The Girl Who Loved Graveyards," and Joyce Carol Oates's "The Premonition" deal with the strange workings of the mind under unbearable stress and with the tricks the mind plays after a trauma.

Family relationships are the stuff of which suspense is built and within these pages you'll find several superb stories of love turned to hatred, trust masking truth, and loneliness leading to murder. The characters and problems vary—from the young family looking for shelter in Christianna Brand's "Bless This House" to the runaway looking for freedom in Sara Paretsky's "The Maltese Cat"—but again and again family is at the heart of the matter.

Master storytellers and expert plotters, the writers in this volume understand the frailties of human nature. They are a credit to the world of suspense writing and I sincerely trust that suspense devotees will be pleased by this collection. I do hope that readers who are new to the world of mystery and suspense will find themselves transported, absorbed, and eager for more.

Happy Reading, one and all!

Thrown-Away Child

Thomas Adcock

THE LITTLE ROOM IN BACK WHERE PERRY STAYED WAS "NOTHIN' but a damn slum the way that no-'count keeps it," according to his aunt Vivian. She had a long list of complaints about her nephew, most of which were shared by most people who knew him. But she and Perry were still family and so she loved him, too, in a quiet and abiding way.

Vivian lived in the rest of the place, a wooden cottage of four narrow connected rooms built up on hurricane stilts with a high pitched roof, batten shutters over the windows, and French louvered doors on either end. The front steps were scrubbed every morning with a ritual mixture of steaming hot water and brick dust to keep evil spirits at bay. The back steps led from Perry's squalor to a tiny fenced garden of thick grass, a chinaberry tree, and a lilac bush. In appearance and infirmity, the cottage was nearly the same as the forty or so others crowded into a rut-filled dirt lane between lower Tchoupitoulas Street and a levee almost crumbled away from years of flood and neglect.

The neighborhood was one of many that tourists in the city were not encouraged to visit, a neighborhood where pain and fears from the hard past overlapped a generally despairing present—a haunted part of New Orleans, some claimed. Which was why, among other customs, the front steps were washed down with brick dust every day.

On most afternoons, the people in the lane would go to the levee for the coolness of the river breezes or to catch themselves a dinner of Mississippi catfish. There, ancient Creole men and widow ladies—their hair covered by *tignons*, the madras handker-chiefs favored by voodoo women with seven points carefully twisted heavenward—would talk until dusk of the old days and the old ways.

Long ago Vivian and her husband had been terribly proud of the cottage. It was truly theirs, no thanks to any of the banks or mortgage companies—bought and paid for with the saved-up wages of a yardman and a cleaning woman whose ancestors had once been shackled to posts in the public squares above Canal Street and sold as slaves. But on a sunny day in March of 1948 Vivian and Willis Duclat took title to a little wood cottage and became the first of their families to own their own home.

It was a long way up in a perilous, hostile world, and Willis and Vivian were pleased to be gracious about their ascent. Almost everyone else in the lane shared generously in their reflected joy. One who did not was a tall, sour-faced woman next door to the Duclats, a spinster known as Miss Toni. "Ain't goin' to be no comfort to you or the rest of us down here to be buyin' your own place when it's the last one that ain't owned yet by Theo Flower. Theo wants the whole lane bad and he means to get it, one way'r other."

Vivian said to pay no mind to Miss Toni. "She only says those poisonous things 'cause she's lonesome and miserable."

The pride of the Duclats was brief.

Toward the end of '48 the parish tax assessor came calling. He smiled quite a bit and seemed genuine. He shook hands with Willis, same as he'd shake a white man's hand. And he addressed Vivian properly as Mrs. Duclat. The assessor was there to explain how he had some important papers for signing, papers that would bring paving and curbing and a sewer hookup. The Duclats didn't understand quite all of the small print on the man's papers, but since he'd been so respectful Willis and Vivian trusted him and signed where it said "Freeholder." Then by Christmas of '49, when they'd fallen impossibly far behind on the special surcharges for modern conveniences levied against them by those important papers, the Duclats' home was seized by the sheriff and put up for sale in tax forfeiture court.

At the auction there was only one bidder—the Church of the Awakened Spirit, in the person of its pastor, the Most Reverend Doctor Theophilus Flower. At last, Theo Flower and his church owned every last cottage in the lane. Pastor Flower wasted no time. He called on the Duclats the very day he put down the cash money to retire the delinquent surcharges, plus the customary plain brown envelope full of money for his friend, the smiling tax assessor.

Pastor Flower drove straightaway from the courthouse to the Duclats' place in his big white Packard motorcar, one of the first postwar models off the Detroit assembly lines. When the neighbors saw the Packard roll in from Tchoupitoulas Street, they went to their homes and shut the doors until they knew Pastor Flower had gone away.

In the parlor of the newly dispossessed Duclats, Theo Flower was courtly and sympathetic. The pastor had no need for meanness when he bought somebody's home out from under them— the law made it all so easy and polite.

"Now, I know you can understand that our church has many missions," he said in his deep, creamy preacher's cadence, "and that among them is providing what we can in the way of housing for our poor and unfortunate brothers and sisters."

Willis sat in a cane-back chair in a sort of shock, still as a stone while Pastor Flower talked. He didn't appear to hear anything. He'd hidden from his wife for days before the court sale so that he could cry, and now his eyes looked like they might rust away with grief. Vivian sat next to him and held his big calloused hands. She looked at the floor, ashamed and resigned, and listened carefully to Theo Flower.

"I surely don't want to see fine people like you having no place to live. You see, though, how we must serve our members first? Now, I've been giving this predicament of yours a lot of my thought and some of my most powerful prayer and I do believe I have come upon a solution—"

When at last Pastor Flower was finished, he collected twenty dollars on account toward the first year's tithe to the Church of the Awakened Spirit. And the church's two newest members, Vivian and Willis Duclat, signed some important papers their new pastor happened to have with him, pressed inside the red leather Bible he always carried. They signed where it said "Tenant."

After scratching his name to Theo Flower's lease, Willis rose from his chair and crossed the room angrily, tearing himself away from Vivian's grip on his shirt. He stood towering over the preacher and his black eyes came alive again. Duclat's huge hands, made hard and heavy from his work with shovels and stone and earth, clenched into dark fists. His voice sounded as if it were a thousand years old.

"I ain't no educated man," he said to Flower, "and I ain't well-spoken like you. But I ain't simple, neither, and I can sure as hell figure you just done somethin' crooked here. I'm goin' to think on this, then I'm goin' to figure some way to bring you down for what you done to me and my wife, and prob'ly other poor folks besides."

The Most Reverend Doctor Theophilus Flower only smiled. When he did, Vivian saw a flash of gold at the back of his dark brown lips. Then Flower stood up, no match in physique to Willis. He folded the lease into his Bible and answered the big angry man with the clenched fists: "It won't do to talk like that, brother. I know you're a troubled man today and I'm sorry for you, truly. But you'd best not take an adversary's tone against a man who knows the mysteries like I do. You understand what I mean, don't you, Brother Willis?"

Willis understood only too well. Since he was a boy, he'd heard of Theo Flower's abilities, how he could call forth the dead from beyond, how he could "fix" an enemy, how his power came from the evil fangs of river snakes. Willis felt something cold on his neck, something like a wet wind.

Then the pastor drove off in his Packard. And later, in the silent night, Willis awoke from a nightmare with a violent fever and pains that shot through his chest and neck.

Willis never worked another day, nor did he sleep well. Then three months into the new year of 1950, on the very day that Perry was born to his younger sister, Willis Duclat dropped dead.

It happened despite his precautions. Convinced that mortal danger lay waiting in the alleyway in the form of water moccasins or copperheads that would sometimes slither up from the levee, Willis had begun a new daily protective routine. He would mix a batch of quicklime and cayenne pepper into the boiling water left over from scrubbing the front steps and pour the potion in two parallel lines along the inside of the fence that enclosed his garden. One of the old *voodooiennes* assured him he would be safe now, back as well as front.

Just before he died Willis was sitting on a step out back smoking a morning pipe of tobacco. Vivian was on her way to a mansion on St. Charles Avenue, where she had a job minding three children, cleaning some, and cooking for a doctor who ate far too much. Across the river, meanwhile, in the parish of Algiers, a midwife pulled an infant boy into the world from between the legs of his very young and frightened mother.

Willis's left leg dangled off the side of the pine steps and his bare foot swung back and forth, toes brushing through the dewy grass that he'd coaxed into growing from muddy soil. Then, suddenly, his body convulsed with a spasm so overwhelming it threw him to the ground, where he twisted around for a few seconds in mute torture before his heart stopped. Vivian found him when she returned home in the afternoon. He was sprawled on his back in the grass, his face covered with bits of blossoms, the white-and-purple petals that fell from the chinaberry tree.

She ran to a confectionery shop where there was a public telephone and rang up the doctor's house. Her employer drove over right away, breaking the speed limit even though Vivian told him that Willis was dead and already cold. The doctor examined the body there in the garden and after a minute or two pointed to a blue-black welt on Willis's left ankle. "He's full of venom more than likely," he said.

"No, sir," said Vivian. "Somebody's gone and hexed my man."

The lane was never paved, nor was it ever so much as named. And through the decades Theo Flower bought up hundreds more ragged neighborhoods in New Orleans, building up his church membership and the sort of respectability money from any source whatever buys in the entrenched power structure of a southern town.

Along about the middle 1970s the federal government mandated sewer hookups for even the lowliest neighborhoods in any city that expected revenue-sharing funds. So New Orleans obliged people like Vivian Duclat, finally. For his part, Theo Flower hiked her rent since the property would become more valuable with the addition of a modern convenience.

In July of 1983 Perry Duclat was paroled out of the Louisiana State Prison at Angola after serving half of a seven-year sentence for grand theft—auto. He'd been convicted of "borrowing" a Rolls Royce that belonged to the doctor where his aunt Vivian worked. In his defense, Perry told the judge, "I was helpin' out my aunt one day at the big house and the man was out of town for the weekend and there was that nice big car of his just sittin' in the garage goin' nowhere. So naturally I borrowed it. How else is a man like me ever goin' to have any style in his life? I put it back right where I found it and I never hurt it one little bit, no sir." Perry had borrowed many things in the past, many of them yet to be returned, so the judge threw the book at him and lectured him on how he'd probably never amount to anything with that sort of thieving attitude. The defendant only smiled.

And even so, even though the doctor told her she could never work at his house again, Vivian took Perry in when he was released from Angola with nowhere to go. She took him in because they were family, no matter what; because he was born on that terrible day her husband died; because in the years he'd been at Angola he'd taken on such a strong resemblance to Willis.

Every day but Sunday Vivian would get up early in the morning and go off to work someplace. Perry would get up right after that and attend to the chores, which included keeping his aunt's part of the cottage meticulously clean and scrubbing down the front steps because she believed most of the old myths even if he didn't. By ten o'clock or so, he would be back in his own room watching television.

In the three months he'd been there, Perry's room had become wall-to-wall beer cans, hundreds of them, under a film of cigarette ash. He would light cigarettes and leave them burning on the windowsill or at the edge of the dresser. Holes were burnt into the sheets of his bed, where he sat day after day watching television game shows, talk shows, soap operas, meaningless news, and witless comedies and endless commercials on a portable black-and-white set with a wire coat hanger for an antenna. He liked to crush the cans after draining them, then he'd toss them aside, anywhere. Mostly he drank Dixie beer in the white cans with red-and-yellow lettering, or Coors in the gold cans when he had a few dollars extra.

Some days he'd stroll down to the levee. But Miss Toni had whispered around that Perry was an escaped convict, so very few neighbors would have anything to do with him. The old-timers talked to him, though, especially the widows in their *tignons*, garrulous old magpies always happy to pass along the legends that meant everything to them and practically nothing to the dis-respectful younger generation.

Sometimes he would tend his late uncle's garden, where Miss Toni would spy on him from a window, ducking out of sight when he turned his face in the direction of her cottage. Or he'd sit on the back steps and read a book, which Miss Toni considered most highly suspicious. Perry had two big stacks of books in his room, one on the dresser and another that filled a corner, floor to ceiling. Sometimes, too, he would write or draw in a tablet. About once a week he would set off by foot all the way up to the library on Rampart Street.

But mostly Perry watched television, drank and smoked, and drowned himself in thought. By noon, his eyes were boozy slits and his fingers stank of nicotine. He would watch the flickering idiot box until it went dark in the wee hours of the next day. He ate very little, though he did enjoy whatever his aunt Vivian cared to cook or bake.

The two of them seldom talked. The chat was pleasant when Vivian spoke of Perry's late uncle, when she'd show him photo-graphs of Willis or bring out a box of Willis's personal effects or tell Perry again about the day he died, what the doctor said, and how she thought that was "nothin' but medical yap." But then it would lead inevitably to the subject of Theo Flower and their chat would quickly become an argument loud enough for Miss Toni next door to hear every word of it, even without her big ears at the window.

"That nigger Flower's nothin' but an old-timey conjure man, nothin' but a slick and cussed old fraud who's got lots of little old ladies like you and Miss Toni and all scared out of your bloomers 'cause he's supposed to 'know the mysteries,'" Perry would say, eyes rolling and his voice heavy with sarcasm. "Haw! Y'all must be crazy."

To which Vivian would reply, her jowls quivering and anger wagging up against her nephew's nose, "You best shut that sassy trap, boy! In the first damn place, we're beholden to Pastor Flower for this house we're in. And in the second damn place, well, let's just say you ain't lived near long enough to understand that precious little in this ol' world is actually what it seems to be."

She never quite told him so, but Vivian thrilled to her nephew's boisterous arrogance on the subject of Theo Flower. She supposed this might be a womanly fault of hers, enjoying the antagonisms of men at dispute where she was concerned, so she kept quiet. But when Perry would inveigh against Pastor Flower and his church, Vivian's eyes would mist over some, and through that prism of tears and remembrance she sometimes thought she was looking at her husband again. *God bless poor black men for what little arrogance they dared show the world*, she thought.

And Vivian didn't care a hoot whether Miss Toni heard them carrying on—which she did, and which she dutifully passed along nearly word for word to Pastor Flower himself, who maintained a pervasive interest in the personal lives of his home-indentured flock.

Perry's irreverence greatly disturbed Theo Flower. His unease was compounded by the unnerving physical resemblance he saw in Perry to the late Willis Duclat, who was about Perry's age when he died. Perry had taken to attending Sunday services of the Church of the Awakened Spirit and he sat right down center and never took his eyes off Pastor Flower, never registered any expression, just stood and sat down when requested. Never had a nickel for the collection plate. But there he sat anyway, unembarrassed, looking for all the world like Willis Duclat with his hot black eyes, taut olive-brown skin, high forehead, and straight hawklike nose. And those wide shoulders and thickly muscled arms, with big hammer hands folded in his lap.

"You better come do somethin' on that boy here," Miss Toni warned Pastor Flower on the telephone. "I tell you, I believe Perry's got some kind of trouble-makin' designs. I see him some days on those back steps, lookin' over to my place and starin' at

me and wonderin' lord only knows what! Now, you know how
we don't want no trouble here. We mean to keep in our houses,
Pastor Flower. Please do somethin' on him!"

"Yes, yes. You're quite right," he told Miss Toni. "We will have
to stop any trouble before it has a chance to begin."

Pastor Flower said yes to a drop of brandy in his coffee and asked
permission to light a cheroot in Vivian Duclat's parlor besides.
"Oh my, yes, go right ahead," she said. "My Willis was a smokin'
man, you know. La, yes, he had to have that pipe of his from
mornin' to midnight."

"Yes, I do recall that." Flower fired a sterling Tiffany lighter
and touched the yellow-blue hiss of flame to the blunt end of his
cigar. In the flash of light Vivian saw again the gold crowns
sparkle in the back of his mouth.

It was a Sunday twilight and a heavy blackness moved across
the sky, overtaking what was left of the day and the week. Perry's
television set droned from the back of the cottage.

"Sister Vivian, I come here to talk with you tonight on a delicate matter, one that causes me grave concern as to your welfare."

"What in the world can that be?" Vivian had enjoyed several
drops of brandy in several cups of coffee before the pastor's call
and her voice was thick.

"Well, Sister Vivian, you know how people will talk. Many of
your neighbors and friends are worried sick about your being all
alone in this house with a man fresh out of prison, a man who I
am told lives like some sort of wild animal in the back room of
this cottage and who does nothing besides drink all day long.
Now, I must worry about this for your sake—and for the sake of
the church's property, after all."

Vivian touched her lips to hide a smile, which she thought
Pastor Flower might well interpret as contemptuous. "I think I
know maybe just one neighbor who'd gab like that and maybe
she's over there listenin' now. Besides, if I had to worry 'bout ev'ry
man round this neighborhood who'd ever been locked up, well,

shoot, I'd be a mighty nervous old hag by now. So don't worry none 'bout my nephew Perry, 'cause *I'm* sure not worryin' and you can tell Miss Toni the same if you want."

"Well, I only mean that your husband, Willis, was a hardworking, sober man and this Perry is a layabout. That is what I'm told." Flower coughed, then opened his red leather Bible and spread it out on the parlor table. "You know very well from the scriptures how the devil works through wicked drinking men and other idle folks."

"Maybe I know that," Vivian said. "I do know for sure that the devil works through schemin' folks."

She poured herself another brandy and spotted it with coffee out of respect for the ministry. The ministry accepted one for himself.

"Let me set your mind at ease some, Pastor Flower. You should know a little of Perry's story, then maybe you'd understand him like I do. He's not a dangerous young man, no more than any other young man. He is sloppy, though. I'd be shamed to have you see where he stays.

"But look here, Perry's been bruised all through his life and them bruises come one right after the other. Ain't none of them healed up completelike, which is maybe why he lays round all the day long. Sometimes he shows some spunk, but if he's dog tired from life most of the time, then I figure he's got the right.

"His mother—that would be Willis's sister—was nothin' but an ignorant teenage girl livin' over in Algiers in a shack all alone near a coal yard. How d'you s'pose a girl like that made out in the world? Well, you can imagine right enough. Anyway, she gets herself in the family way and then come runnin' over here with the baby, not even knowin' her brother Willis had passed on. Not that she'd care 'bout that, mind you, not any more'n she cared for that baby she just plopped down on me.

"But I minded the child for a while and loved him. I named him, too, you know. Maybe I might have gone crazy without the baby round me to take my mind offa how Willis died like he did—" Her shoulders shook and she cried softly. Pastor Flower moved to comfort her with his hands, but she backed away from his touch.

"And you know all 'bout that," she said to Flower. "Anyway, Perry's mama went up to Chicago, so I heard. She wrote how fine she was doin' up north and how she wanted to send for Perry and all. But then the man who did her come by one day with a new wife and says he wants to take his baby and raise him up over to Algiers. That's what he did, took Perry away from me and wasn't nothin' I could do 'bout it.

"But Perry started comin' back here regular when he got older, just as soon as he could get by on the ferry on his own. An' I started noticin' how beat-up lookin' he was. I got it out of him what was goin' on over to his daddy's house. His daddy's lady would be all the time hittin' him, or burnin' him with cigarettes, or shamin' him in front of the other little boys by comin' after him with a belt and whuppin' his head till he'd fall over bloody, then whuppin' some more until he messed his pants.

"I tol' his daddy all this when he would come for him to take him back, and that man said his boy was possessed 'cause he wouldn't never do nothin' right or what was told him. Then he finally put little Perry in a home someplace out in the country.

"Next I heard, Perry'd busted out of that home, which was more like some prison than a home, which it never had any right to be called, and he headed north lookin' for his mama. He found her, too. He come back and tol' me how she was nothin' but a whore and a dope addict, how she looked like death itself and didn't even know Perry was her kin.

"Well, he was right. Later on we heard from some city health official up north how she was dead from heroin and askin' us did we know her birthday. They was so shocked to learn she was only thirty-six.

"Perry figured he'd better stay over with his father, else his daddy'd make trouble for me. But the man tossed him out soon's he showed up over there to Algiers.

"And so, you see, Perry's had trouble all the time in his life. What do you expect? He was nothin' but a thrown-away child. Least that's what he think of himself anytime he's away from here."

Pastor Flower folded his hands over his Bible. Vivian ran her fingers through her hair nervously. From the back of the house where Perry watched television came the added sound of a beer can popping open, an empty being crushed, then the clatter of it when it fell to the littered floor.

"I'm sorry for you, Sister Vivian, but I cannot stand by idly in this matter."

Her voice rising high, Vivian said, "What do you mean? Don't you be takin' my Perry away! Don't you be takin' another man from this place!"

"Quiet, woman!" Flower's voice thundered. There was stillness in the house. "What I shall do here is convene the spirits and consult the wisdom of the other side. I shall call out your own husband, Willis Duclat!"

Vivian shrieked, and her cup and saucer crashed to the floor.

"Yes," Flower said, "I shall call out the spirit of Willis Duclat. He—and only he—shall guide us on the matter of your nephew!"

Pastor Flower closed his Bible and the sound of it echoed in the parlor. He stood up and moved to the door, put on his hat. "I shall request that everybody in this lane come to service next Sunday. You come, too, Sister Vivian. I know you wouldn't want to miss hearing your husband's voice."

The tall dark woman at the side of the altar began chanting in a low, melodious voice. She started in a *Français Africain* dialect—

> *"Danse Calinda, boudoum, boudoum!*
> *Danse Calinda, boudoum, boudoum!"*

Pastor Flower, in a scarlet robe covered with *gris-gris*—dolls made of feathers and hair, skins of snakes, bits of bone—rose from a pit beneath the altar in a great plume of white-and-gray smoke. Beaming at the congregants in front of him, he turned and knelt at the altar as the woman's chanting grew in volume and tempo. He rapped the floor and then lit the black crucifix-shaped candles. He turned again to face his flock and he picked up the chant himself, raising his arms, commanding all to join in the calling out of spirits from beyond life.

Bodies swayed in the pews of the Church of the Awakened Spirit and the chanting rolled in waves, the single line of African French pulsating stronger and stronger through the sanctuary and out the open door into the liquid air of a savagely hot, humid Sabbath morning in New Orleans. Hands kept time and feet moved from muffled accentuation to a steady, rhythmic pounding.

Vivian Duclat, tears streaming down her face, for she had slept little during her week of anticipation, slapped her hands together determinedly and pounded her feet. She would hear her man, maybe she would even see her Willis—it didn't matter if the image were no more real than the times she thought she saw him in Perry's face. But what would Willis say of Perry? Would he send him away from her? Would Willis, too, throw the child away?

The tall dark woman stepped forward from the altar, moved her arms in an arc, and then switched to the Creole patois and to the uninhibited, throaty *canga*—

> "Eh! Eh! Bomba, hen! hen!
> Canga bafio, te,
> Canga moune de le,
> Canga do ki la,
> Canga li!"

All joined the chant, their massed voices now storming and frenzied, so full of pathos and longing that it became impossible for anyone to remain free of the swing and the narcotic influence of the ancient words. Everywhere, people were prepared to believe it all, for the first time in many cases. The eyes of the young were no longer disrespectful, they were full of proper fright—the old-timers clung righteously to *gris-gris* charms of their own they'd brought along to the ceremony, their little "conjure balls" of black wax and bits of their own skin or bleached lizards in glass jelly jars or dried-up rooster hearts—the curious things they kept under lock and key at home, out of embarrassment and fear. Pastor Flower then began the dance of the *voudou*, the leader.

He raised a bottle of brandy from the altar, dashed some of the liquid on each side of a brown bowl full of brick dust, then tossed back his head and took a long pull of the liquor. Then he started the slow hip shuffling, moved his feet backward and then forward, accelerating his movement up to the speed of the hypnotic *canga*. Without ceasing a single step of his dance, Flower poured the rest of the brandy into the bowl, then ignited it with his silver Tiffany lighter. The bowl flared up high over the altar and still he danced the maddening *canga*, his powerful voice starting to rise up over the waning strength of all the others:

"I call out Willis Duclat! *Eh! Eh! Bomba hen! hen!* I call out Willis Duclat! *Eh! Eh! Bomba hen! hen!* Willis Duclat, speak through me—"

And suddenly a tall young man covered in a brilliant red-and-black robe and hood ran crazily from somewhere in the back of the church, whirling and leaping and howling like a dervish until he reached the altar and a stunned Pastor Flower, who tripped and fell to his knees. The mysterious figure then vaulted over a railing and turned to the panicked congregation.

He tore the hood from his head, then the robe from his body, and stood before the assembly, his olive-brown body naked and oiled, his handsome face with the straight hawklike nose held high. Women screamed, but they did not avert their eyes, for the figure before them was a perfect masculine beauty. He raised his big fisted hands and cried out over the nearly hushed church.

"I *am* Willis Duclat! I *am* Willis Duclat!"

And from the pew next to Vivian Duclat, a trembling Miss Toni stood up and screamed, "Jesus, Mary, and Joseph, it's him! Oh la, it's him!"

The old ladies in *tignons* began fainting away and children squealed. Men stared, gape-mouthed, unable to help the women and the young. The tall muscular naked man grasped the shoulders of a terrified Theo Flower and lifted him several inches off the floor, then dropped him, crumpling to a twitching heap. He turned again to the congregation and roared, "I, Willis Duclat, have come out!" He then knelt to Pastor Flower and whispered to him, "Time for you to blow town, chump, 'cause your number's up here."

He stripped Flower's robe of his *gris-gris*, which he dropped into the bowl of flaming brandy with elaborate gesticulation, so that all in the church could see he meant to destroy Theo Flower's control over them. "Be gone, the impostor's fakery!" he shouted.

He asked for silence. Then he raised an arm and slowly directed it toward Miss Toni. "You," he said, "were in league with the impostor cowering at my feet. You placed the snake below the steps where you knew it would strike at me. You murdered me! It could have been no other way!"

Vivian sobbed.

"La, gawd-a-mercy!" Miss Toni screamed.

"Yes, yes, it was you! You and the impostor, this man called Theophilus Flower, who has oppressed you and cheated you all so cruelly for so many years since my death. It was you, Miss Toni, who killed me—to keep me from telling the truth that I do today!"

"La, mercy! Mercy! Oh la, please!" Miss Toni fell to the floor, gasping and writhing and consumed with her guilt, which took the form of what the hospital would later diagnose as massive cerebral hemorrhage.

The man then tore a lock of hair from his head and held it high over him so all could see. "Today I have destroyed the power of the impostor Theophilus Flower, who was foolish enough to call me out. I tell you all now, you must shun him! This hair I hold is the most powerful *gris-gris* of all, the hair of one from beyond. I shall give it to someone who lives amongst you. I shall plant it in his head this very night as he sleeps, and there it will grow. I shall give the power to a thrown-away child, now a grown man in my image, so that you shall always know him!"

Then he disappeared into the pit below the altar.

"Thank you for receiving me here, sir. I would have understood your refusing me."

"Well, son, I look at it this way: you done the crime and you done the time. Now that's just so much water under the bridge, don't you know. B'sides, you intrigue the hell out of me."

"Yes, sir. Thank you again." He brushed lint from the top of his sharply creased charcoal gray slacks, part of a Parisian suit he'd had made for him by a tailor at Gauchaux's on Canal Street.

The fat man offered him one of his cigars, which he declined in favor of a pipe that used to belong to his uncle. He lit the pipe and the fat man's cigar, too, with a sterling lighter that used to belong to Theo Flower.

"Tell me," the fat man said, "how's Vivian doin' for herself these days? We all loved her so much. Damn me for casting her out like I did, just 'cause of what you did."

"Nice of you to inquire, Doctor. My aunt's doin' just fine now. She had a little excitement at church a while back, but she rested lots afterward and I was able to take care of her, now that I'm runnin' the church myself and all."

"She's welcome to come back to me anytime, you know."

"Thanks again, Doctor. I'll send her callin', but, you know, she likes her retirement now and she's earned it, I'd say."

"Of course, of course." The doctor shook his fleshy head. "Damn me again! Perry, I'm sorta sorry now for havin' that judge crack down on you like he did."

"That don't matter much now. You might say you straightened me out by catchin' me. I had lots of time to think things through in prison. It was sorta strange, actually. All kinds of thought just sorta took over me, and I couldn't do much more'n think, day in and day out. Finally, I figured that I had to watch close for somethin' to come along that I could grab on to to make life good for me and my aunt for a change."

"Well, sounds to me like you did a fine piece of thinkin'. Just how'd you manage to take over the church, though? I mean, Theo Flower didn't strike me as a man ready to retire, like your old aunt. All of us fellows downtown were sorta surprised when he lit out for Baton Rouge like he did, without even a bye-you-well."

Perry smiled. "He had a change of spirit, you might say. Decided on greener pastures maybe. Anyway, I was around and interested in the church, you know. Spent lots of time readin' up on it and all and figuring how I might make my contribution. So, the moment come along when I figured I might grab on, so I done that."

He smiled again. "Of course, I had to first prove to Pastor Flower that I understood all the mysteries of his divine work. He musta been satisfied, because he signed everything over to me."

Perry emptied the contents of a satchel onto a table between him and the doctor.

"It's all legal, I didn't have to steal anything—or 'borrow,' I should say." The doctor laughed and Perry went on. "See here, it's all the deeds and titles and bank accounts—everything. That's why I come to you, sir, for some guidance in handling this all."

"You can count on me, Perry."

"I'm so glad."

"Where do you want to start?"

"Well, first thing," Perry said, "I want all the cottages down there in that lane off Tchoupitoulas deeded over to the tenants, maybe for a dollar apiece, some token like that that'd be sure to make it legal, and then—"

The Framing Game

PAUL BISHOP

"**G**O ON, TOMMY. TAKE 'EM!"

"No way, man. We're gonna get caught."

"How? Nobody's looking. Just put 'em on and take 'em."

"If it's that easy, you do it."

"Hey, I'm ready," Spider said, pointing at the new pair of Air Jordans that he had just taken off the store shelf and put on his feet. "But you need the new vrooooms more than me. Look at those things you're wearing."

Tommy Norman looked down at his worn-out canvas high-tops.

Spider nudged him with his elbow. "The only way you're gonna score any hoops against Mansfield in those things is because everyone'll be laughing so hard."

"I don't know." Tommy shook his head. "It ain't right."

"Man, don't be such a wuss," Spider said. "You think the store's gonna miss a couple of pairs of shoes? Just put 'em on your feet and run."

Tommy examined the flashy pair of high-top Air Jordans in his hands. It was as if they had "high-scorer" written all over them. A tiny orange basketball on the side of each shoe acted as a pump to tighten the leather around the foot. Tommy figured that feature alone was worth an extra ten points a game.

The shoes would be like magic. They would make him fly down the court, slash through defenses, and slam-dunk with ease. He was already the top scorer in the toughest high-school league in the Los Angeles area, but these babies would make him an even bigger star. College scouts from all over were going to be in the stands for Friday's league championship game, and Tommy wanted to be sure he made an impression. The game was going to be a monster bash. Tommy and his Franklin High teammates against their crosstown rival, Mansfield. The game was so big that it was going to be played in the Great Western Forum, the home court of the Los Angeles Lakers.

The game was still two days away, but the two boys were already feeling the jitters.

Tommy fingered the price tag. One hundred and twenty-eight bucks. No way did he have that kind of money, and his mom certainly wasn't going to cough up that many dead presidents just so he could score more points on the basketball court. She had too many other things to worry about—like paying the rent.

Spider Thompson was grinning at him, wriggling in anticipation. "You gonna be one awesome dude with them wings on your feet. Even Dolbert won't be able to slow you down."

Tommy's heart jumped. Eddie Dolbert was Mansfield's starting center and had been all-conference for the past three years. He was big, tough, and aggressive and controlled the key like King Kong.

You really think these will help me against Dolbert?"

"Man, I know so. You gonna be like a hot wind. And all you gotta do to own 'em is put 'em on, blast past the cash registers, and keep running."

Tommy looked around again. Anything you could possibly want for any sport was somewhere on the Sports Depot's shelves. The shoe section stocked every brand and style imaginable. Under each style were boxes in different sizes on help-yourself racks. You tried the shoes on and, if they fit, took them up to a register to pay for them—unless you were planning to steal them.

A Sports Depot employee suddenly appeared out of nowhere. "You guys need help?" he asked.

Tommy's heart jumped. "N–n–n–no thanks," he stammered.

The employee took a hard look at both boys before moving away.

"Oh, man," whined Tommy. "That guy figures we're up to something."

"Be cool," Spider said, urgently. "He don't know squat."

"Man, his eyes were all over us," Tommy said, watching the corner where the employee had disappeared. "It was like he knew us or something."

"That's 'cause everybody knows us," Spider said. "We be stylin' on the basketball court and everybody knows we gonna blow the Mansfield team off the court."

"No, man. I know that guy from somewhere, and he spells trouble."

"You're crazy, dude. The only thing that guy can spell is words of three letters or less. If he's such big-time trouble, how come he's working in a square joint like this?"

"I don't know, but I still have a feeling he's bad news."

"Man, you are such a chicken. Are you gonna pick yourself up a new pair of scoots or not? Make up your mind 'cause I'm outta here."

"Wait!" Tommy said, but it was too late. Spider was off and running toward the registers.

With the Air Jordans still in his hands, Tommy followed his teammate out of the shoe section.

The next morning on the school bus, Tommy did not sit with Spider like normal. Spider was at the front of the bus being cool and showing off his new shoes. Tommy sat in the back.

As the bus turned the corner, Tommy could see a huge crowd of kids gathered in front of Franklin High's main entrance. They were upset and it was easy to see why.

During the night somebody had used green and white spray paint on the front doors, walls, and windows. Green and white— the colors of Mansfield High. In several spots Tommy even saw the letters MJAM, the signature of a tagging crew known as the Mansfield Jammers, in green spray paint.

When Tommy stepped off the bus, Coach Jackson and Mr. Smithson, Franklin High School's dean of discipline, were waiting on the sidewalk. Coach Jackson was holding on to the arm of a scared-looking Spider and called Tommy over as soon as he spotted him.

"What's going on?" Tommy asked as he reached Spider's side.

Coach Jackson sighed. "Tommy, I'm very disappointed in you."

"What are you talking about, Coach? Everybody on the team has been real low-key about the rivalry—just like you asked us— This isn't our fault."

"I'm not talking about the graffiti," Coach Jackson said. "I want you in Smithson's office, right now."

As the two boys were escorted through the school's entrance in front of almost the entire student body, Tommy's mind was in a whirl. He hadn't done anything wrong. He couldn't believe he was in trouble.

Once in his office, Mr. Smithson took his place behind his large metal desk. Tommy and Spider sat facing him. Coach Jackson leaned against the closed door of the office as if he expected the boys to make a sudden break for freedom.

Mr. Smithson leaned forward. "Those are pretty fancy shoes you're wearing, Spider. Where did you get them?"

Tommy felt the blood drain out of his face. How could Mr. Smithson know about the shoes Spider snatched?

"I bought them," Spider said. His voice cracked with the lie.

"No, you stole them," Mr. Smithson said calmly, "from the Sports Depot."

Spider looked at Tommy angrily.

"Hey, I didn't say anything," Tommy said defensively.

"No, you certainly didn't," Mr. Smithson said. "Because then you would have to explain these—" From under his desk, he brought out the Air Jordans Tommy had been holding in the Sports Depot.

Tommy looked confused. "Where did those come from?"

"Don't play stupid, Tommy," Coach Jackson said. "We found them in your gym locker."

"But—" Tommy started to defend himself. Mr. Smithson cut him off with a raised hand.

"Don't dig yourself in deeper by lying. The evidence is clear." Mr. Smithson swiveled around in his chair and turned on a television set and a VCR that sat on the shelf behind the desk. He pressed the play button on the VCR's remote control.

A grainy, black-and-white tape began to play on the television screen.

"This is the security tape that was made at the Sports Depot yesterday. Every ten seconds it changes to a camera in a different part of the store."

Tommy and Spider watched the tape in silence. After a few seconds they could see themselves standing in the shoe section of the store. Spider was putting a pair of shoes on his feet and Tommy was holding a pair in his hands. The tape moved off to show ten-second snippets of the camping section, the cash registers, and other parts of the store. After about a minute, it again showed Tommy and Spider in the shoe section. Tommy still had the shoes in his hands, and Spider was waving his arms around talking to him.

The next time the tape showed the shoe section, the Sports Depot employee who had surprised them was standing with the two boys. The tape moved away to the camping section. When the tape moved on to the cash registers, it showed Spider running out the front door. Just before the tape moved on again, it showed Tommy's head and shoulders as he followed Spider.

27

"This tape and the shoes on Spider's feet," Mr. Smithson said, "leave me with little doubt that the shoes found in Tommy's locker are stolen property." He pointed at the pair of beautiful new Air Jordans that sat on his desk like prisoners before a judge.

"But—" Tommy tried again.

"I don't want to hear it," Mr. Smithson said, interrupting.

"Tommy didn't steal—" Spider started, but he too was cut off.

"Spider, unless you can show me a receipt for those shoes, I don't want to hear any more out of you. Take them off now and put them on my desk."

Spider hesitated only for a moment.

"I think both of you boys should consider yourselves lucky. Sports Depot has said that they will not press charges with the police as long as the shoes are returned. But I don't believe we can let things go without some form of punishment."

Tommy and Spider looked at each other.

"As of this moment," Mr. Smithson continued, "you are both suspended from the basketball team."

"Hey! Wait a minute," Tommy stood up as if someone had lit a fire under his seat. "That's not fair. I didn't steal those shoes."

"Are you denying you were in the Sports Depot?"

"No, but—"

"Are you denying these are the shoes you had in your hands on the tape?"

"No, but—"

"Are you calling Coach Jackson and myself liars when we say we found these shoes in your gym locker?"

"No, but—"

"Then I don't think there's anything further to talk about."

"Coach?" Tommy pleaded. He was on the verge of tears. This could ruin everything—the league championship, his scholarship chances—everything.

"I'm sorry, Tommy. There's nothing I can do. You made your choices. Now you have to live with them." Coach Jackson's eyes were as cold as two dead fish. "And so do the rest of us. You not only let yourself down, you let the team down."

"But I didn't, Coach. I didn't steal those shoes."

"Then how did they get in your gym locker?"

"I don't know." Tommy couldn't think, and he couldn't trust himself to say anything more.

"It's not fair," Spider said. He and Tommy were sitting alone at a lunch table.

"Shut up," said Tommy. He couldn't remember anything that had happened in class all morning. All he could think about was being suspended from the basketball team for something he didn't do.

"Man, I couldn't believe Coach Jackson. And that jerk Smithson wouldn't listen to nothing."

"Just shut up," Tommy repeated. "Would you have listened to us? Anyway, you stole the shoes, so you don't have anything to cry about."

"It's not like you weren't thinking about it."

"Right. But the fact is, I didn't steal 'em. So, somebody else put 'em in my locker."

"What are you gonna do about it?"

"I'm gonna find out who did."

Tommy looked around the lunch area. Even here, the vandals had managed to spray paint the walls, and Tommy noticed the MJAM tag signed across one of the lunch tables. He looked away, and then back again.

"Wait a minute," he said to Spider. "The Jammers."

"Yeah? So what?" asked Spider.

"The Jammers, man. The Jammers," Tommy said, sounding excited.

Spider looked confused. "Like I said, so what? Everybody knows they're the only ones who would do something like this. I bet the cops are all over them already."

"Yeah, but you can bet they're clean by now—dumped all the paint cans. And the crew ain't gonna split on each other. They'll walk like they always do."

Spider shrugged. "So what are you getting so excited about?"

"Think, man. Who runs the Jammers?"

"Jammer Dolbert," Spider said without hesitation, "Eddie Dolbert's older brother."

"Now think about yesterday at the Sports Depot. . . ."

Spider looked confused again.

"The guy," Tommy insisted.

"What guy?"

"The guy who almost caught us stealing the shoes."

"Too cool," Spider said as he suddenly understood. "That was Jammer Dolbert!"

"Yeah, yeah!" said Tommy. "I almost didn't recognize him with his hair mowed down and wearing straight clothes, but that was him."

Jammer was a year older than his basketball-playing brother, and as different from him as night is from day. Eddie Dolbert was a tough guy on the basketball court, but he had worked hard to hone his skills and deserved his reputation. Jammer was a different story. Tommy was surprised that Jammer was even working a legitimate job.

"You think he was planning all this when we saw him?" Spider asked, waving a hand at the vandalism.

"Not just this," Tommy said, "but maybe something else as well."

Later that afternoon, Tommy knocked on the door to Coach Jackson's office.

"Come in."

Tommy opened the door and stuck his head around. "I'm sorry to bother you, Coach," he said, gathering up his courage, "but could I please ask you a question?"

Coach Jackson looked at his star center. "What is it?" The coach's voice was flat and calm.

"I wanted to know how you got into my locker today."

Coach Jackson gave Tommy a hard look before answering. "We cut the lock off."

"Do you still have it?"

Coach Jackson pointed to a lump of metal on his desk. The shackle had been cut through on one side.

Tommy took a key out of his pocket. He picked up the lock and examined it. "This isn't my lock, Coach. Mine was a Master Lock." Tommy held up his key. "This one is a Wesloc." He inserted the key into the lock, but it didn't turn.

Coach Jackson raised his eyebrows. "You could have simply brought in a different key."

"I could have, but I didn't," Tommy said defiantly. "I'm telling you I didn't steal those shoes. I thought about it, but I didn't steal 'em."

Coach Jackson shrugged. "You're going to have to do better than that if you expect to convince Mr. Smithson."

"Oh, I'll do better," Tommy said. "But can you please tell me why you checked my locker for the shoes?" Tommy was trying hard to talk polite like his mother had taught him. He needed to get Coach Jackson on his side.

The coach hesitated, then answered. "The security tape was brought to the school this morning by one of the Sports Depot employees. He told us the manager of the store asked that we look at the tape and then check your locker to see if you had hidden the shoes there."

"Did he ask you to check Spider's locker?"

"No," Coach Jackson said thoughtfully. "When we viewed the tape, of course, we recognized Spider. After finding the shoes in your locker, we didn't have time before the buses arrived to check any further. We waited for you and Spider and it was obvious that Spider was wearing the stolen shoes when he came off the bus."

Tommy nodded. "Well," he said, still trying to talk polite, "I called the Sports Depot manager and asked him what they do about guys they catch ripping them off. He said the store always calls the cops."

Coach Jackson continued to look unimpressed, but Tommy was sure his argument was working.

"Spider stole the pair of shoes he was wearing when he ran out of the store," Tommy said. "But that tape just shows my back. You don't get a look at my feet. I was wearing my regular high-tops, not those Air Jordans you found in my locker. I tossed 'em before I left the store. I didn't want to steal 'em. I knew it was wrong."

Coach Jackson shook his head. "Well, if you didn't steal them, then who did? And how did they get in your locker?"

"I think I know. All I have to do now is prove it."

Despite Spider's taunting words when they had been in the Sports Depot, Tommy didn't think of himself as a chicken. Still, as he waited in the parking lot of Mansfield High for school to let out, his stomach hurt with tension. He was in enemy territory, and he knew if he didn't play things right he could end up getting thumped on.

The school bell rang and students started to empty out of buildings. Several people spotted Tommy in his Franklin High letterman's jacket as he leaned against the bumper of Eddie Dolbert's Toyota truck, but they left him alone. Still, Tommy felt their eyes on him. Maybe he shouldn't have come. Maybe this whole thing was a real bad idea. He felt himself start to sweat.

He was about to change his mind about sticking around when Eddie Dolbert and two of his buddies saw him by the truck and walked deliberately toward him.

"Are you crazy, coming here?" Dolbert asked Tommy when he was close enough. "Get off of my truck."

Tommy straightened up. He hoped Eddie and his buddies couldn't see his knees shaking inside his jeans.

"We heard you got yourself bounced off the team," Eddie said.

"Bad news travels fast," Tommy replied.

"Good news for us," said one of Dolbert's buddies.

"We don't like thieves at Mansfield," Eddie said.

"I'm not a thief."

"Oh, yeah. So how come you got bounced?" Eddie asked.

"Because your brother, Jammer, set me up," Tommy said, "at the same time he and his crew vandalized Franklin last night."

Eddie's buddies started to move threateningly toward Tommy. *Here it comes,* Tommy thought.

"Wait a minute," Eddie said. Everyone stopped, and Tommy started to breathe again. "What makes you think my brother is behind this?"

"Come on," Tommy said. "If you didn't know he was behind half the petty trouble around here you wouldn't be asking me that question."

When Eddie didn't say anything, Tommy continued. "Jammer works at Sports Depot, right?"

Eddie nodded.

"He saw me with Spider when Spider took the shoes. He also probably saw me dump the pair I was carrying. He knew I didn't steal 'em, but when he looked at the security videotape, it showed me running out after Spider, but the tape changed to another part of the store before my feet came into the picture. Jammer saw that as a chance to frame me and get me out of Friday's game."

Eddie still didn't look totally convinced. "How do you figure he framed you?"

"He must have snuck that pair of shoes out of the store when he got off work. Then, when he and his crew hit the school last night, I figure he broke into the locker room, cut the lock off of my locker, put the shoes inside, and put his own lock back on. Then he sent the security tape to Mr. Smithson this morning and asked him to check my locker for the shoes as if he was representing the Sports Depot."

"How did he know which locker was yours?"

"Our names are on them, just like yours are here."

Eddie nodded.

Tommy stood looking at Dolbert. "So," he said eventually, "do you want to play this game tomorrow on even terms and let the best team win? Or do you want your brother to have handed you the game on a platter?"

"I ain't afraid of taking you on," Dolbert said.

It was Friday night and the Forum was packed. Tommy was tying the frayed laces on his canvas high-tops and trying to stay calm. He had only gotten word that he would be allowed to play at the end of seventh period, when school let out.

As he stood up, Tommy spotted Spider leaning against his locker. Spider wasn't supposed to be in the locker room, but he had snuck in to talk to Tommy.

"Man, I wish I was going out there with you," Spider said.

"Me too," Tommy told him. "But—"

"I know, I know," Spider interrupted. "I screwed up. But at least the cops nailed Jammer for framing you. How did they know?"

"They found green and white spray-paint cans when they searched his car and then took it from there."

"I can't believe Jammer was stupid enough to keep the paint cans he used," Spider said.

"He wasn't," Tommy told him with a sly smile.

"What do you mean?"

"Well, two can play at the framing game. Eddie Dolbert didn't want to walk off with this game and have everyone say Mansfield was just lucky because you and I weren't playing. So, he gave me the spare key to his brother's car. I put the cans in the car while Jammer was at work. Then I called the cops and tipped 'em off."

"Oh, man," said Spider. "That was really sly."

"After they got the spray cans and started questioning Jammer, he rolled over and told them the whole story. Of course it helped that Eddie talked to his brother and made him come clean about the shoes."

"And Smithson bought off on it?"

"He didn't have much choice," Tommy said. "He talked to the Sports Depot's manager and confirmed they didn't send the tape over here. It was Jammer himself who brought the tape over and gave it to Mr. Smithson. The Sports Depot manager also said that Jammer had been suspected of stealing from the store for a while now, but just hadn't been caught."

"Now that's what I call fighting fire with fire," Spider said.

Coach Jackson gave the team the word to head out to the court for warm-ups. He slapped Tommy on the shoulders as he moved by.

"You're going to smoke 'em tonight, kid," he said.

A moment later Tommy stepped onto the court and looked over at Dolbert. The tall, heavily muscled Mansfield center ignored him.

Yeah, he was going to smoke 'em tonight, all right. And he wasn't going to need a pair of fancy basketball shoes to do it.

Revenge

SAMUEL BLAS

TWILIGHT IS SETTLING IN THE VALLEY. FAR BELOW US PALE LIGHTS ARE *beginning to flicker and the spreading pattern of the city slowly comes alive. As the winding road narrows to the mountaintop the motor sound grows louder in the thin air, within the enclosing silence through which we move.*

In the pale blue haze on my left the deepening dusk mingles with the vast silence that seems to suspend the day. A square yellow sign ahead blazes in our headlights: DANGER! SHARP CURVE AHEAD. The mountain wall leans closer to the road. On Elsa's side the low branches of a solitary tree rush by, scraping the top of the car.

Elsa, too, is part of the surrounding silence. Beside me she stares straight ahead at the highway. For a long time now she has not spoken; she neither smiles nor is sorrowful. Her expression is grave, almost serene, as if there were no such things as tears or laughter.

But this morning she smiled. A half day's journey away, in the cool morning of a quiet glade, she stepped from our trailer door and smiled softly as she waved me off to town. She blushed when I turned back a step to kiss her again. And when I finally drove off, the sweet touch of her hand still tingled in my palm.

Life was wonderful. I drove happily to the small town nearby to buy provisions. We had decided to stay a few days more in this pleasant spot we had found. There could be no better place to finish out our honeymoon. As I neared the town I thought it would be fun to add a gift for Elsa to the stuff that I would carry back to the camp.

It was nearing lunchtime when I started back. I had piled groceries enough in the car to last us a week. While I waited for a traffic light to change, a newsboy came by. I bought a paper. It carried a headline reporting the capture of an escaped convict nearby. The subhead said that his companion was still at large: "Presumed Hiding in Woods near Campbelltown."

I ran quickly through the rest of the item. When the light turned I moved out fast and put on speed. Campbelltown was a place that lay beyond our camp, but too near to suit me, under the circumstances. I felt uneasy, with Elsa alone in the trailer. It was possible, of course, that the fugitive convict might be in our vicinity, but what disturbed me more was the thought that Elsa might have picked up the news on our radio. If she had, she would be frightened. I stepped on the accelerator.

The road twisted and turned around thinly wooded ridges and hills, and as I swung each curve I chided myself for leaving Elsa alone. I reminded myself that she had insisted I shop without her. "I have a surprise for dinner," she had said with the only artfulness she knew—a shy, secret smile. My attention returned to the road.

The winding turns ended and the last stretch was a long, straight drive sheltered by a canopy of tall trees that somehow eased my anxiety. Not much farther now. I imagined the way she would welcome me. She would staunchly deny that she had been afraid, but she would hold my arm tightly. And then all of a sudden she would forget the whole thing. She would smile happily and tell me to close my eyes. How I loved that smile!

In the short while that I had known her and in the single month of our marriage I had grown to cherish that smile and the soft, rich laughter that sometimes accompanied it. So strange, that warm directness with which she shared my life, for in the presence of other men there was only shyness. I think that she was afraid of men. Something in her slender glowing warmth made their blood stir. She knew that, faintly, innocently. When the bold ones stared at her she would ask me to hold her close and never tell me why.

The sun was near high noon when the road broke out of the trees into the clearing. I rolled onto the grass and parked, feeling relieved because I had come so quickly. I pulled up the hand brake and looked to the trailer, expecting to see Elsa's welcoming figure there. My complacency ended. There in the clear fall sunlight I saw wisps of smoke about our home, thin plumes slipping from the unlatched door.

Wild red leaves fluttered across the grass. I listened stupidly to the wavering silence. Then I ran to the door and flung it open violently.

An acrid fog swirled about me, making me choke and cough. A curling mist clung to the ceiling. I swung the door wider and flailed my arms to clear the air. And as the fog lifted and shifted I saw with some relief that there was no fire. Our dinner was smoking and burning on the stove. Three chops—I can see them yet—shriveled and black in a blackened frying pan; string beans in a burning pot, brown where the water had been; and in the oven, where I later found it, a crumbling burnt blob that must once have been Elsa's first cake—the surprise she had promised me.

Panic got hold of me.

"Elsa!" I called.

There was no reply.

"Elsa!" I repeated. "Elsa!"

But only the crackle of the burning pot answered me, and outside a thin echo wandered in the woods. I shut off the burners. The crackling persisted as if in defiance, then it ceased. I turned uneasily toward the door that led to our dining alcove in the rear, stopping short at the sight of the waiting table with its knives and forks and plates in neat array. But no Elsa. But of course. She wouldn't, she couldn't have been there or the dinner would not have burned.

Trying to understand what had happened, I rejected a dozen answers at once. She would never have left the dinner to burn for any sort of errand. Nor were there neighbors about with whom to fall into forgetful conversation. We were alone. Then as I stood there in the silence I suddenly heard the faint sound, a rising and falling as of someone weakly breathing. Behind the curtain that secluded our bed—Elsa!

I faced about and tore aside the curtain.

There she lay. Pale, still. I knelt beside her. She was barely breathing.

"Elsa," I whispered.

She seemed neither to move nor to make any sound, yet I knew she was breathing, for I had heard her. I rubbed her wrists and temples. I shook her gently, then fearfully. She stirred a little.

I wanted to get a doctor, yet I was afraid to leave. Then I remembered the brandy. I fumbled in the cupboard and my hand trembled as I poured a glassful and spooned a little between her lips.

At last it took effect. Her lips moved. Her expression altered, she sputtered, she coughed, and her eyes opened weakly.

At first they were blank. A long second passed while I held her hands tightly. Then, as if awareness had just touched her, horror filled her eyes and she moaned.

As I gathered her into my arms and let the sheet that covered her fall away, I saw that she was naked—completely.

There were bruises on her body, as if someone had beaten her: cruel bruises on her shoulders where callous fingers had pressed; angry marks where heavy fists had struck her.

Those moments beside my wife are not easily recalled, filled as they are with shame and a fierce anger. When at last she stirred again in my arms, I held her tight and looked beyond her so that she would not see the anguish in my eyes. For long minutes she shivered; then she sobbed pitifully. Finally the tears and trembling stopped.

In a flat voice that frightened me she said, *"He killed me . . . he killed me."*

How I gathered the tangled threads of those dreadful hours I cannot entirely remember. For a long time I cradled and comforted her, as though she were a child. After a while she seemed to respond. But then, when she shuddered again, my indignation mounted; I lost control and stormed at her with furious questions: "Who?" I demanded. "Who?" and "When?" and "How?" Until haltingly the brutal story came out. How a salesman knocked—

"A salesman?"

"Yes."

"Are you sure? Did he carry a suitcase, a display?"

"Yes."

A salesman. Then it was not the convict. Nothing reasonable. It was an ordinary man, ordinary.

How he knocked, interrupting her cooking; how he smiled patly and edged inside, eyeing her boldly while he chattered about kitchenware. How he touched her arm and seized her and how, when she resisted, he beat her and—and how she finally fainted away.

As she talked she seemed to fall under a spell of horror that produced in her a curious calm. She repeated, "He killed me, he killed me . . ." until I had to make her stop. Her eyes, I saw, stared straight ahead as she said over those dreadful words and it seemed as though she saw that man, that menacing figure, in the hopeless distance.

I never thought once of the police. Only one impulse was in me, a dreadful agonizing craving for revenge. "I'll find him!" I swore. "I'll kill him."

Her hand clutched mine as if to restrain me, but when she felt the anger in my grip her mood abruptly changed and she said quietly, "Yes . . . yes." And when I hesitantly asked whether she would come with me, help me find him, she nodded, almost eagerly, I thought.

We drove to the outskirts of the town, where she listened carefully to my instructions, nodding with a sort of unearthly calm.

"We'll drive slowly," I told her. And this we did for perhaps half an hour, examining every passerby as we moved back and forth through the unhurried streets. The sun still hung heavy above us as we turned a third time down the town's main artery.

In the wide street were a few parked cars, and a thin afternoon crowd was lazily inspecting the shop windows. A man lounging near the hotel disinterestedly picked his teeth. It seemed to me he observed our slow progress curiously. I directed my wife's attention to him but she gravely shook her head. Then suddenly she gripped my arm. Her lips fell open and her face paled. She pointed at a shabby car parked near the hotel. A man was locking the car door.

"*That's him!*" she whispered.

My blood quickened.

"Are you sure?" I asked finally. Her eyes followed him as he put the keys in his pocket and turned toward the hotel.

"*That's him,*" she insisted, "*that's him . . .*"

I pulled to the curb in front of his car and stepped out quickly. "Wait here," I said. "Don't move—" I looked about me with assumed carelessness. The lounger, I saw, was facing the other way. No one else seemed to notice me. I sauntered into the lobby, a few steps behind my man. I decided to wait for him near the elevator, and sure enough he was soon standing beside me, absently fingering his room key.

Luck was with me, for as the car went up I glimpsed his room number on the key in his hand. I had planned to get out with him and openly follow him to his room. Instead I rode to the floor above his, made my way to the stairwell, down one level, through the hallways to his room, and knocked softly, an unexpected and unknown visitor.

I was calm then as he answered my knock. I spoke to him

through the door and represented myself as a buyer for a local store. He opened the door wide.

"Why, come in," he said; he wore a welcoming grin that infuriated me.

I went in, took the hammer from the waistband of my trousers and, as he turned to walk ahead of me, I smashed him mightily on the back of his head.

A great cry escaped him; then a dismal sigh that collapsed with him to the floor. He lay still.

I stared at the crumpled figure and my fury subsided, spent by that single avenging blow. A clock ticked into my consciousness. My eyes wandered absently to the simple dresser, the bed, the silent telephone. In my hand the hammer was edged with blood. I tucked it back in my trousers and dropped the skirt of my coat over it. With my handkerchief I turned the knob of the door. Curiosity prompted me to glance again at the still figure on the floor, but I no longer cared. It might be hours before anything happened. I might be suspected or I might not. None of these conjectures bothered me. I was reasonably safe from suspicion, that I knew, except perhaps from this—this ordinary individual. I turned and went out quickly, closing the door behind me. And with that closed door behind me, in that quiet carpeted hallway, I at last felt clean, free of obsessing shame.

I went back upstairs, rang for the elevator, and rode down quietly. The very sleepiness of this town made my ambling exit from the hotel unnoticeable.

Elsa was still in the car, gazing straight ahead, just as I had left her.

"It's done," I said.

Her head barely turned in my direction, and she nodded slowly. She said one word: "Good."

Poor Elsa. So altered with shame and shock that she had grown a shell I could not pierce. She sat silently in the car while, back at our camp, I hooked up the trailer and made ready for the journey. Even the lunch I fixed for her she barely touched, nibbling once or twice, then staring into space. Perhaps when we were away from this terrible place . . .

It was evening when we stopped again. I drove furiously past a dozen small villages, hurrying toward the city that lies, now, below and behind us at the foot of the mountain. I hoped to find in its busy streets some distraction from our lonely secret, to lose some of this horror there, perhaps in some lively bar or in a theater, perhaps in a good night's rest. Then the strain of the dreadful day took charge. A good night's sleep was all I craved. But not in the trailer, not yet.

Elsa agreed indifferently. We rolled ahead and merged with the traffic in the city. We would park the trailer and stop at the best hotel. We would have a hot bath, then dinner in our room, and perhaps a bottle of wine. And a good sleep, a good sleep . . . "Would you like that?" I asked her.

I thought her expression softened; certainly a tear glistened in her eye. I wanted right then to hold her in my arms, to caress her and comfort her. I pointed to a hotel we were approaching.

"Would you like that one?" I asked.

Her glance followed my pointing finger. She paled. She gripped my arm tightly and her lips parted. She stared straight ahead. Oh, God! She stared straight ahead and pointed at a man in the street—

"That's him!" she whispered. *"That's him . . ."*

Like a Bug
on a
Windshield

LAWRENCE BLOCK

THERE ARE TWO RODEWAY INNS IN INDIANAPOLIS, BUT WALDRON only knew the one on West Southern Avenue, near the airport. He made it a point to break trips there if he could do so without going out of his way or messing up his schedule. There were eight or ten motels around the country that were favorites of his, some of them chain affiliates, a couple of them independents. A Days Inn south of Tulsa, for example, was right across the street from a particularly good restaurant. A Quality Court outside of Jacksonville had friendly staff and big cakes of soap in the bathroom. Sometimes he didn't know exactly why a motel was on his list, and he thought that it might be habit, like the brand of cigarettes he smoked, and that habit in turn might be largely a matter of convenience. Easier to buy Camels every time than to stand around deciding what you felt like smoking. Easier to listen to WJJD out of Chicago until the signal faded, then dial on down to KOMA in Omaha, than to hunt around and try to guess what kind of music you wanted to hear and where you were likely to find it.

It was more than habit, though, that made him stop at the Indianapolis Rodeway when he was in the neighborhood. They made it nice for a trucker without running a place that felt like a truck stop. There was a separate lot for the big rigs, of course, but there was also a twenty-four-hour check-in area around back just for truckers, with a couple of old boys sitting around in chairs and country music playing on the radio. The coffee was always hot and always free, and it was real coffee out of a Silex, not the brown dishwater the machines dispensed.

Inside, the rooms were large and clean and the beds comfortable. There was a huge indoor pool with Jacuzzi and sauna. A good bar, an okay restaurant—and, before you hit the road again, there was more free coffee and the truckers' room in back.

Sometimes a guy could get lucky at the bar or around the pool. If not, well, there was free HBO on the color television and direct-dial phones to call home on. You wouldn't drive five hundred miles out of your way, but it was worth planning your trip to stop there.

He walked into the Rodeway truckers' room around nine on a hot July night. The room was air-conditioned but the door was always open, so the air-conditioning didn't make much difference. Lundy rocked back in his chair and looked up at him. "Hey, boy," Lundy said. "Where you *been?*"

"Drivin'," he said, giving the ritual response to the ritual question.

"Yeah, I guess. You look about as gray as this desk. Get yourself a cup of coffee. I think you need it."

"What I need is about four ounces of bourbon and half an hour in the Jacuzzi."

"And two hours with the very best TWA has to offer," Lundy said. "What we all need, but meantime, grab some coffee."

"I guess," Waldron said, and poured himself a cup. He blew on the surface to cool it and glanced around the room. Besides Lundy, a chirpy little man with wire-rimmed glasses and a built-up shoe, there were three truckers in the room. Two, like Waldron, were drinking coffee out of Styrofoam cups. The third man was drinking Hudepohl beer out of the can.

Waldron filled out the registration card, paid with his Visa card, pocketed his room key and receipt. Then he sat down and took another sip of his coffee.

"The way some people drive," he said.

There were murmurs of agreement.

"About forty miles out of here," he said, "I'm on the Interstate—what's the matter with me, I can't even think of the goddamned number—"

"Easy, boy."

"Yeah, easy." He took a breath, sipped at his coffee, blew at the surface. It was cool enough to drink, but blowing on it was two reflexive, habitual. "Two kids in a Toyota. I thought at first it was two guys, but it was a guy and a girl. I'm going about five miles over the limit, not pushing it, and they pass me on a slight uphill and then they cut in tight. I gotta step on my brake or I'm gonna walk right up their back bumper."

"These people don't know how to drive," one of the coffee drinkers said. "I don't know where they get their licenses."

"Through the mails," the beer drinker said. "Out of the Monkey Ward catalog."

"So I tapped the horn," Waldron said. "Just a tap, you know? And the guy was driving, he taps back."

"Honks his horn."

"Right. And slows down. Sixty-two, sixty, fifty-eight, he's dying out there in front of me. So I wait, and I flip the brights on and off to signal him, and then I go around him and wait until I'm plenty far ahead of him before I move back in."

"And he passes you again," said the other coffee drinker, speaking for the first time.

"How'd you know?"

"He cut in sharp again?"

Waldron nodded. "I guess I was expecting it once he moved out to pass me. I eased up on the gas, and when he cut in I had to touch the brake, but it wasn't close, and this time I didn't bother hitting the horn."

"I'da used the horn," the beer drinker said. "I'da *stood up* on the horn."

"Then he slowed down again," the second coffee drinker said. "Am I right?"

"What are these guys, friends of yours?"

"They slow down again?"

"To a crawl. And then I *did* use the horn, and the girl turned around and gave me the finger." He drank the rest of the coffee. "And I got angry," he said. "I pulled out. I put the pedal on the floor and I moved out in front of them—and this time they're not gonna let me pass, you know, they're gonna pace me, fast when I speed up, slow when I lay off. And they're looking up at me, and they're laughing, and she's leaning across his lap and she's got her blouse or the front of her dress, whatever it is, she's got it pushed down, you know, like I've never seen it before and my eyeballs are gonna go out on stalks—"

"Like in a cartoon."

"Right. And I thought, You idiots, because all I had to do, you know, was turn the wheel. Because where are they gonna go? The shoulder? They won't have time to get there. I'll run right over them. I'll smear 'em like a bug on a windshield. Splat, and they're gone."

"I like that," Lundy said.

Waldron took a breath. "I almost did it," he said.

"How much is almost?"

"I could feel it in my hands," he said. He held them out in front of him, shaped to grip a steering wheel. "I could feel the thought going into my hands, to turn that wheel and flatten them. I could see it all happening. I had the picture in my mind, and I was seeing myself driving away from them, just driving off, and they're wrecked and burning."

Lundy whistled.

"And I had the thought, That's murder! And the thought like registered, but I was still going to do it, the hell with it. My hands"—he flexed his fingers—"my hands were ready to move on the wheel, and then it was gone."

"The Toyota was gone?"

"The *thought* was gone. I hit the brake and I got behind them and a rest area came up and I took it, fast. I pulled in and cut the engine and had a smoke. I was all alone there. It was empty and I was thinking that maybe they'd come back and pull into the rest area, too, and if they did I was gonna take him on with a tire iron. There's one I keep in the front seat with me and I actually got it down from the rig and walked around with it in one hand, smoking a cigarette and swinging the tire iron just so I'll be ready."

"You see 'em again?"

"No. They were just a couple of kids clowning around, probably working themselves up. Now they'll get into the backseat and have themselves a workout."

"I don't envy them," Lundy said. "Not in the backseat of an effing Toyota."

"What they don't know," said Waldron, "is how close they came to being dead."

They were all looking up at him. The second coffee drinker, a dark-haired man with deep-set brown eyes, smiled. "You really think it was close?"

"I told you, I almost—"

"So how close is almost? You thought about it and then you didn't do it."

"I thought about making it with Jane Fonda," Lundy said, "but then I didn't do it."

"I was going to do it," Waldron said.

"And then you didn't."

"And then I didn't." He shook a cigarette out of his pack and picked up Lundy's Zippo and lit it. "I don't know where the anger came from. I was angry enough to kill. Why? Because the girl shot me a bone? Because she waggled her—?"

"Because you were afraid," the first coffee drinker suggested.

"Afraid of what? I got eighteen wheels under me, I'm hauling building materials, how'm I afraid of a Toyota? It's not my ass if I hit them." He took the cigarette out of his mouth and looked at it. "But you're right," he said. "I was scared I'd hit them and kill them, and that turned into anger, and I almost *did* kill them."

"Maybe you should have," someone said. Waldron was still looking at his cigarette, not noticing who was speaking. "Whole road's full of amateurs and people thinking they're funny. Maybe you got to teach 'em a lesson."

"Swat 'em," someone else said. "Like you said, bug on the windshield."

"I'm just a bug on the windshield of life," Lundy sang in a tuneless falsetto whine. "Now who was it sang that or did I just make it up?" Dolly Parton, the beer drinker suggested. "Now wouldn't I just love to be a bug on her windshield?" Lundy said.

Waldron picked up his bag and went to look for his room.

Eight, ten weeks later, he was eating eggs and scrapple in a diner on Route 1 outside of Bordentown, New Jersey. The diner was called the Super Chief and was designed to look like a diesel locomotive and painted with aluminum paint. Waldron was reading a paper someone else had left in the booth. He almost missed the story, but then he saw it.

A camper had plunged through a guardrail and off an embankment on a branch of the Interstate near Gatlinburg, Tennessee. The driver, an instructor at Ozark Community College in Pine Bluff, Arkansas, had survived with massive chest and leg injuries. His wife and infant son had died in the crash.

According to the driver, an eighteen-wheeler had come up "out of nowhere" and shoved the little RV off the road. "It's like he was a snowplow," he said, "and he was clearing us out of the way."

Like a bug on a windshield, thought Waldron.

He read the story again, closed the paper. His hand was shaking as he picked up his cup of coffee. He put the cup down, took a few deep breaths, then picked up the cup again without trembling.

He pictured them in the truckers' room at the Rodeway, Lundy rocking back in his chair with his feet up, built-up shoe and all. The beer drinker, the two coffee drinkers. Had he even heard their names? He couldn't remember, nor could he keep their images in focus in his memory. But he could hear their voices. And he could hear his own, suggesting an act not unlike the one he had just read about.

My God, had he given someone an idea?

He sipped his coffee, left the rest of his food untouched on the plate. Scrapple was a favorite of his and you could only find it in and around Philadelphia, and they did it right here, fried it crisp and served it with maple syrup, but he was letting the grease congeal around it now. That one coffee drinker, the one with the deep-set eyes, was he the one who'd spoken the words, but he remembered the anger in them, and something else, too, something like a blood lust.

Of course, the teacher could have dreamed the part about the eighteen-wheeler. Could have gone to sleep at the wheel and made up a story to keep him from seeing he'd driven off the road and killed his own family. Pin it on the Phantom Trucker and keep the blame off your own self.

Probably how it happened.

Still, from that morning on, Waldron kept an eye on the papers.

"Hey, boy," Lundy said. "Where *you* been?"

It was a cold December afternoon, overcast, with a raw wind blowing out of the northwest. The daylight ran out early this time of year but there were hours of it left. Waldron had broken his trip early just to stop at the Rodeway.

"Been up and down the Seaboard," he said. "Mostly. Hauling a lot of loads in and out of Baltimore." Of course there'd been some cross-country trips, too, but he'd managed to miss Indianapolis each time, once or twice distorting his schedule as much to avoid Indy as he'd fooled with it today to get here.

"Been a while," Lundy said.

"Six months."

"That long?"

"July, last I was here."

"Makes five months, don't it?"

"Well, early July. Say five and a half."

"Say a year and a half if you want. Your wife asks, I'll swear you was never here at all. Get some coffee, boy."

There was another trucker sitting with a cup of coffee, a bearded longhair with a fringed buckskin jacket, and he'd laughed at Lundy's remark. Waldron poured himself a cup of coffee and sat down with it, sitting quietly, listening to the radio and the two men's light banter. When the fellow in buckskin left, Waldron leaned forward.

"The last time I was here," he said.

"July, if we take your word for it."

"I was wired that night. I'd had a clown playing tag with me on the road."

"If you say so."

"There were three truckers in here plus yourself. One was drinking beer and the other two were drinking coffee."

Lundy looked at him.

"What I need to know," Waldron said, "is their names."

"You must be kidding."

"It wouldn't be hard to find out. You'd have the registrations. I checked the date, it was the ninth of July."

"Wait a minute." Lundy rocked his chair back and put both feet on the metal desk. Waldron glanced at the built-up shoe. "A night in July," Lundy said. "What in hell happened?"

"You must remember. I almost had an accident with a wise-ass, cut me off, played tag, made a game of it. I was saying how angry I was, how I wanted to kill him."

"So?"

"I wanted to kill him with the truck."

"So?"

"Don't you remember? Something I said, you made a song out of it. I said I could have killed him like a bug on the windshield."

"Now I remember," Lundy said, showing interest. "Just a bug on the windshield of life, that's the song that came to me, I couldn't get it out of my head for the next ten or twelve days. Now I'll be stuck with it for the *next* ten or twelve days, like as not. Don't tell me you want to haul my ass down to Nashville and make me a star."

"What I want," Waldron said evenly, "is for you to check the registrations and figure out who was in the room that night."

"Why?"

"Because somebody's doing it."

Lundy looked at him.

"Killing people. With trucks."

"Killing people with trucks? Killing drivers or owners or what?"

"Using trucks as murder weapons," Waldron said. On the radio, David Allen Coe insisted he was an outlaw like Waylon and Willie. "Running people off the road. Flyswatting 'em."

"How d'you know all this?"

"Look," Waldron said. He took an envelope from his pocket, un-folded it, and spread newspaper clippings on the top of Lundy's desk. Without removing his feet from the desk, Lundy leaned forward to scan the clips. "These are from all over," he said after a moment.

"I know."

"Any of these here could be an accident."

"Then somebody's leaving the scene of a lot of accidents. Last I heard, there was a law against it."

"Could be a whole lot of different accidents."

"It could," Waldron admitted. "But I don't believe it. It's murder and it's one man doing it and I know who he is."

"Who?"

"At least I think I know."

"You gonna tell me or is it a secret?"

"Not the beer drinker," Waldron said. "One of the two fellows who were drinking coffee."

"Narrows it down. Not too many old boys drive trucks and drink coffee."

"I can almost picture him. Deep-set eyes, dark hair, sort of a dark complexion. He had a way of speaking. I can about hear his voice."

"What makes you think he's the one?"

"I don't know. You want to get those registrations?"

He didn't, and Waldron had to talk him into it. Then there were three check-ins, one right after the other, and two of the men lingered with their coffee. When they left, Lundy heaved a sigh and told Waldron to mind the store. He limped off and came back ten minutes later with a stack of index cards.

"July the ninth," he announced, sinking into his chair and slapping the cards onto the desk. "You want to deal those, we can play some Five Hundred Rummy. You got enough cards for it."

Not quite. There were forty-three registrations that had come through the truckers' check-in room for that date. Just over half were names that one of the two men recognized and could rule out as the possible identity of the dark-eyed coffee drinker. But there were still twenty possibles, names that meant nothing to either man—and Lundy explained that their man might not have filled in a card.

"He could of shared a room and the other man registered," he said, "or he could have just come by for the coffee and the company. There's old boys every night that pull in for half an hour and the free coffee, or maybe they're taking a meal break and they come around back to say hello. So what you got, you got it narrowed down to twenty, but he might not be one of the twenty anyway. You get tired of driving a truck, boy, you can get a job with Sherlock Holmes. Get you the cap and pipe, nobody'll know the difference."

Waldron was going through the cards, reading the names and addresses.

"Looking through a stack of cards for a man who maybe isn't there in the first place and who probably didn't do anything anyway. And what are you gonna do if you find him?"

"I don't know."

"Where's it your business, come to that?"

Waldron didn't say anything at first. Then he said, "I gave him the idea."

"With what you said? Bug on the windshield?"

"That's right."

"Oh, that's crazy," Lundy said. "Where you been, boy? I hear that same kind of talk four days out of seven. Guy walks in, hot about some fool who almost made him lose it, next thing you know he's saying how instead of driving off the road, next time he'll drive right *through* the mother. Even if somebody's doin' this"—he tapped Waldron's clippings—"which I don't think they are, there's no way it's you gave him the idea. My old man, he'd wash his car and then it'd rain and he'd swear it was him brought the rain on. You're startin' to remind me of him, you know that?"

"I can picture him," Waldron said. "Sitting up behind the wheel, a light rain coming down, the windshield wipers working at the low speed. And he's smiling."

"And about to run some sucker off the road."

"I can just see it so clear. This one time"—he sorted through the newspaper clippings—"downstate Illinois, this sportscar. Witness said a truck just ran right *over* it."

"Like steppin' on it," Lundy said thoughtfully.

"And when I think about it—"

"You don't know it's on purpose," Lundy said. "All the pills some of you old boys take. And you don't know it's one man doing it, and you don't know it's him, and you don't know who he is anyway. And you don't know you gave him the idea, and if there's a God or not you ain't It, so why are you makin' yourself crazy over it?"

"Well, you got a point," Waldron said.

He went to his room, showered, put on swim trunks, and picked up a towel. He went back and forth from the sauna to the pool and into the Jacuzzi and back into the pool again. He swam some laps, then stretched out on a chaise next to the pool. He listened, eyes closed, while a man with a soft hill-country accent was trying to teach his young son to swim. Then he must have dozed off, and when he opened his eyes he was alone in the pool area. He returned to his room, showered, shaved, put on fresh clothes, and went to the bar.

It was a nice room—low lighting, comfortable chairs, and barstools. Some decorator had tricked it out with a library motif, and there were bookshelves here and there with real books in them. At least Waldron supposed they were real books. He'd never seen anyone reading one of them.

He settled in at the bar with bourbon and dry-roast peanuts from the dish on the bartop. An hour later he was in a conversation, and thirty minutes after that he was back in his room, bedded down with an old girl named Claire who said she was assistant manager of the gift shop at the airport. She was partial to truckers, she told him. She'd even married one, and although it hadn't worked out they remained good friends. "Man drives for a living, chances are he's thoughtful and considerate and sure of himself, you know what I mean?"

Waldron saw those deep-set brown eyes looking over the steering wheel. And that slow smile.

After that he seemed to catch a lot of cross-country hauling and he stopped pretty regularly at the Rodeway. It was convenient enough, and the Jacuzzi was a big attraction during the winter months. It really took the road-tension out of you.

Claire was an attraction, too. He didn't see her every visit, but if the hour was right he sometimes gave her a call and they sometimes got together. She'd come by for a drink or a swim, and one night he put on a jacket and took her to dinner in town at the King Cole.

She knew he was married and felt neither jealousy nor guilt about it. "Me and my ex," she said, "it wasn't what he did on the road that broke us up. It was what he didn't do when he was home."

It was mid-March when he found the man. And it was nowhere near Indianapolis.

It was a truck stop just east of Tucumcari, New Mexico, and he'd had no intention of stopping there. He'd had breakfast a while back in a Tex-Mex diner midway between Gallup and Albuquerque, and by the time he hit Tucumcari his gut was rumbling and he was ready for an unscheduled pit stop. He picked a place he'd never stopped at. If it had a name he didn't know what it was. The signs said nothing but DIESEL FUEL and TRUCKERS WELCOME. He clambered down from the cab and used the john, then went in for a cup of coffee he didn't particularly want.

And saw the man right away.

He'd been able to picture the eyes and the smile, and a pair of hands on a wheel. Now the image enlarged to include a round, close-cropped head with a receding hairline, a bulldog jaw, a massive pair of shoulders. The man sat on a stool at the counter, drinking coffee and reading a magazine, and Waldron just stood for a moment, looking at him.

There was a point where he almost turned and walked out. It passed, and instead he took the adjoining stool and ordered coffee. When the girl brought it, he let it sit there. Beside him, the man with the deep-set eyes was reading an article about bonefishing in the Florida Keys.

"Nice day out there," Waldron said.

The man raised his eyes, nodded.

"I think I met you sometime last summer. Indianapolis, the Rodeway Inn."

"I've been there."

"I met you in Lundy's room in the back. There were three men there beside Lundy. One of them was drinking a can of Hudepohl."

"You got a memory," the man said.

"Well, the night stuck in my mind. I had a close one out on the highway, I came in jawing about it. A jerk in a car playing tag with me and I came in mad enough to talk about running him off the road, killing him."

"I remember that night," the man said, and he smiled the way Waldron remembered. "Now I remember you."

Waldron sipped his coffee.

"Like a bug on a windshield," the man said. "I remember you saying that. Next little while, every time some insect went and gummed up the glass, it came to me, you saying that. You ever find them?"

"Find who?"

"Whoever was playing tag with you."

"I never looked for them."

"You were mad enough to," the man said. "That night you were."

"I got over it."

"Well, people get over things."

There was a whole unspoken conversation going on and Waldron wanted to cut through and get to it. "Who I been looking for," he said, "is I been looking for you."

"Oh?"

"I get things in my mind I can't get rid of," Waldron said. "I'll get a thought working and I won't be able to let go of it for a hundred miles. And my stomach's been turning on me."

"You lost me on a curve there."

"What we talked about. What I said that night, just running my mouth, and you picked up on it." Waldron's hands worked, forming into fists, opening again. "I read the papers," he said. "I find stories, I clip them out of the papers." He met the man's eyes. "I know what you're doing," he said.

"Oh?"

"And I gave you the idea," he said.

"You think so, huh?"

"The thought keeps coming to me," Waldron said. "I can't shake it off. I drop it and it comes back."

"You want the rest of that coffee?" Waldron looked at his cup, put it down unfinished. "C'mon then," the man said and put money on the counter to cover both their checks.

Waldron kept his newspaper clippings in a manila envelope in the zippered side pocket of his bag. The bag rode on the floor of the cab in front of the passenger seat. They were standing beside the cab now, facing away from the sun. The man was going through some of the clippings and Waldron was holding the rest of them.

"You must read a lot of papers," the man said.

Waldron didn't say anything.

"You think I been killing people. With my truck."

"I thought so, all these months."

"And now?"

"I still think so."

"You think I did all these here. And you think you started it all by getting mad at some fool driver in Indiana."

Waldron felt the sun on the back of his neck. The world had gone silent and all he could hear was his own breathing.

Then the man said, "This here one was mine. Little panel truck, electrical contractor or some damn thing. Rode him right off a mountain. I didn't figure he'd walk away from it, but then I didn't stay around to find out, you know, and I don't get around to reading the papers much." He put the clipping on the pile. "A few of these are mine," he said.

Waldron felt a pressure in his chest, as if his heart had turned to iron and was being drawn by a magnet.

"But most of these," the man went on, "the hell, I'd have to work night and day and do nothing else. I mean, figure it out, huh? Some of these are accidents, just like they're written up."

"And the rest?"

"The rest are a whole lot of guys like you and me taking a whack at somebody once in a while. You think it's one man doing all of it and you said something to get him started, hell, put your mind at rest. I did it a couple of times before you ever said a word. And I wasn't the first trucker ever thought of it, or the first ever did it."

"Why?"

"Why do it?"

Waldron nodded.

"Sometimes to teach some son of a bitch a lesson. Sometimes to get the anger out. And sometimes—look, you ever go hunting?"

"Years ago, with my old man."

"You remember what it felt like?"

"Just that I was scared all the time," Waldron said, remembering. "That I'd do something wrong, miss a shot or make noise or something, and my dad would get mad at me."

"So you never got to like it."

"No."

"Well, it's like hunting," the man said. "Seeing if you can do it. And there's you and him, and it's like you're dancing, and then he's gone and you're all that's left. It's like a bullfight, it's like shooting a bird on the wing. There's something about it that's beautiful."

Waldron couldn't speak.

"It's just a once-in-a-while thing," the man said. "It's a way to have fun, that's all. It's no big deal."

He drove all day, eastbound on 66, his mind churning and his stomach a wreck. He stopped often for coffee, sitting by himself, avoiding conversations with other drivers. Any of them could be a murderer, he thought, and once he fancied that they were all murderers, unpunished killers racing back and forth across the country, running down anyone who got in their way.

He knew he ought to eat, and twice he ordered food only to leave it untouched on his plate. He drank coffee and smoked cigarettes and just kept going.

At a diner somewhere he reached for a newspaper someone else had left behind. Then he changed his mind and drew away from it. When he returned to his truck he took the manila enve-

lope of newspaper clippings from his bag and dropped it into a
trash can. He wouldn't clip any more stories, he knew, and for
the next little while he wouldn't even read the papers. Because
he'd only be looking for stories he didn't want to find.

He kept driving. He thought about stopping when the sky
darkened but he decided against it. Sleep just seemed out of the
question. Being off the highway for longer than it took to gulp
a cup of coffee seemed impossible. He played the radio once or
twice but turned it off almost immediately; the country music he
normally liked just didn't sound right to him. At one point he
switched on the CB—he hardly ever listened to it these days, and
now the chatter that came over it sounded like a mockery. They
were out there killing people for sport, he thought, and they were
chatting away in that hokey slang and he couldn't stand it. . . .

Four in the morning, or close to it, he was on a chunk of
Interstate in Missouri or maybe Iowa—he wasn't too sure where
he was, his mind was running all over the place. The median strip
was broad here and you couldn't see the lights of cars in the
other lane. The traffic was virtually nonexistent—it was like he
was the only driver on the road, a trucker's Flying Dutchman or
something out of a Dave Dudley song, doomed to ride empty
highways until the end of time.

Crazy.

There were lights in the mirror. High beams, somebody coming
up fast. He moved to his right, hugging the shoulder.

The other vehicle moved out and hovered alongside him. For
a mindless instant he had thought that it was the man with the
deep-set eyes, the killer come to kill him. But this wasn't even a
truck, this was a car, and it was just sort of dipsy-doodling along
next to Waldron. Waldron wondered what was the matter with
the damn fool.

Then the car passed him in a quick burst of speed and Waldron
saw what it was.

The guy was drunk.

He got past Waldron's rig, cut in abruptly, then almost drove off the road before he got the wheel straightened out again. He couldn't keep the car in line, he kept wandering off to the left or right, he was all over the road.

A fucking menace, Waldron thought.

He took his own foot off the gas and let the car pull away from him, watching the taillights get smaller in the distance. Only when the car was out of sight did Waldron bring his truck back up to running speed.

His mind wandered then, drifting along some byway, and he came back into present time to note that he was driving faster than usual, pushing past the speed limit. He found he was still doing it even after he noticed it.

Why?

When the taillights came into view, he realized what he'd subconsciously been doing all along. He was looking for the drunk driver, and there he was. He recognized the taillights. Even if he hadn't, he'd recognize the way the car swung from side to side, raising gravel on the shoulder, then wandering way over into the left-hand lane and back again.

Drivers like that were dangerous. They killed people every day and the cops couldn't keep the bastards off the roads. Look at this crazy son of a bitch, look at him, for God sake, he was all over the place, he was sure to kill himself if he didn't kill someone else first.

Downhill stretch coming up. Waldron was loaded up with kitchen appliances, just a hair under his maximum gross weight. Give him a stretch of downhill loaded like that, hell, wasn't anyone could run away from him going downhill.

He looked at the weaving car in front of him. Nobody else out in front, nobody in his mirror. Something quickened in his chest. He got a flash of deep-set eyes and a knowing smile.

He put the gas pedal on the floor.

Bless This House

CHRISTIANNA BRAND

THEY WERE BEAUTIFUL; AND EVEN IN THAT FIRST MOMENT, THE OLD
woman was to think later, she should have known, should have
recognized them for what they were. Standing there so still and
quiet in the face of her own strident aggression, the boy in the
skintight blue jeans, with his mac held over his head against
the fine drizzle of the evening rain—held over his head like a
mantle—the girl with her long hair falling straight as a veil down
to the pear-shaped bulge of her pregnancy. But though suspicion
died in her, she would not be done out of her grievance. "What
you doing here? You got no right here, parking outside my
window."

They did not reply that after all the street did not belong to
her. The girl said only, apologetically, "We got nowhere else
to sleep."

"Nowhere to sleep?" She glanced at the ringless hand holding
together the edges of the skimpy coat. "Can't you go home?"

"Our homes aren't in London," said the boy.

"You slept somewhere last night."

"We had to leave. The landlady—Mrs. Mace—she went away
and her nephew was coming home and wanted the place. We've
been hunting and hunting for days. No one else will take us in."

"Because of the baby," said the girl. "In case it comes, you see."

Suspicion gleamed again. "Well, don't look at me. I got nothin', only my one bed-sit, here in the basement—the other rooms are used for storage, all locked up and bolted. And upstairs—well, that's full."

"Oh, of course," said the girl. "We didn't mean that at all. We were sleeping in the car."

"In the car?" She stood at the top of the area steps peering at them in the light of the streetlamp, shawled, also against the rain. She said to the boy, "You can't let her sleep in that thing. Not like she is."

"Well, I know," he said. "But what else? That's why we came to this quiet part."

"We'll move along, of course," said the girl, "if you mind us being here."

"It's a public street," she said illogically. But it was pitiful, poor young things; and there was about them this—something: so beautiful, so still and quiet, expressionless, almost colorless, like figures in some dim old church, candlelit at—yes, Christmastime. Like figures in a Christmas crèche. She said uncertainly, "If a few bob would help—"

But they disclaimed this at once. "No, no, we've got money; well, enough anyway. And he can get work in the morning, it's nothing like that. It's only . . . well," said the girl, spreading slow, explanatory hands, "it's like we told you. The baby's coming and no one will take us in. They just say, sorry—no room."

Was it then that she had known?—when she had heard herself saying, almost without her own volition, "Out in the back garden—there's a sort of a shed . . ."

It was a strain, perhaps—the uncertainty, the long day's search for accommodation, the fading hope—but the baby came that night. No time for doctor or midwife; but Mrs. Vaughan was experienced in such matters, delivered the child safely, dealt with the young mother—unexpectedly resilient despite her fragile look, calm, uncomplaining, apparently impervious to the pain—settled her comfortably at last on the old mattress in the shed, covered over with clean bedclothes. "When you're fit to be moved—we'll see." And to the boy she said sharply, "What you got there?"

He had employed the waiting time in knocking together a sort of cradle out of a wooden box; padded it round and fitted it with a couple of down-filled cushions from their car. Taken nothing of hers; all the things were their own. "Look, Marilyn—for the baby."

"Oh, Jo," she said, "you always were a bit of carpenter! You always were good with your hands."

Joseph. And Marilyn. And Joseph a bit of a carpenter, clever with his hands. And a boy child born in an outhouse because there was no room elsewhere for his coming. . . . She got down slowly onto her thick, arthritic knees beside the mattress and, with something like awe in her heart, gathered the baby from his mother's arms. "I'll lay him in the box. It'll do him lovely." And under her breath, "He won't be the first," she said.

The boy left money with her the next day for necessities and went out and duly returned that evening with news of a job on a building site, carrying in one scarred hand a small, drooping bunch of flowers which he carefully divided between them, half for Marilyn, half for Mrs. Vaughan—"till I can get you something better"—and one violet left over to place in the baby's tiny mottled fist. "And till I can get *you* something better," he said.

They gave him no name. . . . Other young couples, she thought, would have spent the idle hours trying to think up "something different" or christened him after a pop star, some loose-mouthed, long-haired little good-for-nothing shrieking out nonsense, thin legs kept jerking by drugs in an obscene capering. But no—it was "the baby," "the little one." Perhaps, she thought, they dared not name him, dared not acknowledge, even to themselves. . . .

For the huge question in her mind was: *how much do they know?*

For that matter—how much did she herself know? And what?— what in fact did she know? The Holy Child had been born already, had been born long ago. Vague thoughts of a Second Coming wandered through her brain, but was that not to be major, a clearly recognizable event, something terrible, presaging the end of all things? The End. And the other had been the Beginning. *Perhaps,* she thought, *there could be a Beginning—Again? Perhaps with everything having gone wrong with the world, there was going to be a second chance . . . ?*

It was a long time since she had been to church. In the old days, yes; brought up the two girls to be good Catholics, washed and spruced-up for mass every Sunday, convents, catechism, the lot. And much good it had done her—married a couple of heathen GIs in the war and gone off to America for good—for good or ill, she did not know and could no longer care; for years she had heard not a word from either of them. But now . . . she put on her crumpled old hat and, arthritically stumping, went off to St. Stephen's.

It was like being a schoolgirl again, all one's childhood closing in about one: to be kneeling there in the stuffy, curtained darkness, to see the outlined profile crowned by the black hump of the biretta with its pom-pom atop, leaning against the little iron-work grille that was all that separated them. "In the name of the Father and of the Son and of the Holy Ghost . . . Yes, my child?"

He talked to her quietly and kindly, while waiting penitents shifted restlessly outside, and thought, among their Firm Purposes of Amendment, that the old girl must be having a right old load of sins to cough up. About chance, he spoke, and about coincidence, about having the Holy Child in one's heart and not trying to—well—rationalize things. . . . She thanked him, made of old habit the sign of the cross, and left. "Them others—*they* didn't recognize Him either," she said to herself.

And she came to her room and saw the quiet face bent over the sleeping baby lying in its wooden cradle; and surely—surely—there was a light about its head?

On payday, Jo brought in flowers again. But the vase got knocked over almost at once, and the flowers and water spilled—there was not room for even the smallest extras in the close little room now

that Marilyn was up and sitting in the armchair with the wooden
box beside her and the increasing paraphernalia of babyhood taking up so much of the scanty space. The car was being used as
a sort of storage dump for anything not in daily use. "During the
weekend," said Jo, "I'll find us a place."

"A place?" she said, as though the idea came freshly to her. But
she had dreaded it. "Marilyn can't be moved yet."

"By the end of the week?" he said.

"You've been so good," said Marilyn. "We can't go on taking
up your room. We'll have to get somewhere."

But it wasn't so easy. He spent all his evenings, after that,
tramping round, searching; but as soon as he mentioned the baby,
hearts and doors closed against him. She protested, "But I don't
want you to go. I got none of my own right now, I like having
you here," and she knelt, as so often she did, by the improvised
wooden-box cradle and said, worshiping, "And I couldn't lose—
Him." And she went out and bought a secondhand bed and fixed
that up in the shed, brought Marilyn into her own bed, was happy
to sleep on a mattress on the floor, the box-cradle close to her
so that if the child stirred in the night, it was she who could
hush it and croon to it and soothe it to sleep again. *Is He all-
knowing?* she would wonder to herself in the dark. *Does He understand, even though He's so small, does the Godhead in Him understand that
it's I who hold Him? Will I one day sit at the right hand of the Father
because on this earth I nursed His only begotten Son . . . ? (Well, His—second
begotten Son . . . ?)* It was all so difficult. And she dared not ask.

She had no close friends these days, but at last, one night, a
little in her cups, she whispered it to Nellie down at the Dog.

"You'll never guess who I got at my place."

Nellie knocked back her fifth brown ale and volunteered a
bawdy suggestion. "A boy and a girl," said Mrs. Vaughan, ignoring
it. "And a Baby." And she thought of him lying there in his
wooden bed. "His little head," she said. "Behind His little head,
you can see, like—a light. Shining in the darkness—a kind of a
ring of light."

"You'll see a ring of light round *me*," said Nellie, robustly, "if you put back another of them barley wines." And to the landlord she confided, when Mrs. Vaughan, a little bit tottery, had gone off home, "I believe she's going off her rocker, honestly I do."

"She looked all right to me," said the landlord, who did not care for his regulars going off their rockers.

"They're after her stocking," said Nellie to the pub at large. "You'll see. Them and their Baby Jesus! They're after what she's got."

And she set a little trap. "Hey, Billy, you work on the same site as this Jo of hers. Give him a knock someday about the old girl's money. Got it in a stocking, saving up for her funeral. Worried, she is, about being put in the common grave. Well, who isn't? But she, she's proper scared of it."

So Billy strolled up to Jo on the site, next break-time. "I hear you're holed up with old Mother Vaughan, down near the Dog. After her stocking then, are you?" And he pretended knowledge of its place of concealment. "Fill it up with something; she'll never twig till after you've gone. Split me a third to two-thirds if I tell you where it's hid?"

And he looked up for the first time into Jo's face and saw the look that he gave him: a look almost—terrible. "He come straight home," Mrs. Vaughan told Nellie in the pub that night, "and—'they're saying you got money, Mrs. V,' he says. 'If you have, you should stash it away somewhere,' he says, 'and let everyone know you've done it. Living here on your tod, it isn't safe for you, people thinking you are worth robbing.'" And he had explained to her how to pay it into the post office so that no one but herself could ever touch it. Only a few quid it was, scrimped and saved for her funeral. "I couldn't a'bear to go into the common grave, not with all them strangers. . . ."

"Never mind the common grave, it'll be the common bin for *you*, if you don't watch out," said Nellie. "You and your Mary and Joseph—they come in a car, didn't they, not on a donkey?"

"You haven't got eyes to see. You don't live with them."

"They've lived other places before you. Did them other land-ladies have eyes to see?"

What was that name—Mrs. Mace? Had Mrs. Mace had eyes to see, had she recognized, even before the baby came—? "Course not," said Nellie, crossly. "She chucked 'em out, didn't she?"

"No, she never. She was moving out herself to the country, her son or someone needed the flat." But if one could have seen Mrs. Mace, consulted with her . . . "Don't you ever visit your last landlady?" she asked them casually. "Does she live too far?"

"No, not far; but with the baby and all . . . All the same, Mari-lyn," said Jo, "we ought to go someday soon, just to see she's all right. Take you along," he suggested to Mrs. Vaughan. "You'd enjoy the drive and it's a lovely place, all flowers and trees and a little stream."

"Oh, I wouldn't half like that. I dare say," said Mrs. Vaughan, craftily, "she thought a lot of you, that Mrs. Mace?"

"She was very kind to us," said Marilyn. "Very kind."

"And the baby? She wasn't, like—shocked?"

"Shocked? She was thrilled," said Jo. And he used an odd ex-pression: "Quietly thrilled."

So she *had* known. Mrs. Mace had known. The desire grew strong within Mrs. Vaughan's anxious breast to see Mrs. Mace, to discuss, to question, to talk it all over. With familiarity, with the lessening of the first impact of her own incredulous wonder, it became more difficult to understand that others should not share her faith. "I tell you, I see the light shining behind His head!"

She confided it to strangers on buses, to casual acquaintances on their way to the little local shops. They pretended interest and hastily detached themselves. "Poor thing—another of them loonies," they said with the mirthless snickers of those who find themselves outside the normal experience, beyond their depths. She was becoming notorious, a figure of fun.

The news reached the ears of the landlord, a local man. He

came round to the house and afterward spoke to the boy. "I've told her—you can't go on living in that one little room, it's not decent."

"There's the shed," said Jo. "I sleep out in the shed."

"You won't like that for long," said the man with a leer.

Billy had seen that look, on the building site. But the boy only said quietly: "You couldn't let us have another room? She says they're only used for storage."

"They're let—storage or not, no business of mine. For that matter," said the man, growing cunning, "it's no business of mine how you live or what you do. Only . . . well, three and a kid for the price of one—"

"I'll pay extra if that's it," said Jo. "I could manage that. It's only that I can't find anywhere else, not for the price I could afford."

"Just between the two of us, then. Though how you put up with it," he said, as the boy sorted through his pocketbook, "I don't know. The old girl's round the bend. What's this about your kid got a light around its head?—and your girl's a—" But the look came once more. A strange look almost—frightening. "Well, like that other lot, Jesus and all. She's mad."

"She has some ideas," said the boy. "That doesn't make her mad."

But not everyone agreed with him. The greengrocer's wife tackled Marilyn one day when she went out for the shopping, Mrs. Vaughan left worshiping the baby at home. "They're all saying she's going off her rocker. You shouldn't be there, with the baby and all. It could be dangerous."

So still and beautiful, the quiet face framed in a veil of long, straight hair. "Mrs. Vaughan—dangerous? She's kind. She'd do us no harm; she loves us."

"She told us last time that the baby lies with its arms stretched out like a—well, like a cross. She said it knows how it's going to die. Well, I *mean!* It's blasphemous."

"He does lie with his arms stretched out."

"Any baby does, sometimes. And she says he shines. She says there's always a light around his head."

"I put a lamp on the floor once to keep the brightness out of his eyes. It did sort of gleam through a crack in the wood. We explained it to her."

"Well, she never listened then. And I say it's not right. Everyone's talking. They say . . ." It took a little courage to persist, in the face of that quiet calm. "They're saying you ought to fetch a doctor to her."

Mrs. Vaughan rebelled, predictably, against any suggestion of seeing a doctor. "What for? I'm not ill. Never better." But it alarmed her. "You don't think there's something wrong with me?"

"We just thought you looked a bit pale, that's all."

"I'm not pale, I'm fine, never been better in my life. Even them arthritics nearly gone, hardly any pain these days at all." And she knew why. Alone with Him, she had taken the little hand and with it touched her swollen knees, had moved it, soft and firm, across her own gnarled fingers. "Look at 'em," she had insisted to Nellie the next evening at the pub. "Half the size. All them swollen joints gone down."

"They look the same to me," said Nellie, and suddenly saw Mrs. Hoskins through in the Private and had to hurry off and join her. "Barmy!" she said to Mrs. Hoskins. "I don't feel safe with her. How do I know she won't suddenly do her nut and start bashing me? It should be put a stop to."

Only one thing seemed to threaten Mrs. Vaughan with any suggestion of doing her nut and that was mention of her precious little family going away. If Jo searched for rooms now, he kept very quiet about it. To outside representations that she ought to let him go, that young people should be together in a place of their own, she replied that it wasn't "like that" between them; that Marilyn was "different." All the same, they were young and shouldn't always be cooped up with an old woman, and she fought to be allowed to move out to the shed and let them have her room; there was a bed out there now and in this weather it was warm and dry—she'd like it. In other days, she would have gone off to the pub in the evenings and left them free, but the Dog wasn't what it had been; people didn't seem so friendly, they looked at her funny, and sometimes, she suspected, made mock behind her back of her claim to be housing God. Not that that worried her too much. In them old days, no one had believed in Him then, either. *And I'll prove it to them,* she thought, and she would watch the children playing in the street and when she saw a tumble, bring in the poor victim with its bruises and scratches and cajole it into letting the baby touch the sore places with its little hand. "Now you feel better, love, don't you?" she would anxiously say. "Now it's stopped bleeding, hasn't it?—when the Baby touched you, it was all better in a minute? Now you tell me— wasn't it?" "Yes," the children would declare, wriggling from her grasp, intent only upon getting away. "It's dangerous," said their mothers, gathering outside the shops in anxious gossip. "You don't know what she might do, luring them inside like that." And a deputation at last sought out Jo. "You ought to clear out, you two, and leave her alone. You're driving her up the wall with these ideas."

"That's just what we can't do now," said Jo. "She gets upset if we even mention it."

"It could be the last straw," admitted Mrs. Hoskins, who knew all about it from Nellie at the Dog. "Properly finish her off."

"And then she'd be there without us to look after her."

"You can't spend your whole lives in that one room."

"If we could get a place and take her with us . . . But we can't find anywhere, not that we could possibly afford, let alone where she could come too."

"What?—you two kids, saddle yourselves forever with a mad old woman? You couldn't do that."

"She saddled herself with us," said Jo. "Where'd we be now, but for her?"

All the same, clearly something must be done. With every day of her life with them, Mrs. Vaughan's obsession increased. She could not bear the baby out of her sight, would walk with Marilyn when she carried it out for a breath of fresh air and almost threateningly warn off the curious who tried for a glimpse of the now quite famous child. If they came to worship, well and good. If not . . . "If you don't make some arrangement about her," said the greengrocer's wife at last to Jo, "I will. She's terrorizing the whole neighborhood."

"She wouldn't hurt a fly. She believes our baby's—something special. What harm does that do anyone else?"

"You never know," said the greengrocer, supporting the missus, though in fact he was fond of Mrs. Vaughan—as indeed everyone had been in easier days. "They do turn queer, sometimes. Why not just take her to the doctor and ask him, or take her to the hospital?"

"She won't go to any hospital; she won't go to any doctor."

"They can be forced," said the wife. "Straitjackets and that. They come and fetch them in a padded van." But anyway, she repeated, if something were not done and soon, she herself would ring up the police and let *them* deal with it. "She's keeping custom from the shop. It can't go on."

He promised hastily and later convened a little meeting of the malcontents. "Well, I've done what you said. I went to the hospital and they sent me to some special doctor and I told him all about it. They're going to send her to a place where she won't be too suspicious, and they'll have her under observation there, that's what they call it, and then there'll be psychiatrists and that, and she can have treatment. He says it's probably only a temporary thing, she can be cured all right."

"Well, there you are! You and Marilyn can be finding somewhere else in the meantime, and when she gets back and you're not there, she'll just settle down again."

"We'll go anyway even if we don't find anywhere. We couldn't let it start all over again."

"These things aren't as quick as all that. You'll have time to look around."

"It's not very nice," he said, "us there in her room and her in the bin."

"If you ever get her there. How'll you persuade her to go?"

"I've thought of that," he said. "Our last landlady—"

"Oh, yes, that Mrs. Mace she's always talking about! 'Mrs. Mace would understand,' she keeps saying. 'Mrs. Mace knew all about it.' . . . You tell her she's going to see Mrs. Mace."

"That's what I thought. Mrs. Mace is out in the country now and so's this place, fifteen, twenty miles. I can drive her there in the car. She'll go if she thinks Mrs. Mace is there. I think it'll work."

And it worked. Mrs. Vaughan was prepared to leave even the precious Baby for a while, if she could go and talk to Mrs. Mace. So many puzzling things that Mrs. Mace might be able to help her with. That about the Second Coming, for example, and then no Kings had arrived, not even a shepherd carrying a woolly lamb; and what about Herod killing off all them boy babies? Of course, these were modern days, what would they have done with a live lamb, anyway?—and people didn't go around killing babies anymore. But you'd think there'd be something to take the place of these events, something—well, sybollick, or whatever the word was, and it might be important to recognize it. Mrs. Mace would understand, would at least be sympathetic and talk it all over; she had known them since before the baby even started, had been brushed by the very wings of Gabriel bringing the message; Hail Mary, full of grace, the Lord is with thee. . . . She could hardly wait to gather up her few shabby clothes and pack them into the cardboard suitcase. "You'll look after things, Marilyn, love, just for a couple of days? I'd like to have some good long talks with Mrs. Mace. Do you think she'll let me stay?"

"It's a big place; like, sort of, a hotel," said Jo. "But lovely, all them trees and flowers. And lots of nice people," he added, cautiously.

"I thought it was a cottage? It's only Mrs. Mace I want to see. I can be with her?"

"Oh, yes, of course. We've written and told her," fibbed Jo, "how good you've been to us."

"Me—good?" she said. "When you think what you've done for *me*. Me being chosen. But still, there—the last time it was only a pubkeeper, wasn't it?" The thought struck her that perhaps, in fact, it had been meant that they should park outside the Dog that night, only a few doors down—that only through an error had they come to her. "Well, never mind, even if I wasn't worthy to be chosen, the fact remains it was me that got you—and reckernized you. First minute I saw you. I'll never forget it." So beautiful, so quiet and undemanding, standing out there in the drizzle of the evening rain, Mary and Joseph and the promise of the Holy Child. And as they had been then, so had they remained: quiet, considerate, gentle; reserved, unemotional as she was emotional and outgiving; almost colorless; almost impersonal—a little apart from other human beings, from ordinary people like herself; and yet living with herself close together in that little place with her for their only friend—the Mother and the Guardian of the Son of God; and the Word made flesh. She knelt and kissed the tiny hand. "I'll come back to you, my little Lord. I'll always love You and serve You, You know that. It's only just that I want to know everything about You; I want to get things right, I want to ask Mrs. Mace." And all unaware of eyes watching from behind window curtains, balefully or pityingly or only with relief, she climbed into the battered old car with Jo and drove away.

Marilyn was nursing the baby when he got home. "You've got the place all cleared up," he said, astonished at the change in it. "You must have been slaving."

"It kept my mind off things," she said. But still she did not ask what must be uppermost there. "Without Mrs. Vaughan here, I must say there's more room. Not as much as we had at Mrs. Mace's—"

"We couldn't stay at Mrs. Mace's once the nephew was coming home."

"No, I know, I was only saying." And now she did ask at last, "Did it go all right?"

"Yes, not a murmur. A bit surprised when we got there, of course, but I kept urging her on, saying she'd be with Mrs. Mace."

"You found the place again, no trouble?"

"Yes, I found it. A lovely spot, perfect, in the middle of all those woods."

"And Mrs. Mace?"

"Still there, quite OK. A bit lonely, I daresay. She'll be glad of company."

"They should get on fine." She smiled her own cool, quiet, impersonal little smile, shifting the baby on her shoulders so that its fluffy head pressed, warm and sweet, against her cheek. "Well, she got her wish. You couldn't call that a common grave."

"No, just her and Mrs. Mace; and right in the middle of them lovely woods like I told her, and all them flowers and the stream and all." He came across and ran a bent forefinger up the little channel at the back of the baby's tender neck. "A shame to have to bash her. She was a kind old thing. But there you are; it's so hard to find anywhere—we had to have the place."

"Yes," she said. "Especially now we got the kid."

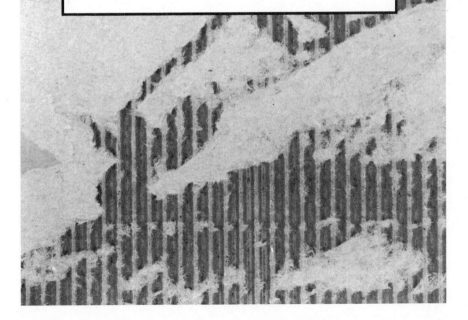

The Gun

ANN CAROL

"HE RUNS!" DEREK SAID, DRIBBLING THE BASKETBALL DOWN THE cracked cement of the empty school yard. "He jumps!" Quick and agile, he sidestepped his friend Jerry and leaped into the air. "He shoots, and—" he watched as the ball dropped through the hoop, then finished his commentary with a grin "—nothing but net!"

"Nothing but trouble, you mean." Jerry grabbed the ball and tucked it under his arm. "Look over there."

Turning, Derek saw two men coming through the gate of the school yard. It was a drizzly March day and both of them wore trench coats. Their faces were calm, and they walked casually, like maybe they were out for a stroll. But Derek knew they weren't. Even before the taller one reached into his pocket, he knew they were cops.

It was about the gun, Derek thought. It had to be. He felt panicky for a second, and had to remind himself that he'd thrown it away.

"Derek Robinson?" the tall one said.

"Yeah?"

"Detectives Kramer and Reed." His hand came all the way out of his pocket and he flashed his badge. "Can we talk to you for a minute? We have a few questions."

"What about?"

"Why don't you step into our office?" Reed motioned to a bench on the other side of the school yard.

Derek's heart sped up. *Definitely the gun,* he thought. With a quick glance at Jerry, he followed the officers across the yard and sat down on the bench. Kramer sat next to him. Reed stayed on his feet, looking around.

Kramer came right to the point. "It's about the gun, Derek."

Derek felt his face get hot, but he asked, "What gun?"

Kramer sighed. "The one you were flashing around in school yesterday."

His eyes on the building across the street, Reed said, "And before that, the one Max Cooper saw you stuffing under your jacket."

Max Cooper owned the deli that Derek passed every day on his way to school. *Great,* Derek thought. *The guy had seen him.*

"Plenty of people saw you with it," Kramer said. "And we'll find it, Derek, you can count on that. So do yourself a favor and cooperate."

"OK . . . OK," Derek said. "I had a gun."

"Right. Where'd you get it?"

"I found it. In a lot." Derek shook his head, remembering the fear and excitement he'd felt when he saw it. "I couldn't believe it. A .38, just lying there!"

"You knew the caliber?" Kramer raised an eyebrow. "Where'd you learn about guns?"

"Where do you think? It's not the first gun I've seen in this neighborhood."

"Just the first one you found lying in a vacant lot."

"Yeah."

Kramer raised his eyebrow again. "So you took it to school?"

"Yeah. Look," Derek said, sitting up straighter on the hard bench. "It was dumb, OK? I know it. That's why I got rid of it. I dumped it on my way home, right back where I found it."

"Where's this lot?" Reed asked, getting out a notebook.

"Corner of Fourth and Cooper," Derek said. "Nothing there but weeds. That's where I picked it up and that's where I put it back. All you have to do is look and you'll find it."

"We'll find it, all right," Kramer said. "But let's back up a little. You still had the gun with you after school. That's what . . . three, three-thirty?"

Derek nodded. "Three."

"So you left school. Then what'd you do?"

"Shot some hoops. Had some pizza," Derek said. "The usual stuff."

Reed slipped the notebook back in his pocket. "Does the usual stuff include holding up a hardware store at four-thirty?" His voice was quiet, almost conversational. But his eyes were as gray and chilly as the sky.

Derek's face got hot again and his heart started hammering. He wanted to stand but he was afraid his legs might shake. "That's crazy!" He wanted to sound cool, but he knew he sounded scared. "I never held up any hardware store! That's crazy," he said again.

"Seventeen or eighteen. Brown hair." Kramer was reading from a little notepad. "About five-eleven, approximately a hundred and fifty pounds. Wearing jeans and a hooded, black-and-red Bulls jacket." He stopped and eyed Derek's jacket. "Black-and-white high-tops." He glanced down at Derek's shoes, then closed the notepad. "And carrying a .38 caliber revolver."

"It fits pretty well," Reed commented quietly. "Don't you think, Derek?"

Derek knew he didn't have any reason to be so scared, but when he spoke, his voice shook. He couldn't help it. "Yeah, it fits. But it wasn't me. I had nothing to do with any robbery."

"Maybe you didn't," Kramer admitted. "So let's go back over what you did after school, OK?"

"I told you." Derek looked at Jerry standing on the other side of the yard, shooting hoops and missing them all because he was keeping one eye on the little gathering by the bench. Suddenly,

Derek's fear left him. When he spoke again, his voice was strong and confident because he was telling the truth. "We left school at three," he said. "We shot a few hoops, then we had some pizza."

"We?"

"Me and Jerry." Derek nodded toward his friend. "We had some pizza at Luigi's, you can ask Jerry. That was about four." He stood up now, knowing that his knees wouldn't quiver like an old man's. "And then we went down by the train tracks."

There was a pause as the two detectives eyed each other. Then Reed asked, "With the gun?" His voice was quieter than ever.

Derek nodded.

"And what were you doing there?"

"Shooting at tin cans," Derek said. He hadn't told them before because he didn't want to admit any more about the gun than he had to. But it didn't matter now. They were after a hold-up guy; they wouldn't care about a little target practice. Especially since Derek didn't have the gun anymore.

"Let's see if I've got this straight," Kramer said. "You left Luigi's and went to the train tracks and shot at tin cans with the .38 you found."

"Yeah, it was about four-thirty, quarter to five," Derek said.

"Did you shoot at anything besides tin cans?"

"Bottles and cans. That's all."

"Weren't you afraid somebody would hear the gunshots?" Kramer asked.

Derek shook his head. "We waited for the trains to pass through."

Kramer nodded. "Very clever. Did Jerry fire the gun, too?"

"No. Only me."

"And then what?" Reed asked.

"When the gun was empty, we split. Jerry went home and so did I," Derek told him. "And I threw the gun back in the lot where I found it." He shoved his hands in his pockets. "Look, ask Jerry. He was with me at Luigi's. Plenty of other people saw me there, too. And Jerry was with me at the tracks."

"About four-thirty, quarter to five?" Kramer asked.

"Yeah."

As Kramer got up from the bench and headed over to Jerry, Derek took a deep breath and let it out. He might still be in trouble about the gun. But no way could they pin the robbery on him. He hadn't done it and he'd just proved it.

When Kramer came back, he nodded at Reed. "It checks out," he said.

Derek let out a sigh of relief. "OK if I go now?"

"I don't think so," Reed said.

"But I told you what happened and you said it checked out!" Derek cried. "I didn't rob anyone!"

"No, we know you didn't," Reed said.

"So?"

"So at four-forty yesterday afternoon, a stray bullet from a .38 caliber revolver smashed through the window of the D train and into the head of a young woman." Reed looked at Derek with cold eyes. "You didn't rob anyone, Derek," he said. "You killed someone."

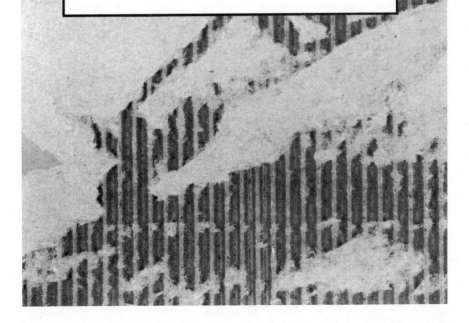

Lucky Dip

LIZA CODY

HE WAS SITTING AGAINST A BIT OF BROKEN WALL, LOOKING almost normal. I could see him because of the full moon. It was a lovely moon with wispy clouds like old ladies' hair across its face.

I watched the man for a couple of minutes but he didn't move. Well, he wouldn't, would he? I could see he didn't belong—he was far too well-dressed—and I wondered how he got there. This is not a part of the city men dressed like him go.

He had not been dead long. You could tell that at a glance because he still had his shoes on. If you die here you won't keep your shoes for ten minutes. You won't keep your wallet for ten seconds, dead or alive.

With this in mind I had a quick look, right and left, for anyone lurking in the shadows. If I'd seen anyone bigger than me I'd have stayed where I was. Moon shadows are blacker than hearses and I knew I wasn't the only one out that night. But in the Trenches only the big are bold, and someone big would have been rummaging in the remains already. So I hopped out from behind my pile of rubble and made a run for it.

I reached him in no time at all and grabbed his left lapel. Seven out of ten men are right-handed, and the chances are seven to three anything valuable will be in a left-hand inside pocket. I took a swift dip and came up with the winnings.

By now I could hear stirrings—a snap of rotten wood, a slide of brick dust. I flicked his watch off his wrist and almost in the same motion made a dive into his jacket pocket. Then I got on my toes and legged it.

I legged it out of the Trenches completely, because, although there are plenty of places to hide, the people I wanted to hide from know them as well as I do. The Trenches are useful as long as it's only the Law you want to avoid. Robbing a corpse isn't nice and I didn't want to take all that trouble only to be robbed myself.

It was just a quick jog to the High Street. On the way, I stopped under a streetlamp to look at what I had in my hand. The wallet was fat snakeskin, the watch was heavy gold, and the loose change was all pound coins and fifty-pence pieces. For once in my short life I'd struck oil.

All the same, you don't break old habits for the sake of one lucky dip, and when I saw all those plump taxpayers doing their late Christmas shopping on the High Street, I stuck out my hand as usual.

"Got any spare change, please?" I said, as always. "For a cup of tea. For a bed for the night. For a hot meal."

And as always they coughed up like princes or told me to get myself a job. It was nice that night. I perform best when there's no pressure, and by the time I'd worked my way down to the station I'd made a nice little pile. But it doesn't do to loll around and count your takings in public, so I jumped a tube to Paddington.

My sister has this room in Paddington. She lives in Camberwell with her boyfriend so this room's just for business. I don't trust my sister's boyfriend but I do trust my sister, up to a point, which was why I went to her business address. You may meet all sorts of funny blokes there, but you won't meet her boyfriend, and that suits me. It suits him, too, if you want to know the truth: he doesn't like me any more than I like him.

When we first came down to the city, Dawn and me, we relied

on each other; we didn't have anyone else to turn to. But after she took up with him and he set her up in business she didn't need me like she used to, and we drifted apart.

The trouble with Dawn is she always needs a man. She says she doesn't feel real without one. Feeling real is important to Dawn so I suppose I shouldn't criticize. But her men have been nothing but a disappointment. You could say I'm lucky to have an older sister like Dawn: she's an example to me. I'd rather die than turn out like her.

Still, she is my sister, and we've been through a lot together. Especially in this last year when we came down to the city together. And before that, when our mum kicked us out, or rather, kicked Dawn out because of the baby. And after that when Dawn's boyfriend kicked Dawn out because of the baby.

I have never been hungrier than I was last year trying to look after Dawn. She lost the baby in the end, which was a bit of a relief to me. I don't know how we would have managed if she'd had it. I don't think she would have coped very well either. It's much harder to get a man when you've got a little baby to look after.

Anyway, that's all in the past, and now Dawn has business premises in Paddington.

I waited outside until I was sure she was alone and then I went up and knocked on the door.

"Crystal!" she said when she opened the door. "What you doing here? You got to be more careful—I might've had company."

"Well, you haven't," I said. And she let me in, wrinkling her nose and pulling her kimono tight. I don't like that kimono—it's all hot and slippery. Since she got her hair streaked, Dawn has taken to wearing colors that would look all right on a tree in autumn but which turn her hard and brassy.

"Gawd," she said, "you don't half look clatty. Can't you get your hair cut? That coat looks like it's got rats living in it."

I took the coat off, but she didn't like the one underneath either.

"What a pong," she said.

"I had a wash last week," I told her. "But I would like to use your bathroom." I wanted somewhere private to look at what I'd got off the dead man.

"You can't stop around here," she said, worried. "I got someone coming in half an hour." She looked at her watch.

I sat in her bathroom and looked at the dead man's watch. It had Cartier written on the face, and it really was proper gold. *Quality*, I thought, and felt a bit sad. By rights a man with a watch like that shouldn't end up in the Trenches without a stitch on. Because that's how he'd be by now, pale and naked in the moonlight. Nobody would recognize him without his coat and suit and shoes. He'd just look like anyone. We're into recycling in the Trenches.

To cheer myself up I looked at his wallet, and when I counted up I found I had seven hundred and forty-three pounds and eighty-nine pence. And I couldn't use half of it.

Imagine me trying to change a fifty-pound note! There's a chance in a million a cat with cream on his whiskers milked a cow, but that's good odds compared to the chance I'd come by a fifty-quid note honestly. I couldn't even pop the watch. One look at a watch like that and any honest pawnbroker would turn me in. A dishonest one would rip me off quick as a wink. Either way the watch was no good for me.

I borrowed my sister's toothbrush and had a fast swipe with her deodorant before I joined her again. You never know when you're going to find clean water next so it pays to make use of what there is.

"Do me a favor, Crystal," she said, when she saw me. "Bugger off before you frighten the horses."

"Brought you a Christmas present," I said and handed her the watch.

"You're barmy, Crystal." She stared at the watch like it was a spider in her bed. "Who'd you nick this off?"

"I never," I told her. "I found it." And it was true because the feller was dead. It wasn't as if it was his property because there wasn't a him anymore for it to belong to. When you're dead you're gone. And that's final. Dead men don't own watches.

Even with a Christmas present, Dawn wouldn't let me stop for the night. It's a funny thing, if I hadn't had seven hundred and forty-three pounds, eighty-nine pence in my pocket, I wouldn't have wanted to. If it had just been the eighty-nine pence I'd've been quite happy sleeping out.

But having things is dangerous. Having things makes you a mark. It's like being pretty. If you don't believe me, look at Dawn. She's pretty and she's been a mark from the time she was eleven. Being pretty brought her nothing but trouble. She's always had to have someone to protect her. I'm glad I'm not pretty.

There's a hospital down the Harrow Road, so I went there. I couldn't decide what to do, so I sat in casualty till they chucked me out. It's a pity there aren't more places you can go and sit in at night to have a quiet think. It's hard to think on the hoof, and if you are cold or hungry thinking is not on your mind at all.

It seemed to me, after a while, that the best place to go was where I slept last night. Some might say it was a daft idea to go back to a place that was rousted, but I thought if the police had been there last night it would be deserted tonight.

Twenty-seven Alma-Tadema Road is a condemned house. They say it's unsafe. There are holes in the roof and holes in the floors but it is perfectly safe if you are sober, tread carefully, and don't light fires. That was what went wrong last night: we had a couple of winos in and one of them got cold just before daybreak.

When I got there I saw that they had nailed more boards across the front door and downstairs windows. I could get in but it would take time. There were still people up and about so, to be on the safe side, I would have to come back later if I wanted more than a few minutes' kip.

I walked on past and went down to the Embankment. It is quite a long walk and by the time I got there I was hungry. Actually, I'm hungry all the time. Dawn says she thinks I must have worms and I probably do, but mostly I think it's just my age. Someone like Bloody Mary does almost as much walking as I do but she doesn't seem to need half the fuel. She stopped growing years ago.

There are a lot of women like Bloody Mary but I mention her because she was the one I picked up on the Embankment that night, huffing and puffing along with her basket on wheels.

"Oh, me poor veins," she said, and we walked on together. I slowed down a bit so she could keep up.

"There's a stall open by the Arches," she said. "Couldn't half murder a cuppa."

She used to sing in the streets—walk up and down Oxford Street bellowing "It's Only a Paper Moon" with her hand held out—but after a bad dose of bronchitis last year her voice went.

At the Arches I got us both a cup of tea and a sausage sandwich.

"Come into money, Crys?" Johnny Pavlova asked. It is his stall and he has a right to ask because now and then when there's no one around to see he gives me a cup free. As he always says, he's not a charitable institution, but catch him in the right mood and he'll slip you one like the best of them.

All the same it reminded me to be careful.

"Christmas," I said. "They were feeling generous down the High Street."

"Down the High Street?" he said. "You ain't been on that demolition site, have you? I heard they found this stiff bollock-naked there this evening."

"Did they?" I said as if I couldn't care less. "I didn't hear nothing. I was just working the High Street."

I went over and sat with Bloody Mary under the Arches. Johnny Pavlova doesn't like us hanging too close round his stall. He says we put the respectable people off their hot dogs.

"Will you look at that moon," Bloody Mary said, and she pulled her coats tight.

It was higher in the sky now and smaller, but there was still a good light to see by.

"Where you kipping tonight, Crystal?" she asked. I knew what she meant. A moon like that is a freezing moon this time of year.

Just then, Brainy Brian came slithering in beside us, so I didn't have to answer. He was coughing his lungs out as usual and he didn't say anything for a while. I think he's dying. You can't cough like that and live long. He used to go to college in Edinburgh but then he started taking drugs and he failed all his exams. He did all right down here in the city because to begin with he was very pretty. But druggies don't keep their looks any longer than they keep their promises. Now he's got a face like a violin and ulcers all over his arms and legs.

When he recovered his breath he said, "Share your tea, Crystal?"

We'd already finished ours so we didn't say anything for a while. But Brian was so sorry-looking, in the end I went to get another two, one for him and one for Bloody Mary. While they were sucking it up I slipped away.

"Watch yourself, Crys," Johnny Pavlova said as I went by. He gave me a funny look.

The first thing you do when you break into a house is find another way out. A good house has to have more than one way out because you don't want to go running like the clappers to get out the same door the Law is coming in.

The house on Alma-Tadema Road has a kitchen door through to the garden. I loosened the boards on that before lying down to sleep. I also made sure I had the snakeskin wallet safe.

I had made the right decision: there was no one but me there. A heap of damp ashes marked the spot where the winos had lit their fire and they blew in little eddies from the draft. Otherwise nothing stirred.

I went over the house collecting all the paper and rags I could find to build myself a nest, then I curled up in it and shut my eyes.

Nighttime is not the best time for me. It's when I can't keep busy and in control of my thoughts that bad memories and dreams burst out of my brain. It's hard to keep cheerful alone in the dark, so I need to be very, very tired before I'll lie down and close my eyes. Sometimes I say things over and over in my head until I get to sleep—things like the words of a song or a poem I learned at school—over and over so there's no spare room in my brain for the bad stuff.

That night I must have been very tired because I only got part of the way through "What's Love Got to Do with It" when I dropped off. Dawn used to play that song all the time when we were still living at home. She played it so often it used to drive me up the wall. But it is songs like that, songs I didn't even know I'd learned the words to, which help me through the night nowadays.

The next thing I knew someone was coughing. I opened my eyes but it was still dark, and there was this cough, cough, cough coming my way. *Brainy Brian,* I thought, and relaxed a bit. It's something you have to watch out for—people coming up on you when you're alone in the dark.

"It's cold," he said when he found me. "It's hard, hard cold out there." He crawled into my nest. I was quite warm and I didn't want to leave but I knew his coughing would keep me awake.

"Give us a cuddle, Crystal," he said. "I got to get warm."

"Shove off," I said. His hands remind me of a fork. Some people do it to keep warm. Not me. I've seen too much and I want to die innocent.

He started coughing again. Then he said, "You got any dosh, Crystal?"

"Enough for a tea in the morning," I said. I really did not want to go. It was one of my better nests and it didn't seem fair to give it up to Brian.

"They're looking for you," he said. "Someone saw you in the Trenches."

"Not me," I said. "Who saw me?"

"You know that little kid?" he said. "Marvin, I think he's called. Well, they hurt him bad. He said he saw you."

"Who wants to know?" I sat up.

"Lay down," he said, "I got to get warm." He grabbed me and pulled me down, but he didn't start anything so I kept still.

After a while he said, "Johnny Pavlova says you got dosh. They asked him too."

I waited till he finished coughing. Then I said, "Who's asking? The Law?"

"Not them," he said. *He knew something*, I thought. And then I thought, *he talked to Johnny Pavlova, he's talked to Marvin, and Marvin saw me in the Trenches. Maybe Brian talked to whoever is looking for me.*

I said, "Did they send you, Brian? Did they send you to find me?"

He doubled over, coughing. Later he said, "You don't understand, Crystal. I got to get some money. I lost my fixings, and I haven't scored for days."

So that was that. I left him and went out the kitchen way. Brian was right—it was hard cold outside. And I was right too—having things makes you a mark. I dumped the snakeskin wallet in the garden before I climbed over the fence. And then I climbed right back and picked it up again. Dumping the wallet wouldn't stop anyone looking for me. Not having it would be no protection. Marvin didn't have it and he got hurt. I wondered why they picked on Marvin to clobber. Perhaps he got the dead man's shoes, or his coat. Perhaps they saw a little kid in a big thick coat and they recognized the coat.

No one ever looked for me before. There was no one interested. I thought maybe I should run away—somewhere up north, or maybe to the West Country. But when I ran away the first time it was me and Dawn together. And it was difficult because we didn't know the city. It took us ages to get sorted.

I thought about it walking down the road. The moon had gone and the sky had that dirty look it gets just before day. My nose was running from the cold and I was hungry, so I went to the Kashmir take-away. The Kashmir is a good one because it has a bin not twenty paces away. What happens is that when the pubs close a lot of folks want an Indian take-away, but because they've been drinking they order too much and chuck what's left over in this bin. I've had breakfast there many times. The great thing about a Kashmir breakfast is that although the food is cold by the time you get it, the spices are still hot, and it warms you up no end. From this point of view Indian food is the best in the city.

I felt much more cheerful after breakfast and I found a lighted shop window with a doorway to sit in. It was there I had a proper look at the wallet. Before, at Dawn's business premises, I only counted the money and redistributed it in the pockets of my coats. Now I studied the credit cards, library cards, and business stuff.

These are not things I am normally interested in. I can't use them. But this time, it seemed to me, the only way out of trouble was to give them back. The dead man in the Trenches might be dead but he was still dangerous.

His name was Philip Walker-Jones. He belonged to a diners' club, a bridge club, and a chess club. He had two business cards—Data Services Ltd. and Safe Systems Plc. He was managing director twice over, which seemed quite clever because both companies had the same address in Southwark Road. Southwark Road is not far from where I found him. Maybe he walked out of his office and died on the way to the station. But that didn't explain what he was doing in the Trenches. Nobody like him goes in the Trenches.

I thought about Philip Walker-Jones sitting in the moonlight against the broken brickwork. He had looked as if he'd just sat down for a bit of a breather. But he wasn't resting. He was dead. There wasn't a mark on him that I could see. It didn't look as if anyone had bumped him—he was just sitting there in all his finery. Quite dignified, really.

Little Marvin would have been there watching like I was, and probably a few others too—waiting to see if it was safe to take a dip. We were wrong, weren't we?

I didn't want to go back too close to the Trenches, but if I

was going to give the wallet back I had to. It was too early yet
for public transport so I started walking. A good breakfast does
wonders for the brain, so while I was walking I went on thinking.

I didn't know anything about "data" and "systems" except that
they sounded like something to do with computers, but I do know
that dining, bridge, and chess are all things you do sitting down.
Philip Walker-Jones didn't have any cards saying he belonged to
a squash club or a swimming club, and if he spent all that time
sitting down maybe he wasn't very fit. If he wasn't very fit, and
he started to run suddenly, he could have had a heart attack.

It was a satisfying bit of thinking, which took me down to the
river without really noticing. Crossing over, it occurred to me
that computers, bridge, and chess were things that really brainy
people did, and in my experience brainy people all wear glasses
and don't run around much. A really brainy man would not go
running into the Trenches after dark unless he was being chased.
A scared, unfit man running in the Trenches would have no bother
getting a heart attack. Easy.

The wind off the river was sharp and cold, but it wasn't the
only thing making me shiver. Because if Philip Walker-Jones had
a reason to be scared to death, so did I.

Give the rotten wallet back, I thought, *and do it double quick. Say,*
"Here's your money, now leave me be." And then do a runner. I'm good
at that.

I stopped for a pint of milk to fuel up. And I went through my
pockets to find some of the fifty pound notes, which I stuffed
back in the wallet to make it look better.

I felt quite good. I had made my plan and it was almost as if
I didn't have the wallet anymore. It was as good as gone, and by
the time I reached Southwark Road I wasn't bothering much about
keeping out of sight. It was daylight now and there were other
people in the streets, and cars on the roads, and as usual no one
seemed to notice me.

All the same, I gave the Trenches a miss. I walked down

Southwark Road bold as brass looking at numbers and signs. And when I found one which read Safe Systems Plc., I walked right up to the door.

It was a new door in an old building, and it was locked. Perhaps it was too early. Not having a watch myself, I don't keep track of office hours. I stood there wondering if I should hike on to the station where there's a clock and a cup of tea, and just then the door opened from the inside. It gave me such a fright I nearly legged it. But the person opening the door was a young woman, and usually women don't give me much trouble. This one had red rims to her eyes and a really mournful expression on her face. She also had a nasty bruise on her cheekbone, which made me think of Little Marvin.

She said, "Where do you think you're going?" She wasn't friendly but she looked as if she had other things on her mind.

"Safe Systems Plc.," I said.

"What do you want?" she said. "The office is closed. And haven't you heard of a thing called soap and water?"

"I've got something for Safe Systems," I said and held out the wallet.

"Jesus Christ!" she said and burst into tears.

We stood there like that—me holding the wallet and her staring at it, crying her eyes out.

At last, she said, "I don't want it. Take it away." And she tried to slam the door.

But I stuck my foot in there. "What do I do with it?" I said.

"Lose it," she said, and because I wouldn't let her close the door, she went on, "Look, you silly little cow, don't you come near me with that thing. Drop it in the river—you can give it to Steve for all I care. I'm finished with all that."

She started banging the door on my foot so I hopped back. The door crashed shut and she was gone.

I was so surprised I stood there gawping at the door and I didn't see the big feller coming up behind until he dropped a hand on my shoulder.

"You the one they call Crystal?" he said, from a great height.

"Not me," I said. "Never heard of her." I got the wallet back under my top coat without him noticing.

"What are you doing at that office then?" he said, not letting go.

"The lady sometimes gives me her spare change," I said and watched his feet. It's no good watching their eyes. If you want to know what a bloke's going to do, watch his feet. The big man's feet were planted. I did not like him knowing my name.

"What is your name then?" he said.

I nearly said, "Dawn," but I bit it off just in time.

"What?" he said.

"Doreen," I said. "Who's asking?" If he was Steve I would give him the wallet and run.

"Detective Sergeant Michael Sussex," he said. It was even worse than I thought. Now even the Law knew my name. It made me sweat in spite of the cold.

"I've got a few questions for you," he said, and he tightened his hand on my shoulder.

"I don't know anything," I said. "What about?"

"About where you was last night," he said. "And who you saw."

"I never saw nothing," I said, really nervous.

"Course you didn't," he said. "Come on. I'll buy you breakfast and then we can talk." And he smiled.

Never, never trust the Law when it smiles.

None of this had ever happened to me before. If you must know, I've hardly ever talked to a policeman in my life. I'm much too fast on my feet.

"Where do you live, Crystal?" he said, starting to walk.

"The name's Doreen," I said, and tried to get out from under the big hand.

"Where do you live . . . Doreen?" he said.

The thing you have to know about the Law is that they ask questions and you answer them. You've got to tell them something or they get really upset. It's the same with social workers. If they want an answer, give them an answer, but keep the truth to yourself. I told Detective Sergeant Michael Sussex the address of a hostel in Walworth.

He was walking us in the direction of the Trenches, and I didn't want to go there. So I said, "I've had my breakfast and I ought to go because I've got an appointment with my social worker."

It was a mistake because then he wanted to know who my social worker was and what time I had to be there. Lies breed. It's much better if you don't talk to the Law because then you can keep to the truth.

After a while he said, "Aren't you a bit young to be living on your own . . . Doreen?"

"I'm eighteen," I said. I felt depressed. I hadn't spoken one honest word to the man since he dropped his big hand on my shoulder. Well, you can't, can you? I talked to a social worker once and she tried to put Dawn and me in care. Never again. They would have split us up and then Dawn would never have found herself a man. Say what you like about Dawn's boyfriend, but he did set her up in business, and she does make good money. She feels real. No one can feel real in care.

We were right next to the Trenches by now. For a change it looked completely deserted—no winos, no bonfires, none of us picking through the rubbish dumped there in the night. It's just a big demolition site really, but since no one is in any hurry to build there, it's become home to all sorts of people.

Detective Sergeant Michael Sussex stopped. He said, "We found a body in there last night."

I said nothing. I couldn't see the bit of wall the dead man had been sitting by, but I knew where it was.

"Yes," he said, as if he was thinking about something else. "Stripped clean, he was. When it comes my turn I'd like to be somewhere no one can get their thieving hands on me."

I was still watching his feet, and now even his boots looked as if they were thinking about something else. So I took off.

I broke clear of his hand. I dodged between two people passing by and hopped over the wire. Then I dropped down into the Trenches.

It was the last place I wanted to be, but it was the only place I could go.

I heard him come down behind me, and as I ran through the rubble I could feel his feet thudding onto the ground. He was awfully fast for a big man.

"Stop!" he yelled, and I kept running. This way, that way, over the brickwork, round the rubbish tips, into cellars, up steps. And all the time I could hear his feet and his breath. I couldn't get free of him.

I was getting tired when I saw the drain. I put on one more sprint and dived headfirst into it. It was the only thing I could think of to do. It was the only place he couldn't come after me.

It was the only place I couldn't get out of.

I know about the drain. I've been in there before to get out of the wind, but it doesn't go anywhere. There is a bend about ten yards from the opening and after that it's very wet and all stopped up with earth.

Anyway, like it or not, I dived straight in and crawled down. There wasn't much room even for me. I had to get all the way to the bend before I could turn round.

It was totally dark in the drain. There should have been a circle of light at the opening but Detective Sergeant Michael Sussex had his head and shoulders wedged in it.

He said, "Don't be a fool, Crystal. Come out of there!" His voice boomed.

"Look, I only want a chat," he said. "I'm not going to hurt you."

He wasn't going to hurt me as long as I stayed in the drain and he stayed out of it.

"Come and get me," I said. I would have felt quite cheerful if it hadn't been so dark and wet.

"I don't know what you think you're up to, Crystal," he said. "But you're in a lot of trouble. I can help you."

I nearly laughed. "I don't know any Crystals," I said. "How can you help me?"

"You've got enemies," he said. "The bloke who died had the same enemies. You took something off him and now they're looking for you. They're rough people, Crystal, and you need my help."

"I don't know any dead blokes," I said. "I didn't take anything. What am I supposed to have nicked?"

"You're wasting my time," he said.

"All right," I said. "Then I'll go." There wasn't anywhere to go, but I didn't think he'd know that.

"Wait," he said. "Don't go anywhere till you've heard what I have to say." He fell silent. It was what I always thought. You tell them things. They'd rather eat worms before they tell you something back.

After a bit he said, "You still there?"

"I'm still here," I said. "But not for long. I'm getting wet."

"All right," he said. "You won't understand this, but I'll tell you anyway. The dead bloke was a systems analyst."

"What's one of them?" I asked.

"He was a computer expert." Detective Sergeant Michael Sussex sighed. I could hear it from my end of the drain. Sound travels in a drain.

"He wrote programs for computers. He debugged programs. But most of all he wrote safe programs." He sighed again.

"This doesn't mean anything to you," he said. "Why don't you just come out of there like a good girl and give me the number."

"What number?" I said. He was right. I didn't understand. I was very confused. I thought I was in trouble because I'd taken the wallet. I tried to give it back but the woman wouldn't take it. That was confusing. Whoever heard of anyone not taking money when it was offered.

"It doesn't matter what number," he said, sounding angry. "This bloke, this Philip Walker-Jones, he worked for some very funny types. These types don't keep their dealings in books or ledgers anymore. Oh no. They stick them on computer tape, or disks where your average copper won't know how to find them. It's all bleeding high tech now."

He sounded very fed up, and I couldn't tell if it was because I was in a drain out of reach, or because he didn't understand high tech any more than I did.

Just then I heard footsteps, and someone said, "What you doing down there, boss?"

"Taking a bleeding mudbath," Detective Sergeant Michael Sussex said. "What does it look like I'm doing?"

"Did you lose her, then?" the other voice said.

"Course not. This is a new interview technique. Orders from on high: 'Do it in a bleeding land-drain.'" He sounded so down I almost laughed.

"Are you still there?" he said.

"No," I said. "Good-bye." And I scrambled into the bend of the pipe and pulled my knees up to my chest so that I couldn't be seen.

"Shit!" Detective Sergeant Michael Sussex said. "You've scared her off, you bleeding berk."

I could hear him heaving and cursing, and then he said, "You'd better give me a pull out of here, Hibbard."

There was some more heaving and cursing, and then I heard his voice from farther off saying, "Where does this bleeding drain come out?"

"Buggered if I know, boss," Hibbard said. "Could be the river for all I know."

"Well, bleeding go and look," Detective Sergeant Michael Sussex said. "And if you find her don't lose her or I'll have you back in uniform quicker than you can say 'crystal balls.'"

"You sure you had the right one?" Hibbard said. He sounded reluctant to go tramping around the Trenches looking for the other end of a drain.

"You saw the description—there can't be two like her."

I didn't like the way he said that, and I didn't like the way he made fun of my name. I was freezing cold and soaked through, but I wasn't going to come out for anyone with that sort of attitude.

So that's where we stayed: him outside in the Trenches and me scrunched up at the end of the drain waiting for him to give up and go away. Sometimes he shone a torch in—to keep himself busy, I suppose. But I stayed stone-still and never made a sound.

Sometimes he paced up and down and muttered foul language to himself. He reminded me of our mum's boyfriend when he thought I'd pinched something off him. We were all at it in those days. He'd pinch things out of our mum's handbag and Dawn and me pinched things off him. We used to hide under the stairs, Dawn and me, while he raged around swearing he'd leather the lights out of us. Sometimes I'd hide from the truant officer too.

I'm used to hiding. All it takes is a bit of patience and a good breakfast in your belly. Don't try it somewhere wet and cold though—that calls for real talent and I wouldn't recommend it to beginners.

At one stage Hibbard came back. He didn't sound half so cocky now.

"She'll be long gone," he said. "I can't find where this thing comes out."

"It's got to come out somewhere," Detective Sergeant Michael Sussex said. "Use your radio. Get more bodies. Make a bleeding effort."

He stayed where he was, and I stayed where I was.

Another time, Hibbard said, "Why don't we get in the Borough Engineers to dig this whole fucking site up and be done with it?"

And another time Detective Sergeant Michael Sussex said, "Comb the bleeding area. She could've dropped it or stashed it." He was sounding cold and tired too.

"All this for a bleeding number," he said. "And if we don't get it our whole case goes down the bleeding bog. Why couldn't the silly sod pick somewhere else to pop his clogs?"

Hibbard said, "Why are we so sure he had it on him? And why are we so sure she's got it now?"

"We know he had it because he was bringing it to me," Detective Sergeant Michael Sussex said. "And we know she got it because she swiped his wallet. We've got everything else back except that and unless he had the number tattooed to his bleeding skull under his bleeding hair that's where it is."

"Couldn't he have just had it in his head?" Hibbard said. "Remembered it?"

"Twenty-five bleeding digits? Do me a favor. He said it was written down and he said I could have it. You just want to go indoors for your dinner. Well, no one gets any dinner till I get that kid."

So we all sat there without our dinners. Detective Sergeant Michael Sussex made everyone go hungry for nothing. Because I didn't have any number twenty-five digits long.

But it's no use worrying about what you don't have, especially when what really worries you is what you might get. I was worried I might get pneumonia. If you get sick you can't feed yourself. If you can't feed yourself you get weak, and then either the officials grab you and put you in a hospital, or you die. I've seen it happen.

And I'll tell you something else—a very funny thing happened when I got out of the drain. Well, it wasn't a thing, and it didn't really happen. But I thought it did and it really frightened me.

I became an old woman.

It was when I looked round the bend and couldn't see the circle of light at the end of the drain. I strained my ears and I couldn't hear anything moving out there. And suddenly I thought I'd gone deaf and blind.

I tried to move, but I was so stiff with cold it took me ages to inch my way along to the opening. I didn't care if Detective Sergeant Michael Sussex caught me. In fact, I called out to him, and my voice had gone all weak and husky. I wanted him to be there, if you can believe that. I actually wanted him to help me, see, because I thought I'd gone blind, and I was scared.

But he wasn't there, and it was dark and teeming down with rain. And I couldn't straighten up. My back was bent, my knees were bent. There was no strength in my legs. I couldn't have run if they'd set the dogs on me.

I was an old woman out there in the dark—looking at the puddles in the mud, shuffling along, bent over. And I thought about Bloody Mary and the way she is first thing of a morning. There are some of them even older than she is who never have to bend over to look in dustbins because that's the shape they always are.

Of course, I come to my senses soon enough. I got my circulation back and I rubbed the stiffness out of my legs. And I knew it was truly dark. I hadn't gone blind. But I did not stop being scared.

Even standing upright I felt helpless. Even with seven hundred and forty-three pounds, eighty-nine pence in my pockets. The Law was after me. The bastards who beat up little Marvin were after me. And I had nowhere to go. I was sick and old, and I needed help. What I needed, I thought, was a mark of my own.

Once having thought that, I became a little more cheerful. Not a lot, mind, because I hadn't had anything to eat since that curry before daybreak and being hungry brings on the blues like nothing else can. But I pulled myself together and went looking for my mark.

I didn't know her name, but I knew where to find her. It was up the other end of the northern line. I couldn't have walked it that night, not for love nor money. So I caught the tube to Chalk Farm, and I hung around outside one of those bookshops.

I thought I had her once, but she tightened her grip on her shopping and hurried away. It was a mistake I put down to hunger. Usually I don't go wrong on middle-aged women.

But I saw her at last. She was wearing a fawn-colored raincoat and a tartan scarf. She had a green umbrella and she was struggling with her Christmas shopping.

I said, "Carry your bags for you, Missus?"

She hesitated. I knew her. She's the one who has her handbag open before you even ask. She doesn't give you any mouth about finding a job or spending money on drink. She just looks sort of sorry and she watches you when you walk away.

She hesitated, but then she gave me a bag to carry. Not the heaviest one either. She's nice. She wants to trust me. At least she doesn't want to distrust me. I knew her. She was my mark.

She said, "Thank you very much. The car is just round the corner."

I followed her and stood in the rain while she fumbled with her umbrella and car keys. I put her bag in the boot and helped her with the other one.

She looked at me and hesitated again. Not that she'd dream of going off without giving me something. This one just wants to find a polite way of doing it.

She said, "Well, thanks very much," and she started to fumble in her handbag again. I let her get her money out, and then I said, "I don't want your money, Missus, thanks all the same for the thought."

She said, "Oh, but you must let me give you something."

I just stood there shaking my head, looking pitiful.

"What is it?" she asked, with that sorry expression on her face.

It was the crucial time. I said. "I've got some money, Missus, but I can't spend it." And I held out one of the fifty-pound notes.

She looked at the money and she looked at me.

I said, "I know what you're thinking. That's why I can't spend it. I want to get some decent clothes because I can't get a job looking like this. But every time I try they look at me like I stole the money and they go to call the Law. No one trusts people like me."

She went on looking first at me and then at the money, and said, "I don't mean to sound suspicious, but where *did* you get a fifty-pound note?"

"A nice lady give it to me," I said. "She must've thought it was a fiver. She was a really nice lady because no one's ever given me a fiver before. But when I went in to buy a cup of tea and some chips the man went to call the Law and I saw she must have made a mistake."

"I see," she said.

"You don't," I said. "Having this money is worse than not having anything."

"I can see that," she said. "How can I help?"

I had her. "Please, Missus," I said. "Please help me spend it. All I want's a good coat and some shoes. There's a charity shop just round the corner and I been hanging around for ages but I can't bring myself to go in on my own."

She was good as gold, my lady mark. She bought me a big wool coat for only a couple of quid and she talked to the women in the shop while I looked for jeans and jerseys.

It was all quality stuff and probably it was all donated to the charity by women like her. They don't give any old rubbish to charity. And I'll tell you something else—my lady mark was having the time of her life. It was like a dream come true to her. Someone really and truly wanted her help with something she approved of. She didn't have to worry I was spending her money on drink or drugs because it wasn't her money and I was there under her nose spending it on warm clothes.

Even the women behind the counter had a sort of glow on them when I came out from behind the racks with my arms full. She'd probably told them my story in whispers when my back was turned. And that was why I really had needed her help. Because those nice ladies behind the counter would have chased me out if I'd gone in on my own. They'd have been afraid I'd pinch their charity.

It was still coming down in buckets when we left the shop. This time it was me carrying all the bags.

I was about to go when she said, "Look, don't be insulted, but what you need is a hot bath and somewhere to change." She said it in a rush as if she really was afraid of hurting my feelings.

"I live up the hill," she said. "It won't take any time at all."

"Nah," I said. "I'll get your car seats all dirty."

"It doesn't matter," she said. "Please."

And I thought, *Why not?* She deserved the satisfaction.

She ran me a hot bath and squirted loads of scented oil in. She gave me her shampoo and a whole heap of clean towels. And then my lovely lady mark left me alone in her bathroom.

I swear she had tears in her eyes when I came out in my new clothes.

"Crystal," she said, "you look like a new person." This was just what I wanted to hear.

"You look quite like my own daughter when she was younger," she said. Which was a good thing because the Law and the bastards who beat Marvin up weren't looking for someone who looked like my lady mark's daughter. And no one would bat an eyelash if she had a fifty-pound note. My lady mark's daughter would not turn into an old woman who didn't have to bend over to root around in dustbins.

And nor, I thought, *would I, if I could help it.*

She cooked me eggs and potatoes for my tea, and when I left she gave me a fiver and her green umbrella.

It was a shame, really, to have pinched her soap. But you can't break old habits all at once.

She even wanted to give me another ride in her car. But I wouldn't let her. She was a lovely lady, but I didn't think she'd understand about Dawn. Lovely ladies don't.

I could give lessons about what to do when you find your mark, and the last one would be: Don't push your luck. Because if you push your luck and let them take over they start giving you what they think you need instead of what you want. If my lady mark knew too much about Dawn and what was really going on she'd have got in touch with the Social Services all over again. And far from being a lovely lady she'd have turned into an interfering old cow.

I was doing her a favor really. I'm sure she'd rather be a lovely lady than an interfering old cow.

No one who saw me knocking at Dawn's door in Paddington would have known I'd spent all day down a drain. Dawn didn't.

" 'Struth, Crystal," she said when she opened up. "You look like one of those girls from that snob school up the hill from ours."

I knew what she meant and I didn't like it much. But I was lucky really. I'd caught her at a slack time when she was just lying around reading her comics and playing records. And now I was all clean and respectable she didn't mind if I sat on her bed.

"You still need your hair cut," Dawn said.

She got out her scissors and manicure set, and we sat on her bed while she cut my hair and did my nails. Dawn could be a beautician if she wanted. The trouble is she'd never stand for the training and the money wouldn't be enough. She's used to her creature comforts now, is Dawn.

It was a bit like the old days—Dawn and me together listening to records, and her fiddling with my hair. I didn't want to spoil it but I had to ask about the watch.

Because when I was in the lovely lady's bathroom I'd had another search through Philip Walker-Jones's wallet.

Dawn said, "What about the watch?" And she rubbed round my thumb with her little nail file.

"It was real gold," I said, to remind her. "Your Christmas present."

"I can't wear a man's watch," she said. Dawn likes to be very dainty sometimes.

"Where is it?" I said.

"You want it back?" she asked. "Fine Christmas present if you want it back."

I looked at her and she looked at me. Then she said, "Well, Crystal, if you must know, I was going to give it to my boyfriend for Christmas."

"It wasn't for him," I said. "It was for you."

"A man's watch?" she said, and laughed. "I was going to get his name engraved on the back. 'Eternal love, from Dawn.' But there wasn't room. There were all these numbers on the back, and the man at the jewelers said I'd lose too much gold having them rubbed down."

"Hah!" I said. I felt clever. Because all it takes is some good hot food to help you think. And it had come to me in a flash just after I'd put down my last mouthful of egg and potato.

I said, "Bet there were twenty-five of them."

"Loads of numbers," she said. She put the nail file back in her manicure set.

"If you must know, Crystal," she said, "I popped it. And I bought him a real gold cigarette lighter instead."

And she gave me the pawn ticket.

She hadn't got much for a solid gold watch. Dawn isn't practical like I am, so the pawnbroker cheated her. Not that it mattered. It wasn't her watch in the first place, and besides, it would cost me less to get back. If I wanted it back.

Poor Dawn. She needs me to take care of her. She doesn't think she does because she thinks her boyfriend's doing it. She's not like me. She doesn't want to look after herself. That's not her job. And if I told her what I'd been through today to solve my own problems she'd say I was a fool.

But look at it this way—I'd given Detective Sergeant Michael Sussex the slip. I'd dressed up so he wouldn't know me again if I ran slap-bang into him. Nor would Brainy Brian. So he couldn't finger me to the bastards who beat up little Marvin. I'd had a bath and I'd had eggs and potatoes for my tea. I had enough money to sleep in a bed for as many nights as I wanted. And now I had the watch.

Or I could have it any time I wanted. But it was safer where it was. I still didn't know why the number was so important but I was sure it would be worth something to me sooner or later.

I saw Dawn looking at me.

"Don't get too cocky, Crystal," she said. "You might *look* like a girl from the snob school but you're still just like me."

That's how much she knew.

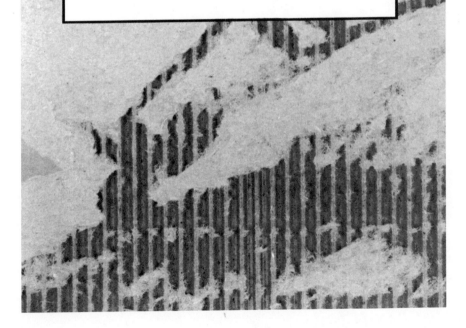

Death of the
Right Fielder

STUART DYBEK

AFTER TOO MANY BALLS WENT OUT AND NEVER CAME BACK WE went out to check. It was a long walk—he always played deep. Finally we saw him, from the distance resembling the towel we sometimes threw down for second base.

It was hard to tell how long he'd been lying there, sprawled on his face. Had he been playing infield his presence, or lack of it, would, of course, have been noticed immediately. The infield demands communication—the constant, reassuring chatter of team play. But he was remote, clearly an outfielder (the temptation is to say *outsider*). The infield is for wisecrackers, pepper-pots, gum-poppers; the outfield is for loners, onlookers, brooders who would rather study clover and swat gnats than holler. People could pretty much be divided between infielders and outfielders. Not that one always has a choice. He didn't necessarily choose right field so much as accept it.

There were several theories as to what killed him. From the start the most popular was that he'd been shot. Perhaps from a passing car, possibly by that gang calling themselves the Jokers who played sixteen-inch softball on the concrete diamond with painted bases, in the center of the housing project, or by the Latin Lords who didn't play sports, period. Or maybe some pervert with a telescopic sight from a bedroom window, or a mad sniper from a water tower, or a terrorist with a silencer from the expressway overpass, or maybe it was an accident, a stray slug from a robbery, or shoot-out, or assassination attempt miles away.

No matter who pulled the trigger it seemed more plausible to ascribe his death to a bullet than to natural causes like, say, a heart attack. Young deaths are never natural; they're all violent. Not that kids don't die of heart attacks. But he never seemed the type. Sure, he was quiet, but not the quiet of someone always listening to the heart murmur his family has repeatedly warned him about since he was old enough to play. Nor could it have been leukemia. He wasn't a talented enough athlete to die of that. He'd have been playing center, not right, if leukemia was going to get him.

The shooting theory was better, even though there wasn't a mark on him. Couldn't it have been, as some argued, a high-powered bullet traveling with such velocity that its hole fuses behind it? Still, not everyone was satisfied. Other theories were formulated; rumors became legends over the years: he'd had an allergic reaction to a bee sting; been struck by a single bolt of lightning from a freak, instantaneous electric storm; ingested too strong a dose of insecticide from the grass blades he chewed on; sonic waves; radiation; pollution; etc. And a few of us liked to think it was simply that chasing a sinking liner, diving to make a shoestring catch, he broke his neck.

There *was* a ball in the webbing of his mitt when we turned him over. His mitt had been pinioned under his body and was coated with an almost luminescent gray film. There was the same gray on his black, high-top gym shoes, as if he'd been running through lime, and along the bill of his baseball cap—the blue felt one with the red C, which he always denied stood for the Chicago Cubs. He may have been a loner, but he didn't want to be identified with a loser. He lacked the sense of humor for that, lacked the perverse pride that sticking up for losers season after season breeds, and the love. He was just an ordinary guy, .250

at the plate, and we stood above him not knowing what to do next. By then the guys from the other outfield positions had trotted over. Someone, the shortstop probably, suggested team prayer. But no one could think of a team prayer. So we all just stood there silently, bowing our heads, pretending to pray while the shadows moved darkly across the outfield grass. After a while the entire diamond was swallowed and the field lights came on.

In the bluish squint of those lights he didn't look like someone we'd once known—nothing looked quite right—and we hurriedly scratched a shallow grave, covered him over, and stamped it down as much as possible so that the next right fielder, whoever he'd be, wouldn't trip. It could be just a juvenile, seemingly trivial stumble that would ruin a great career before it had begun, or hamper it years later the way Mantle's was hampered by bum knees. One can never be sure the kid beside him isn't another Roberto Clemente; and who can ever know how many potential Great Ones have gone down in the obscurity of their neighborhoods? And so, in the catcher's phrase, we "buried the grave" rather than contribute to any further tragedy. In all likelihood the next right fielder, whoever he'd be, would be clumsy too, and if there was a mound to trip over he'd find it and break *his* neck, and soon right field would get the reputation as haunted, a kind of sandlot Bermuda Triangle, inhabited by phantoms calling for ghostly fly balls, where no one but the most desperate outcasts, already on the verge of suicide, would be willing to play.

Still, despite our efforts, we couldn't totally disguise it. A fresh grave is stubborn. Its outline remained visible—a scuffed bald spot that might have been confused for an aberrant pitcher's mound except for the bat jammed in earth with the mitt and blue cap fit over it. Perhaps we didn't want to eradicate it completely—a part of us was resting there. Perhaps we wanted the new right fielder, whoever he'd be, to notice and wonder about who played there before him, realizing he was now the only link between past and future that mattered. A monument, epitaph, flowers wouldn't be necessary.

As for us, we walked back, but by then it was too late—getting on to supper, getting on to the end of summer vacation, time for other things, college, careers, settling down and raising a family. Past thirty-five the talk starts about being over the hill, about a graying Phil Niekro in his forties still fanning them with the knuckler as if it's some kind of miracle, about Pete Rose still going in headfirst at forty-two, beating the odds. And maybe the talk is right. One remembers Mays, forty-two and a Met, dropping that can-of-corn fly in the '73 Series, all that grace stripped away and with it the conviction, leaving a man confused and apologetic about the boy in him. It's sad to admit it ends so soon, but everyone knows those are the lucky ones. Most guys are washed up by seventeen.

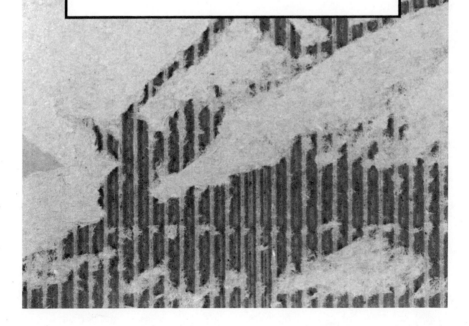

The Dare

CAROL ELLIS

"**Y**OU'RE NOT GOING TO CHICKEN OUT, ARE YOU?" JIM'S VOICE was taunting.

Phil jammed his fists into his armpits. "I'm thinking," he whispered.

"Yeah, well don't," Jim said. "Just do it."

Phil gritted his teeth and stared at the back of the house. He'd seen it from the front plenty of times, but never from the back, at night.

It was a skinny old house, two stories high. It sat on top of a rise at the end of the street, a little apart from the rest of the neighborhood, and it had been empty for more than a year. Then this morning, according to Jim, a moving van had arrived. The movers had unloaded boxes and rugs and furniture and then left. Now the house was dark again.

"Perfect timing," Jim had said in homeroom earlier that day. "Whoever bought it's not going to be there tonight. Probably moving in tomorrow. Now's our chance to give 'em a little welcome."

The welcome Jim had in mind had nothing to do with giving. For the past few weeks, he and his two buddies, Denny and Mike, had been bragging to Phil about their latest form of recreation:

They'd cruise around, pick a house they were sure was empty, break in, and take something. Nothing major, like a TV or a VCR. Not even money. Just something small—a vase, maybe, or a photograph. Something to prove they'd done it. Jim got a kick out of imagining the owners accusing each other of moving the vase or wondering what had happened to that little dog statue. He and Denny and Mike called the stuff they took their trophies.

Phil thought they were crazy, and he'd made the mistake of telling them so.

"Yeah, but that's the point," Jim had said. His brown eyes glittered as he smiled. "It's a crazy, risky kick, don't you get it?"

"Nah, he doesn't get it, Jim," Mike had said. "Phil's idea of a risk is not doing his homework. He'd be too scared to do what we do."

Denny made chicken sounds and snickered.

"I wouldn't be too scared," Phil said without thinking.

"You wouldn't?" Jim's smile widened into a grin. "Then prove it, Phillie. Tonight."

Phil could have backed out, but he didn't. He'd taken Jim up on the dare. And now here he was, standing at the back of the house, trying to convince himself it was the night air that was making him shiver.

Jim nudged him with his shoulder. "Go on," he whispered. "Show me how brave you are, Phillie. It's only an empty house."

Phil shoved him away and pushed through a hedge into the backyard. It was overgrown and littered with dry leaves that crunched under his feet. Phil kept his eyes on the back door and tried to ignore the noise he was making. He kept telling himself there was nobody inside and no neighbors near enough to hear.

When he reached the wooden back steps, he stopped and looked over his shoulder. Jim's face was a pale blur at the far end of the yard. He was watching, waiting for Phil to cut and run.

Phil put one foot on the bottom step, then slowly brought his other foot up. As his weight shifted, the wood creaked, and his heart knocked against his chest so hard it made him dizzy.

The next two steps were silent. As Phil curled his fingers around the screen-door handle, the sweat started trickling down his back and the sides of his face. Gingerly, he pulled on the door, and it opened with a loud whine. Phil's breath came out in a rush. His back and face were slick with sweat, but his mouth was so dry he could hardly swallow.

He counted to ten, listening. He heard a dog barking somewhere far away and the rustle of leaves and branches in the wind.

Cautiously, Phil tested the handle on the inside door. It turned with a snap that sounded like a firecracker and the door swung in on its hinges. They'd forgotten to lock it.

Phil grabbed it before it banged against a wall. His knees felt wobbly. He strained his ears, listening for sounds. The dog had stopped barking. All he heard was the wind and his heartbeat.

Get it over with, he thought. *Just go in and get it over with.* Turning sideways, still holding onto the door, Phil slipped through the narrow opening and found himself in inky darkness. He was inside the house.

He stood perfectly still and listened. A branch scraping on the roof. His heart thudding in his ears. The regular, monotonous tick of a clock.

Easing the door in a little more, Phil took one step, then another. The floor was hard under his sneakers. No rug to cushion any sound he made. He still couldn't see anything. He held one arm out, let go of the back door, and took a third step.

The floor creaked and he froze. There was a click, and he gasped out loud, already turning, ready to run. But the click was followed by a low, mechanical whir, and he suddenly knew what it was. The refrigerator. Not in this room, though. Farther inside the house.

Phil took another step. His outstretched hand bumped against something. He pulled back, then reached out again. It was a box, maybe a stack of them. Carefully, he felt along the edges of the box, up to the top. The flaps were folded in, but all he had to do was pry them open and pull out the first thing he touched.

129

Slowly, he lifted the edge of a flap. The cardboard shrieked. Wincing at the noise, Phil pulled all the flaps up at once and plunged his hand into the box. His fingers closed around something smooth and square. He didn't know what it was, didn't care. He was getting out.

Turning, he took a step away from the box. The floor squeaked again. And suddenly the darkness disappeared. Light spilled into the room from another door, and a shadow, a human shadow, loomed on the wall.

"Who's there?" a voice cried. It was a woman's voice, frightened but strong. "Is someone there?"

Before the woman had finished calling out, Phil was through the back door and stumbling down the steps. He raced through the crackling leaves, tore through the hedge, and then let out a yelp of fear as a figure rose up before him.

"Hey, Phillie!" Jim reached out and grabbed Phil's arm. "What's your rush?"

"There was a woman in there!" Phil gasped. "You said it was empty!"

"Wrong. I said it was *probably* empty." Jim leaned closer. "Hey, I thought you were going to be brave, but you look like you're ready to wet your pants. Better get on home." Laughing softly, he shot out his hand and grabbed the object Phil had taken from the box. "Thanks for the trophy," he said. Then he ran off, leaving Phil to walk home alone.

Phil finally saw what he'd stolen the next morning in homeroom before their teacher came in. It was a small wooden plaque with a tennis racket carved into it. The metal strip at the bottom was engraved with the words "Doubles. First Place. Eva Morrisey."

Jim had waved it in front of Phil's face when he first walked in. Now he was huddled with Denny and Mike and taking credit for the whole thing. "It was great!" he crowed. "I could hear her snoring while I was creeping around in the dark. I even started upstairs. I thought I'd swipe a bedroom slipper or something, but I didn't want to push my luck." He laughed. "Next time, for sure."

Denny and Mike grinned and shook their heads in admiration, and then Jim glanced at Phil. "Not bad, huh?" he said. He turned back to his buddies. "Phillie chickened out, surprise, surprise."

Phil started to say something, to tell them Jim was a liar, but just as he opened his mouth, the teacher came in.

She started toward her desk, smiling around the room. Then she changed direction.

She stopped in front of Jim. Her smile had faded. In a voice Phil had heard before, she said, "I'm your substitute this morning. My name is Miss Morrisey." She took the plaque from Jim's hand, looked at it, then looked back at Jim. "Eva Morrisey," she said.

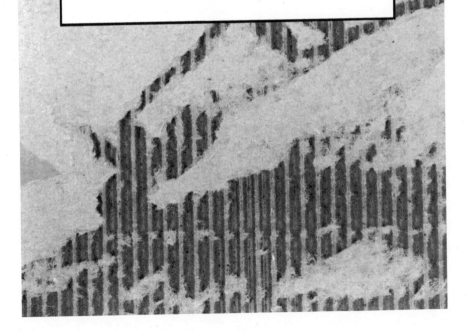

Why Herbert
Killed
His Mother

WINIFRED HOLTBY

ONCE UPON A TIME THERE WAS A MODEL MOTHER WHO HAD A Prize Baby. Nobody had ever had such a Baby before. He was a Son, of course. All prize babies are masculine, for should there be a flaw in their gender this might deprive them of at least 25 percent of the marks merited by their prize-worthiness.

The Mother's name was Mrs. Wilkins, and she had a husband called Mr. Wilkins, but he did not count much. It is true that he was the Baby's father, and on the night after the child was born he stood Drinks All Round at the Club; though he was careful to see that there were only two other members in the bar at the time he suggested it, because although one must be a Good Father and celebrate properly, family responsibilities make a man remember his bank balance. Mr. Wilkins remembered his very often, particularly when Mrs. Wilkins bought a copy of *Vogue*, or remarked that the Simpsons, who lived next door but one, had changed their Austin Seven for a Bentley. The Wilkinses had not even an old Ford; but then the buses passed the end of their road, and before the Prize Baby arrived, Mrs. Wilkins went to the stores and ordered a very fine pram.

Mrs. Wilkins had determined to be a Real Old-Fashioned Mother. She had no use for these Modern Women who Drink

Cocktails, Smoke Cigarettes, and dash about in cars at all hours with men who are not their husbands. She believed in the true ideal of Real Womanliness, Feminine Charm, and the Maternal Instinct. She won a ten-shilling prize once from a daily paper, with a circulation of nearly two million, for saying so, very prettily, on a postcard.

Before the Baby came she sat with her feet up every afternoon sewing little garments. She made long clothes with twenty tucks round the hem of each robe and embroidered flannels, fifty inches from hem to shoulder tape, and fluffy bonnets and teeny-weeny little net veils; she draped a bassinet with white muslin and blue ribbons, and she thought a great deal about violets, forget-me-nots, and summer seas in order that her baby might have blue eyes. When Mrs. Burton from The Acacias told her that long clothes were unhygienic, and that drapery on the bassinet held the dust, and that heredity had far more to do with blue eyes than thoughts about forget-me-nots, she shook her head charmingly and said, "Ah, well. You *clever* women know so much. I can only go by what my darling mother told me." Mrs. Burton said, "On the contrary. You have a lot of other authority to go by nowadays," and she produced three pamphlets, a book on infant psychology, and a program of lectures on "Health, Happiness, and Hygiene in the Nursery." But Mrs. Wilkins sighed, and said, "My poor little brain won't take in all that stuff. I have only my Mother Love to guide me." And she dropped a pearly tear onto a flannel binder.

Mrs. Burton went home and told Mr. Burton that Mrs. Wilkins was hopeless, and that her baby would undoubtedly suffer from adenoids, curvature of the spine, flat feet, halitosis, bow legs, indigestion, and the Oedipus complex. Mr. Burton said, "Quite, quite." And everyone was pleased.

The only dissentient was the Wilkins baby, who was born without any defect whatsoever. He was a splendid boy, and his more-than-proud parents had him christened Herbert James Rodney Stephen Christopher, which names they both agreed went very well with Wilkins. He wore for the ceremony two binders, four flannels, an embroidered robe with twenty handmade tucks, a woolly coat, two shawls, and all other necessary and unnecessary garments, and when he stared into the rector's face and screamed lustily, his aunts said, "That means he'll be musical, bless him." But his mother thought, *What a strong will he has! And what sympathy there is between us! Perhaps he knows already what I think about the rector.*

As long as the monthly nurse was there, Mrs. Wilkins and Herbert got along very nicely on Mother Love; but directly after she left the trouble began.

"My baby," Mrs. Wilkins had said, "shall never be allowed to lie awake and cry like Mrs. Burton's poor little wretch. Babies need cuddling." So whenever Herbert cried at first, she cuddled him. She cuddled him in the early morning when he woke up Mr. Wilkins and wanted his six o'clock bottle at four. She cuddled him at half past six and half past seven and eight. She cuddled him half-hourly for three days and then she smacked him. It was a terrible thing to do, but she did it. She fed him when he seemed hungry and showed him to all the neighbors who called and kept him indoors when it rained, which it did every day, and nursed him while she had her own meals and when she didn't give him Nestlé's. And he still flourished.

But what with the crying and the washing that hung in the garden, the neighbors began to complain, and Mrs. Burton said, "Of course, you're killing that child."

Mrs. Wilkins knew that the Maternal Instinct was the safest guide in the world; but when her husband showed her an advertisement in the evening paper which began: "Mother, does your child cry?" she read it. She learned there that babies cry because their food does not agree with them. "What-not's Natural Digestive Infants' Milk solves the Mother's problem." Mrs. Wilkins thought that no stone should be left unturned and bought a specimen tin of What-not's Natural Digestive Infants' Milk and gave it to Herbert. Herbert flourished. He grew larger and rounder and pinker and more dimpled than ever. But he still cried.

So Mrs. Wilkins read another advertisement in the evening paper. And there she learned that when babies cry it is because they are not warm enough, and that all good mothers should buy Flopsy's Fleecy Pram Covers. So, being a good mother, she bought a Flopsy's Fleecy Pram Cover and wrapped Herbert in it. And still Herbert flourished. And still he cried.

So she continued to read the evening papers, for by this time both she and Mr. Wilkins were nearly distracted, and one of the neighbors threatened to complain to the landlord, and Mrs. Simpson kept her loudspeaker going all night and day to drown the noise, she said. And now Mrs. Wilkins learned that the reason her baby cried was because his Elimination was inadequate, so she bought him a bottle of Hebe's Nectar for the Difficult Child and gave him a teaspoon every morning. But still he cried.

Then the spring came, and the sun shone, and the bulbs in the garden of Number Seven were finer than they had ever been before, and Mrs. Wilkins put Herbert out in the garden in his pram, and he stopped crying.

She was such a nice woman and such a proud mother that she wrote at once to the proprietors of What-not's Natural Digestive Infants' Milk and Flopsy's Fleecy Pram Covers and Hebe's Nectar for the Difficult Child and told them that she had bought their things for Herbert and that he had stopped crying.

Two days later a sweet young woman came to the Wilkins' house, and said that What-not's Limited had sent her to see Herbert, and what a fine baby he was, and how healthy, and could she take a photograph? And Mrs. Wilkins was very pleased and thought, *Well, Herbert is the most beautiful baby in the world, and won't this be a sell for Mrs. Burton,* and was only too delighted. So the young woman photographed Herbert in his best embroidered robe drinking Natural Digestive Infants' Milk from a bottle and went away.

The next day a kind old man came from Flopsy's Fleecy Pram Covers Limited and photographed Herbert lying under a Fleecy Pram Cover. It was a hot afternoon and a butterfly came and settled on the pram; but the kind old man said that this was charming.

The next day a scientific-looking young man with horn-rimmed spectacles came from Hebe's Nectar Limited and photographed Herbert lying on a fur rug wearing nothing at all. And when Mr. Wilkins read his Sunday paper, there he saw his very own baby, with large black capitals printed above him, saying: "My Child Is Now No Longer Difficult, declares Mrs. Wilkins, of Number 9, The Grove, SW10."

Mrs. Burton saw it too, and said to Mr. Burton, "No wonder, when at last they've taken a few stones of wool off the poor little wretch."

But Mr. and Mrs. Wilkins saw it differently. They took Herbert to a Court photographer and had him taken dressed and undressed, with one parent, with both parents, standing up and sitting down; and always he was the most beautiful baby that the Wilkinses had ever seen.

One day they saw an announcement in a great Sunday paper of a £10,000 prize for the loveliest baby in the world. "Well, dear, this will be nice," said Mrs. Wilkins. "We shall be able to buy a saloon car now." Because, of course, she knew that Herbert would win the prize.

And so he did. He was photographed in eighteen different poses for the first heat; then he was taken for a personal inspection in private for the second heat; then he was publicly exhibited at the Crystal Palace for the semifinals, and for the Final Judgment he was set in a pale blue bassinet and examined by three doctors, two nurses, a child psychologist, a film star, and Mr. Cecil Beaton. After that he was declared the Most Beautiful Baby in Britain.

That was only the beginning. Baby Britain had still to face Baby France, Baby Spain, Baby Italy, and Baby America. Signor Mussolini sent a special message to Baby Italy, which the other national competitors thought unfair. The Free State insisted upon sending twins, who were disqualified. The French president cabled inviting the entire contest to be removed to Paris, and the Germans declared that the girl known as Baby Poland, having been born in the Polish Corridor, was really an East Prussian and should be registered as such.

But it did not matter. These international complications made no difference to Herbert. Triumphantly he overcame all his competitors and was crowned as World Baby on the eve of his first birthday.

Then, indeed, began a spectacular period for Mr. and Mrs. Wilkins. Mrs. Wilkins gave interviews to the press on "The Power of Mother Love," "The Sweetest Thing in the World," and "How I Run My Nursery." Mr. Wilkins wrote some fine manly articles on "Fatherhood Faces Facts," and "A Man's Son"—or, rather, they were written for him by a bright young woman until Mrs. Wilkins decided that she should be present at the collaborations.

Then a firm of publishers suggested to Mr. Wilkins that he should write a Christmas book called *Herbert's Father*, all about what tender feelings fathers had and what white, pure thoughts ran through their heads when they looked upon the sleeping faces of their sons and about how strange and wonderful it was to watch little images of themselves growing daily in beauty and how gloriously unspotted and magical were the fairylike actions of little children. Mr. Wilkins thought that this was a good idea if someone would write the book for him, and if the advance royalties were not less than £3,000 on the date of publication; but he would have to ask Mrs. Wilkins. Mrs. Wilkins was a trifle hurt. Why *Herbert's Father*? What right had Paternity to override Maternity? The publisher pointed out the success of Mr. A. A. Milne's *Christopher Robin*, and Mr. Lewis Hind's *Julius Caesar*, and of Mr. A. S. M. Hutchinson's *Son Simon*, to say nothing of Sir James Barrie's *Little White Bird*. "But none of these children was my Herbert," declared Mrs. Wilkins— which, indeed, was undeniable. So the contract was finally signed for *The Book of Herbert* by His Parents.

It was a success. Success? It was a Triumph, a Wow, a Scream, an Explosion. There was nothing like it. It was The Christmas Gift. It went into the third hundredth thousand before December 3. It was serialized simultaneously in the *Evening Standard, Home Chat,* and *The Nursery World.* Mr. Baldwin referred to it at a guild-hall banquet. The prince used a joke from it in a broadcast speech on England and the Empire. The Book Society failed to recommend it, but every bookstall in the United Kingdom organized a display stand in its honor, with photographs of Herbert and copies signed with a blot "Herbert, His Mark" exquisitely arranged.

The Herbert boom continued. Small soap Herberts (undressed for the bath) were manufactured and sold for use in delighted nurseries. Royalty graciously accepted an ivory Herbert, designed as a paperweight, from the loyal sculptor. A Herbert Day was instituted in order to raise money for the children's hospitals of England, and thirty-seven different types of Herbert calendars, Christmas cards, and pen wipers were offered for sale—and sold.

Mrs. Wilkins felt herself justified in her faith. This, she said, was what mother love could do. Mr. Wilkins demanded 10 percent royalties on every Herbert article sold. And they all bought a country house near Brighton, a Bentley car, six new frocks for Mrs. Wilkins, and an electric refrigerator and lived happily ever after until Herbert grew up.

But Herbert grew up.

When he was four he wore curls and a Lord Fauntleroy suit and posed for photographers. When he was fourteen he wore jerseys and black fingernails and collected beetles. When he left one of England's Great Public Schools he wore plus fours and pimples and rode a motorcycle and changed his tie three times in half an hour before he called on the young lady at the tobacconist's round the corner. He knew what a Fella does, by Jove, and he knew what a Fella doesn't. His main interests in life were etiquette, Edgar Wallace, and the desire to live down his past. For on going to a preparatory school he had carefully insisted that his name was James. His father, who knew that boys will be boys, supported him, and as he grew to maturity, few guessed that young James Wilkins, whose beauty was certainly not discernible to the naked eye, was Herbert, the Loveliest Baby in the

World. Only Mrs. Wilkins, in a locked spare bedroom, cherished a museum of the Herbert photographs, trophies, first editions, soap images, ivory statuettes, silver cups, and Christmas cards. The Herbert vogue had faded, as almost all vogues do, until not even a gag about Herbert on the music hall stage raised a feeble smile.

But Mrs. Wilkins found the position hard to bear. It is true that the fortunes of the family were soundly laid, that Mr. Wilkins had invested the profits of his son's juvenile triumphs in trustee stock, and that no household in South Kensington was more respected. But Mrs. Wilkins had tasted the sweet nectar of publicity and she thirsted for another drink.

It happened that one day, when (Herbert) James was twenty-three, he brought home the exciting news that he had become engaged to Selena Courtney, the daughter of Old Man Courtney, whose office in the city Herbert adorned for about six hours daily.

Nothing could have been more fortunate. Mr. Wilkins was delighted, for Courtney, of Courtney, Gilbert, and Co., was worth nearly half a million. Herbert was delighted, for he was enjoying the full flavor of Young Love and Satisfied Snobbery combined, which is, as everyone knows, the perfect fulfillment of a True Man's dreams. The Courtneys were delighted, because they thought young Wilkins a very decent young man, with none of this damned nonsense about him. And Mrs. Wilkins—well, her feelings were mixed. It was she, after all, who had produced this marvel, and nobody seemed to remember her part in the production nor to consider the product specially marvelous. Besides, she was a little jealous, as model mothers are allowed to be, of her prospective daughter-in-law.

The engagement was announced in the *Times*—the reporters came, rather bored, to the Kensington home of Mrs. Wilkins. She was asked to supply any details about her son's career. "Any adventures? Any accidents? Has he ever won any prizes?" asked a reporter.

This was too much. "Come here!" said Mrs. Wilkins, and she led the reporters up to the locked spare bedroom.

What happened there was soon known to the public. When (Herbert) James, two evenings later, left the office on his way to his future father-in-law's house in Belgrave Square, hoping to take his fiancée after dinner to a dance given by Lady Soxlet, he was confronted by placards announcing "The Perfect Baby to Wed." Taking no notice he went on to the tube station, but there he saw yet further placards. "The World's Loveliest Baby Now a Man," and "Little Herbert Engaged."

Still hardly conscious of the doom awaiting him, he bought an evening paper, and there he saw in black letters across the front page: "Herbert's Identity at Last Discovered," and underneath the fatal words: "The young City man, Mr. James Wilkins, whose engagement to Miss Selena Courtney, of 299 Belgrave Square, was announced two days ago, has been revealed by his mother, Mrs. Wilkins, to be Herbert, the Wonder Baby." There followed descriptions of the Perfect Childhood; stories taken from the Herbert Legend; rapid advertisements rushed out by What-not's Natural Digestive Infants' Milk, Flopsy's Fleecy Pram Covers, and Hebe's Nectar for the Difficult Child, illustrated by photographs of the Infant Herbert. The publishers of *The Book of Herbert* announced a new edition, and a famous daily paper, whose circulation was guaranteed to be over two million, declared its intention of publishing a series of articles called "My Herbert Is a Man, by Herbert's Mother."

Herbert did not proceed to Belgrave Square. He went to Kensington. With his own latchkey he opened the door and went up to his mother's boudoir. He found her laughing and crying with joy over the evening paper. She looked up and saw her son.

"Oh, darling," she said. "I thought you were taking Selena to a dance."

"There is no Selena," declared Herbert grimly. "There is no dance. There is only you and me."

He should, doubtless, have said "You and I," but among the things a Fella does, correct grammar is not necessarily included.

"Oh, Herbert," cried Mrs. Wilkins, with ecstatic joy. "My mother instinct was right. Mother always knows, darling. You have come back to me."

"I have," said Herbert.

And he strangled her with a rope of twisted newspapers.

The judge declared it justifiable homicide, and Herbert changed his name to William Brown and went to plant tea or rubber or something in the Malay states, where Selena joined him two years later—and Mr. Wilkins lived to a ripe old age and looked after his dividends, and everyone was really very happy after all.

The Girl
Who Loved
Graveyards

P. D. James

S HE COULDN'T REMEMBER ANYTHING ABOUT THE DAY IN THE HOT August of 1956 when they first brought her to live with her aunt Gladys and uncle Victor in the small East London house at 49 Alma Terrace. She knew that it was three days after her tenth birthday and that she was to be cared for by her only living relations now that her father and grandmother were dead, killed by influenza within a week of each other. But those were just facts which someone, at some time, had briefly told her. For her, memory and childhood both began with that moment when, waking in the small unfamiliar bedroom with the kitten, Sambo, still curled asleep on a towel at the foot of her bed, she had walked barefoot to the window and drawn back the curtain.

And there, stretched beneath her, lay the cemetery, luminous and mysterious in the early morning light, bounded by iron railings and separated from the rear of Alma Terrace only by a narrow path. It was to be another warm day, and over the serried rows of headstones there lay a thin haze pierced by the occasional obelisk and by the wing tips of marble angels whose disembodied heads seemed to be floating on particles of shimmering light. And as she watched, motionless in an absorbed enchantment, the mist began to rise and the whole cemetery was revealed to her, a miracle of stone and marble, bright grass and summer-laden trees, flower-bedecked graves and intersection paths stretching as far as her eyes could see. In the far distance she could just make out the top of the Victorian chapel gleaming like the spire of some magical castle in a long-forgotten fairy tale. In those moments of growing wonder she found herself shivering with delight, an emotion so rare that it stole through her thin body like a pain. And it was then, on that first morning of her new life, with the past a void and the future unknown and frightening, that she made the cemetery her own. Throughout her childhood and youth it was to remain a place of delight and mystery, her habitation and her solace.

It was a childhood without love, almost without affection. Her uncle Victor was her father's elder half-brother; that, too, she had been told. He and her aunt weren't really her relations. Their small capacity for love was expended on each other, and even here it was less a positive emotion than a pact of mutual support and comfort against the threatening world that lay outside the trim curtains of their small claustrophobic sitting room.

But they cared for her as dutifully as she cared for the cat Sambo. It was a fiction in the household that she adored Sambo, her own cat, brought with her when she arrived, her one link with the past, almost her only possession. Only she knew that she disliked and feared him. But she brushed and fed him with conscientious care as she did everything and, in return, he gave her a slavish allegiance, hardly ever leaving her side, slinking through the cemetery at her heels, and only turning back when they reached the main gate. But he wasn't her friend. He didn't love her, and he knew that she didn't love him. He was a fellow conspirator, gazing at her through slits of azure light, relishing some secret knowledge that was her knowledge too. He ate voraciously yet he never grew fat. Instead his sleek black body lengthened until, stretched in the sunlight along her windowsill, his sharp nose turned always to the cemetery, he looked as sinister and unnatural as a furred reptile.

It was lucky for her that there was a side gate to the cemetery from Alma Terrace and that she could take a shortcut to and from school across the graveyard, avoiding the dangers of the main road. On her first morning her uncle had said doubtfully, "I suppose it's all right. But it seems wrong somehow, a child walking every day through rows of the dead."

Her aunt had replied, "The dead can't rise from their graves. They lay quiet. She's safe enough from the dead."

Her voice had been unnaturally gruff and loud. The words had sounded like an assertion, almost a defiance. But the child knew that she was right. She did feel safe with the dead, safe and at home.

The years in Alma Terrace slipped by, bland and dull as her aunt's blancmange, a sensation rather than a taste. Had she been happy? It wasn't a question which it had ever occurred to her to ask. She wasn't unpopular at school, being neither pretty nor intelligent enough to provoke much interest either from the children or the staff; an ordinary child, unusual only because she was an orphan but unable to capitalize even on that sentimental advantage. Perhaps she might have found friends, quiet unenterprising children like herself who might have responded to her unthreatening mediocrity. But something about her repelled their timid advances, her self-sufficiency, the bland uncaring gaze, the refusal to give anything of herself even in casual friendship. She didn't need friends. She had the graveyard and its occupants.

She had her favorites. She knew them all, when they had died, how old they had been, sometimes how they had died. She knew their names and learned their memorials by heart. They were more real to her than the living, those rows of dearly loved wives and mothers, respected tradesmen, lamented fathers, deeply mourned children. The new graves hardly ever interested her, although she would watch the funerals from a distance then creep up later to read the mourning cards. But what she liked best were the old neglected oblongs of mounded earth or chipped stones, the tilted crosses, the carved words almost erased by time. It was

round the names of the long dead that she wove her childish
fantasies.

Even the seasons of the year she experienced in and through
the cemetery. The gold and purple spears of the first crocuses
thrusting through the hard earth. April with its tossing daffodils.
The whole graveyard *en fête* in yellow and white as mourners
dressed the graves for Easter. The smell of mown grass and the
earthy tang of high summer as if the dead were breathing the
flower-scented air and exuding their own mysterious miasma.
The glare of sunlight on stone and marble as the old women in
their stained cotton dresses shuffled with their vases to fill them
at the tap behind the chapel. Seeing the cemetery transformed
by the first snow of winter, the marble angels grotesque in their
high bonnets of glistening snow. Watching at her window for the
thaw, hoping to catch that moment when the edifice would slip
and the shrouded shapes become themselves again.

Only once had she asked about her father and then she had
known as children do that this was a subject which, for some
mysterious adult reason, it was better not to talk about. She had
been sitting at the kitchen table with her homework while her
aunt busied herself cooking supper. Looking up from her history
book she had asked, "Where is Daddy buried?"

The frying pan had clattered against the stove. The cooking
fork dropped from her aunt's hand. It had taken her a long time
to pick it up, wash it, clean the grease from the floor. The child
had asked again, "Where is Daddy buried?"

"Up north. At Creedon outside Nottingham with your mum
and gran. Where else?"

"Can I go there? Can I visit him?"

"When you're older, maybe. No sense is there, hanging about
graves. The dead aren't there."

"Who looks after them?"

"The graves? The cemetery people. Now get on with your
homework, do, child. I'll be wanting the table for supper."

She hadn't asked about her mother, the mother who had died

when she was born. That desertion had always seemed to her willful, a source of secret guilt. "You killed your mother." Someone, sometime, had spoken those words to her, had laid on her that burden. She wouldn't let herself think about her mother. But she knew that her father had stayed with her, had loved her, hadn't wanted to die and leave her. Someday, secretly, she would find his grave. She would visit it, not once but every week. She would tend it and plant flowers on it and clip the grass as the old ladies did in the cemetery. And if there wasn't a stone, she would pay for one, not a cross but a gleaming obelisk, the tallest in the graveyard, bearing his name and an epitaph she would choose. She would have to wait until she was older, until she could leave school and work and save enough money. But one day she would find her father. She would have a grave of her own to visit and tend. There was a debt of love to be paid.

Four years after her arrival in Alma Terrace her aunt's only brother came to visit from Australia. Physically he and his sister were alike, the same stolid short-legged bodies, the same small eyes set in square pudgy faces. But Uncle Ned had a brash assurance, a cheerful geniality which was so alien to his sister's unconfident reserve that it was hard to believe that they were siblings. For the two weeks of his visit he dominated the little house with his strident alien voice and assertive masculinity. There were unfamiliar treats, dinners in the West End, a visit to a greyhound stadium, a show at Earl's Court. He was kind to the child, tipping her lavishly, even walking through the cemetery with her one morning to buy his racing paper. And it was that evening, coming silently down the stairs to supper, that she overheard disjointed scraps of conversation, adult talk, incomprehensible at the time but taken into her mind and stored there.

First the harsh boom of her uncle's voice, "We were looking at this gravestone together, see. Beloved husband and father. Taken from us suddenly on 14 March 1892. Something like that. Marble chips, cracked urn, bloody great angel pointing upwards. You know the kind of thing. Then the kid turned to me. 'Daddy's death was sudden, too.' That's what she said. Came out with it cool as you please. Now what in God's name made her say that? I mean, why then? Christ, it gave me a turn, I can tell you. I didn't know where to put my face. And what a place to choose, the bloody cemetery. I'll say one thing for coming out to Sydney. You'll get a better view, I can promise you that."

Creeping closer, she strained her ears vainly to catch the indistinct mutter of her aunt's reply.

Then came her uncle's voice again, "That bitch never forgave him for getting Helen pregnant. No one was good enough for her precious only daughter. And then when Helen died having the kid she blamed him for that, too. Poor sod, he bought a packet of trouble when he set eyes on that girl. Too soft, too romantic. That was always Martin's trouble."

Again the murmur of indistinguishable voices, the sound of her aunt's footsteps moving from table to stove, the scrape of a chair. Then her uncle Ned's voice again.

"Funny kid, isn't she? Old-fashioned. Morbid you might say. Seems to live in that boneyard, she and that damned cat. And the split image of her dad. Christ, it turned me up I can tell you. Looking at me with his eyes and then coming out with it. 'Daddy's death was sudden, too.' I'll say it was! Influenza? Well, it's as good a name for it as any if you can get away with it. Helps having such an ordinary name, I suppose. People don't catch on. How long ago is it now? Four years? It seems longer."

Only one part of this half-heard, incomprehensible conversation had disturbed her. Uncle Ned was trying to persuade them to join him in Australia. She might be taken away from Alma Terrace, might never see the cemetery again, might have to wait for years before she could save enough money to return to England and find her father's grave. And how could she visit it regularly, how could she tend and care for it from the other side of the world? After Uncle Ned's visit ended it was months before she could see one of his rare letters with the Australian stamp drop through the letter box without the cold clutch of fear at the heart.

But she needn't have worried. It was October 1966 before they left England, and they went alone. When they broke the news to her one Sunday morning at breakfast it was apparent that they had never even considered taking her with them. Dutiful as ever, they had waited to make their decision until she had left school and was earning her living as a shorthand typist with a local firm of estate agents. Her future was assured. They had done all that conscience required of them. Hesitant and a little shame-faced they justified their decision as if they believed that it was important to her, that she cared whether they left or stayed. Her aunt's arthritis was increasingly troublesome; they longed for the sun; Uncle Ned was their only close relation and none of them was getting any younger. Their plan, over which they had agonized for months in whispers behind closed doors, was to visit Sydney for six months and then, if they liked Australia, to apply to emigrate. The house in Alma Terrace was to be sold to pay the airfare. It was already on the market. But they had made provision for her. When they told her what had been arranged, she had to bend her face low over her plate in case the flood of joy should be too apparent. Mrs. Morgan, three doors down, would be glad to take her as a lodger if she didn't mind having the small bedroom at the back overlooking the cemetery. In the surging tumult of relief she hardly heard her aunt's next words. There was one small problem. Everyone knew how Mrs. Morgan was about cats. Sambo would have to be put down.

She was to move into 43 Alma Terrace on the afternoon of the day on which her aunt and uncle flew from Heathrow. Her two cases, holding all that she possessed in the world, were already packed. In her handbag she carefully stowed the meager official confirmations of her existence: her birth certificate, her medical card, her post office savings book showing the £103 painstakingly saved toward the cost of her father's memorial. And, the next day, she would begin her search. But first she took Sambo to the vet to be destroyed. She made a cat box from two cartons fitted together, pierced it with holes, then sat patiently in the waiting room with the box at her feet. The cat made no sound and this patient resignation touched her, evoking for the first time a spasm of pity and affection. But there was nothing she could do to save him. They both knew it. But then, he had always known what she was thinking, what was past and what was to come. There was something they shared, some knowledge, some common experience which she couldn't remember and he couldn't express. Now with his destruction even that tenuous link with her first ten years would go forever.

When it was her turn to go into the surgery she said, "I want him put down."

The vet passed his strong experienced hands over the sleek fur. "Are you sure? He seems quite healthy still. He's old, of course, but he's in remarkably good condition."

"I'm sure. I want him put down."

And she left him there without a glance or another word.

She had thought that she would be glad to be free of the pretense of loving him, free of those slitted accusing eyes. But as she walked back to Alma Terrace she found herself crying; tears, unbidden and unstoppable, ran like rain down her face.

There was no difficulty in getting a week's leave from her job. She had been husbanding her holiday entitlement. Her work, as always, was up to date. She had calculated how much money she would need for her train and busfares and for a week's stay in modest hotels. Her plans had been made. They had been made for years. She would begin her search with the address on her birth certificate, Cranstoun House, Creedon, Nottingham, the house where she had been born. The present owners might remember her and her father. If not, there would be neighbors or older inhabitants of the village who would be able to recall her father's death, where he was buried. If that failed she would try the local undertakers. It was, after all, only ten years ago. Someone locally would remember. Somewhere in Nottingham there would be a record of burials. She told Mrs. Morgan that she was taking a week's holiday to visit her father's old home, packed a hold-all with overnight necessities and, next morning, caught the earliest possible fast train from St. Pancras to Nottingham.

It was during the bus ride from Nottingham to Creedon that she felt the first stirrings of anxiety and mistrust. Until then she had traveled in calm confidence, but strangely without excitement, as if this long-planned journey was as natural and inevitable as her daily walk to work, an inescapable pilgrimage ordained from that moment when a barefooted child in her white nightdress had drawn back her bedroom curtains and seen her kingdom spread beneath her. But now her mood changed. As the bus lurched through the suburbs she found herself shifting in her seat as if mental unease were provoking physical discomfort. She had expected green countryside, small churches guarding neat domestic graveyards patterned with yew trees. These were graveyards she had visited on holidays, had loved almost as much as she loved the one she had made her own. Surely it was in such bird-loud sanctified peace that her father lay. But Nottingham had spread during the past ten years and Creedon was now little more than an urban village separated from the city by a ribbon development of brash new houses, petrol stations, and parades of shops. Nothing in the journey was familiar, and yet she knew that she had traveled this road before and traveled it in anxiety and pain.

But when, thirty minutes later, the bus stopped at its terminus at Creedon she knew at once where she was. The Dog and Whistle still stood at one corner of the dusty litter-strewn village green with the same bus shelter outside it. And with the sight of its graffiti-scrawled walls memory returned as easily as if nothing had ever been forgotten. Here her father used to leave her when he brought her to pay her regular Sunday visits to her grandmother. Here her grandmother's elderly cook would be waiting for her. Here she would look back for a final wave and see her father patiently waiting for the bus to begin its return journey. Here she would be brought at six-thirty when he arrived to collect her. Cranstoun House was where her grandmother lived. She herself had been born there but it had never been her home.

She had no need to ask her way to the house. And when, five minutes later, she stood gazing up at it in appalled fascination, no need to read the name painted on the shabby padlocked gate. It was a square-built house of dark brick standing in incongruous and spurious grandeur at the end of a country lane. It was smaller than she now remembered, but it was still a dreadful house. How could she ever have forgotten those ornate overhanging gables, the high pitched roof, the secretive oriel windows, the single forbidding turret at the east end? There was an estate agent's board wired to the gate and it was apparent that the house was empty. The paint on the front door was peeling, the lawns were overgrown, the boughs of the rhododendron bushes were broken, and the gravel path was studded with clumps of weed. There was no one here who could help her to find her father's grave. But she knew that she had to visit, had to make herself pass again through that intimidating front door. There was something the house knew and had to tell her, something that Sambo had known. She couldn't escape her next step. She must find the estate agent's office and get a permit to view.

She had missed the returning bus and by the time the next one had reached Nottingham it was after three o'clock. She had eaten nothing since her early breakfast but she was too driven now to be aware of hunger. But she knew that it would be a long day and she ought to eat. She turned in to a coffee bar and bought a toasted cheese sandwich and a mug of coffee, grudging the few minutes which it took to gulp them down. The coffee was hot but almost tasteless. Flavor would have been wasted on her, but she realized as the hot liquid stung her throat how much she had needed it.

The girl at the cash desk was able to direct her to the house agent's office. It seemed to her a happy augury that it was within ten minutes' walk. She was received by a sharp-featured young man in an over-tailored pinstripe suit who, in one practiced glance at her old blue tweed coat, the cheap hold-all, and bag of synthetic leather, placed her precisely in his private category of client from whom little can be expected and to whom less need be given. But he found the particulars for her and his curiosity sharpened as she merely glanced at them, then folded the paper away in her bag. Her request to view that afternoon was received, as she expected, with politeness but without enthusiasm. But this was familiar territory and she knew why. The house was unoccupied. She would have to be escorted. There was nothing in her respectable drabness to suggest that she was a likely purchaser. And when he briefly excused himself to consult a colleague and returned to say that he could drive her to Creedon at once, she knew the reason for that too. The office wasn't particularly busy and it was time that someone from the firm checked up on the property.

Neither of them spoke during the drive. But when they reached Creedon and he turned down the lane to the house the apprehension she had felt on her first visit returned, but deeper and stronger. Yet now it was more than the memory of an old wretchedness. This was childish misery and fear relived, but intensified by a dreadful adult foreboding. As the house agent parked his Morris on the grass verge she looked up at the blind windows and was seized by a spasm of terror so acute that, momentarily, she was unable to speak or move. She was aware of the man holding open the car door for her, of the smell of beer on his breath, of his face, uncomfortably close, bending on her a look of exasperated patience. She wanted to say that she had changed her mind, that the house was totally wrong for her, that there would be no point in viewing it, that she would wait for him in the car. But she willed herself to rise from the warm seat and scrambled out under his supercilious eyes, despising herself for her gracelessness. She waited in silence as he unlocked the padlock and swung open the gate.

They passed together between the neglected lawns and the spreading rhododendron bushes toward the front door. And suddenly the feet shuffling the gravel beside her were different feet and she knew that she was walking with her father as she had walked in childhood. She had only to stretch out her hand to feel the grasp of his fingers. Her companion was saying something about the house but she didn't hear. The meaningless chatter faded and she heard a different voice, her father's voice, heard for the first time in over ten years.

"It won't be for always, darling. Just until I've found a job. And I'll visit you every Sunday for lunch. Then, afterward, we'll be able to go for a walk together, just the two of us. Granny has promised that. And I'll buy you a kitten. I'll bring it next weekend. I'm sure Granny won't mind when she sees him. A black kitten. You've always wanted a black kitten. What shall we call him? Little black Sambo? He'll remind you of me. And then, when I've found a job, I'll be able to rent a little house and we'll be together again. I'll look after you, my darling. We'll look after each other."

She dared not look up in case she should see again those desperately pleading eyes, begging her to understand, to make things easy for him, not to despise him. She knew now that she ought to have helped him, to have told him that she understood, that she didn't mind living with Granny for a month or so, that everything would be all right. But she hadn't managed so adult a response. She remembered tears, desperate clingings to his coat, her grandmother's old cook, tight-lipped, pulling her away from him and bearing her up to bed. And the last memory was of watching him from her room above the porch, of his drooping defeated figure making its way down the lane to the bus stop.

As they reached the front door she looked up. The window was still there. But, of course, it was. She knew every room in this dark house.

The garden was bathed in a mellow October sunlight, but the hall struck cold and dim. The heavy mahogany staircase led up from gloom to a darkness that hung above them like a pall. The estate agent felt along the wall for the light switch. But she didn't wait. She felt again the huge brass doorknob that her childish fingers had hardly encompassed and moved unerringly into the drawing room.

The smell of the room was different. Then there had been a scent of violets overlaid with furniture polish. Now the air smelled cold and musty. She stood in the darkness shivering but perfectly calm. It seemed to her that she had passed through a barrier of fear as a tortured victim might pass through a pain barrier into a kind of peace. She felt a shoulder brush against her as the man went across to the window and swung open the heavy curtains.

He said, "The last owners have left it partly furnished. Looks better that way. Easier to get offers if the place looks lived in."

"Has there been an offer?"

"Not yet. It's not everyone's cup of tea. Bit on the large size for a modern family. And then, there's the murder. Ten years ago, but people still talk in the neighborhood. There's been four owners since then and none of them stayed long. It's bound to affect the price. No good thinking you can hush up murder."

His voice was carefully nonchalant, but his gaze never left her face. Walking to the empty fire grate, he stretched one arm along the mantelpiece and followed her with his eyes as she moved as if in a trance about the room.

She heard herself asking, "What murder?"

"A sixty-four-year-old woman. Battered to death by her son-in-law. The old cook came in from the back kitchen and found him with the poker in his hand. Come to think of it, it could have been one like that."

He nodded to a collection of brass fire irons resting against the fender. He said, "It happened right where you're standing now. She was sitting in that very chair."

She said in a voice so gruff and harsh that she hardly recognized it, "It wasn't this chair. It was bigger. Her chair had an embroidered seat and back and there were armrests edged with crochet and the feet were like lions' claws."

His gaze sharpened. Then he laughed warily. The watchful eyes grew puzzled, then the look changed into something else. Could it have been contempt?

"So you know about it. You're one of those."

"One of those?"

"They aren't really in the market for a place. Couldn't afford one this size anyway. They just want a thrill, want to see where it happened. You get all sorts in this game and I can usually tell. I can give you all the gory details if you're interested. Not that there was much gore. The skull was smashed but most of the bleeding was internal. They say there was just a trickle falling down her forehead and dripping onto her hands."

It came out so pat that she knew that he had told it all before, that he enjoyed telling it, this small recital of horror to titillate his clients and relieve the boredom of his day. She wished that she wasn't so cold. If only she could get warm again her voice wouldn't sound so strange.

She said through her dry and swollen lips, "And the kitten. Tell me about the kitten."

"Now that was something! That was a touch of horror if you like. The kitten was on her lap, licking up the blood. But then you know, don't you? You've heard all about it."

"Yes," she lied. "I've heard all about it."

But she had done more than that. She knew. She had seen it. She had been there.

And then the outline of the chair altered. An amorphous black shape swam before her eyes, then took form and substance. Her grandmother was sitting there, squat as a toad, dressed in her Sunday black for morning service, gloved and hatted, prayer book in her lap. She saw again the glob of phlegm at the corner of her mouth, the thread of broken veins at the side of the sharp nose. She was waiting to inspect her grandchild before church, turning on her again that look of querulous discontent. The witch was sitting there. The witch who hated her and her daddy, who had told her that he was useless and feckless and no better than her mother's murderer. The witch who was threatening to have Sambo put down because he had torn her chair, because Daddy had given him to her. The witch who was planning to keep her from Daddy forever.

And then she saw something else. The poker was there, too,

just as she remembered it, the long rod of polished brass with its heavy knob.

She seized it as she had seized it then and, with a high scream of hatred and terror, brought it down on her grandmother's head. Again and again she struck, hearing the brass thudding against the leather, blow on splitting blow. And still she screamed. The room rang with the terror of it. But it was only when the frenzy passed and the dreadful noise stopped that she knew from the pain of her torn throat that the screaming had been hers.

She stood shaking, gasping for breath. Beads of sweat stood out on her forehead and she felt the stinging drops seeping into her eyes. Looking up she was aware of the man's eyes, wide with terror, staring into hers, of a muttered curse, of footsteps running to the door. And then the poker slid from her moist hands and she heard it thud softly on the rug.

He had been right, there was no blood. Only the grotesque hat knocked forward over the dead face. But as she watched, a sluggish line of deep red rolled from under the brim, zigzagged down the forehead, trickled along the creases of the cheeks, and began to drop steadily onto the gloved hands. And then she heard a soft mew. A ball of black fur crept from behind the chair and the ghost of Sambo, azure eyes frantic, leapt as he had leapt ten years earlier delicately up to that unmoving lap.

She looked at her hands. Where were the gloves, the white cotton gloves the witch had always insisted must be worn to church? But these hands, no longer the hands of a nine-year-old child, were naked. And the chair was empty. There was nothing but the split leather, the burst of horsehair stuffing, a faint smell of violets fading on the quiet air.

She walked out of the front door without closing it behind her as she had left it then. She walked as she had walked then, gloved and unsullied, down the gravel path between the rhododendrons, out of the ironwork gate and up the lane toward the church. The bell had only just started ringing; she would be in good time. In the distance she had glimpsed her father climbing a stile from the water meadow into the lane. So he must have set out early after breakfast and had walked to Creedon. And why so early? Had he needed that long walk to settle something in his mind? Had it been a pathetic attempt to propitiate the witch by coming with them to church? Or, blessed thought, had he come to take her away, to see that her few belongings were packed and ready by the time the service was over? Yes, that was what she had thought at the time. She remembered it now, that fountain of hope soaring and dancing into glorious certainty. When she got home all would be ready. They would stand there together and defy the witch, would tell her that they were leaving together, the two of them and Sambo, that she would never see them again. At the end of the road she looked back and saw for the last time the beloved ghost crossing the lane to the house, toward that fatally open door.

And after that? The vision was fading now. She could remember nothing of the service except a blaze of red and blue shifting like a kaleidoscope then fusing into a stained-glass window, the Good Shepherd gathering a lamb to his bosom. And afterward? Surely there had been strangers waiting on the porch, grave concerned faces, whispers and sidelong glances, a woman in some kind of uniform, an official car. And after that, nothing. Memory was a blank.

But now, at last, she knew where her father was buried. And she knew why she would never be able to visit him, never make that pious pilgrimage to the place where he lay because of her, the shameful place where she had put him. There could be no flowers, no obelisk, no loving message carved in marble for those who lay in quicklime behind a prison wall. And then, unbidden, came the final memory. She saw again the open church door, the trickle of the congregation filing in, inquiring faces turning toward her as she arrived alone on the porch. She heard again that high childish voice speaking the words which more than any others had slipped that rope of hemp over his shrouded head.

"Granny? She isn't very well. She told me to come on my own. No, there's nothing to worry about. She's quite all right. Daddy's with her."

The Green Killer

Killer

M. E. KERR

"BE NICE TO HIM," MY FATHER SAID. "HE'S YOUR COUSIN, AFTER all."

"He takes my things."

"Don't be silly, Alan. What of yours could Blaze possibly want? He has everything . . . *everything*," my father added with a slight tone of disdain, for we all knew how spoiled my cousin was.

But he did take my things. Not things he wanted because he needed them, but little things like a seashell I'd saved and polished, an Indian head nickel I'd found, a lucky stone shaped like a star. Every time he came from New York City with his family for a visit, some little thing of mine was missing after they left.

We were expecting them for Thanksgiving that year. It was our turn to do the holiday dinner with all our relatives. Everyone would be crowded into our dining room with extra card tables brought up from the cellar, and all sorts of things borrowed from the next-door neighbors: folding chairs, extra serving platters, one of those giant coffee pots that could serve twenty . . . on and on.

It was better when it was their turn and everyone trooped into New York for a gala feast in their Fifth Avenue apartment overlooking Central Park. They had a doorman to welcome us, a cook to make the turkey dinner, maids to serve us.

Blaze's father was the CEO of Dunn Industry. My father was the principal of Middle Grove High School on Long Island. About the only thing the two brothers had in common was a son apiece: brilliant, dazzling Blaze Dunn, seventeen; and yours truly, Alan Dunn, sixteen, average.

But that was a Thanksgiving no one in the family would ever get to enjoy or forget. An accident on the Long Island Expressway caused the cherry black Mercedes to overturn, and my cousin Blaze was killed instantly.

I had mixed emotions the day months later when I was invited into New York to take what I wanted of Blaze's things.

Did I want to wear those cashmere sweaters and wool jackets and pants I'd always envied, with their Ralph Lauren and Calvin Klein labels? The shoes—even the shoes fit me, British-made Brooks Brothers Church's. Suits from Paul Stuart. Even the torn jeans and salty denim jackets had a hyperelegant "preppy" tone.

Yes!

Yes, I wanted to have them! It would make up for all the times my stomach had turned over with envy when he walked into a room, and the niggling awareness always there that my cousin flaunted his riches before me with glee. And all the rest—his good looks (Blaze was almost beautiful with his tanned perfect face, long eyelashes, green eyes, shiny black hair); and of course he was a straight-A student. He was at ease in any social situation. More than at ease. He was an entertainer, a teller of stories, a boy who could make you listen and laugh. Golden. He was a golden boy. My own mother admitted it. Special, unique, a winner—all of those things I'd heard said about Blaze. Even the name, never mind it was his mother's maiden name. Blaze Dunn. I used to imagine one day I'd see it up on the marquee of some Broadway theater, or on a book cover, or at the bottom of a painting in the Museum of Modern Art. He'd wanted to be an actor, a writer, a painter. His only problem, he had always said, was deciding which talent to stress.

*   *   *

While I packed up garment bags full of his clothes, I pictured him leering down from that up above where we imagine the dead watching us. I thought of him smirking at the sight of me there in his room, imagined him saying, "It's the only way *you'd* ever luck out like this, Snail!" He used to call me that. Snail. It was because I'd take naps when he was visiting. I couldn't help it. I'd get exhausted by him. I'd curl up in my room and hope he'd be gone when I'd wake up. . . . He said snails slept a lot, too. He'd won a prize once for an essay he'd written about snails. He'd described how snails left a sticky discharge under them as they moved, and he claimed that because of it a snail could crawl along the edge of a razor without cutting itself. . . . He'd have the whole dining table enthralled while he repeated things like that from his prize-winning essays. And while I retreated to my room to sleep—that was when he took my things.

All right. He took my things; I took *his* things.

I thought I might feel weird wearing his clothes, and even my mother wondered if I'd be comfortable in them. It was my father who thundered, "Ridiculous! Take advantage of your advantages! It's an inheritance, of sorts. You don't turn down *money* that's left you!"

Not only did I not feel all that weird in Blaze's clothes, I began to take on a new confidence. I think I even walked with a new, sure step. I know I became more outgoing, you might even say more popular. Not dazzling, no, not able to hold a room spellbound while I tossed out some information about the habits of insects, but in my own little high-school world out on Long Island I wasn't the old average Alan Dunn plodding along snaillike anymore. That spring I got elected to the prom committee, which decides the theme for the big end-of-the-year dance, and I even found the courage to ask Courtney Sweet out.

The only magic denied me by my inheritance seemed to be

whatever it would take to propel me from being an average student with grades slipping down too often into Cs and Ds, up into Blaze's A and A-plus status. My newfound confidence had swept me into a social whirl that was affecting my studies. I was almost flunking science.

When I finally unpacked a few boxes of books and trivia that Blaze's mother had set aside for me, I found my seashell, my Indian head nickel, and my lucky stone. . . . And other things: a thin gold girl's bracelet, a silver key ring from Tiffany, initials H. J. K. A school ring of some sort with a ruby stone. A medal with two golf clubs crossed on its face. A lot of little things like that . . . and then a small red leather notebook the size of a playing card.

In very tiny writing inside, Blaze had listed initials, dates, and objects this way:

A.D.	December 25	Shell
H.K.	March 5	Key ring
A.D.	November 28	Indian nickel

He had filled several pages.

Obviously, I had not been the only one whose things Blaze had swiped. It was nothing personal.

As I flipped the pages, I saw more tiny writing in the back of the notebook.

A sentence saying: *"Everything is sweetened by risk."*

Another: *"Old burglars never die, they just steal away. (Ha! Ha!)"*

And: *"I dare, you don't. I have, you won't."*

Even today I wonder why I never told anyone about this. It was not because I wanted to protect Blaze or to leave the glorified memories of him undisturbed. I suppose it comes down to what I found at the bottom of one of the boxes.

The snail essay was there, and there was a paper written entirely in French. There was a composition describing a summer he had spent on the Cape, probably one of those "What I Did Last Summer" assignments unimaginative teachers give at the beginning of fall terms. . . . I did not bother to read beyond the opening sentences, which were "The Cape has always bored me to death for everyone goes there to have fun, clones with their golf clubs, tennis rackets, and volleyballs! There are no surprises on the Cape, no mysteries, no danger."

None of it interested me until I found "The Green Killer." It was an essay with an A-plus marked on it, and handwriting saying, "As usual, Blaze, you excel!"

The title made it sound like a Stephen King fantasy, but the essay was a description of an ordinary praying mantis . . . a neat and gory picture of the sharp spikes on his long legs that shot out, dug into an insect, and snap went his head!

"You think it is praying," Blaze had written, *"but it is waiting to kill!"*

My heart began pounding as I read, not because of any blood-thirsty instinct in me, but because an essay for science was due, and here was *my* chance to excel!

Blaze had gone to a private school in New York that demanded students handwrite their essays, so I carefully copied the essay into my computer, making a little bargain with Blaze's ghost as I printed it out: *I will not tell on you in return for borrowing your handiwork. Fair is fair. Your golden reputation will stay untarnished, while my sad showing in science will be enhanced through you.*

"The Green Killer" was an enormous hit! Mr. Van Fleet, our teacher, read it aloud, while I sat there beaming in Blaze's torn Polo jeans and light blue cashmere sweater. Nothing of mine had ever been read in class before. I had never received an A.

After class, Mr. Van Fleet informed me that he was entering the essay in a statewide science contest, and he congratulated me, adding, "You've changed, Alan. I don't mean just this essay—but *you*. Your personality. We've all noticed it." Then he gave me a friendly punch, and grinned slyly. "Maybe Courtney Sweet has inspired you."

And she was waiting for me by my locker, looking all over my face as she smiled at me, purring her congratulations.

Ah, Blaze, I thought, finally, my dear cousin, you're my boy . . . and your secret is safe with me. That's our deal.

Shortly after my essay was sent off to the science competition, Mr. Van Fleet asked me to stay after class again.

"Everyone," he said, "was impressed with 'The Green Killer,' Alan. Everyone agreed it was remarkable."

"Thank you," I said, unbuttoning my Ralph Lauren blazer, breathing a sigh of pleasure, rocking back and forth in my Church's loafers.

"And why not?" Mr. Van Fleet continued. "It was copied word for word from an essay written by Isaac Asimov. One of the judges spotted it immediately."

So Blaze was Blaze—even dead he'd managed to take something from me once again.

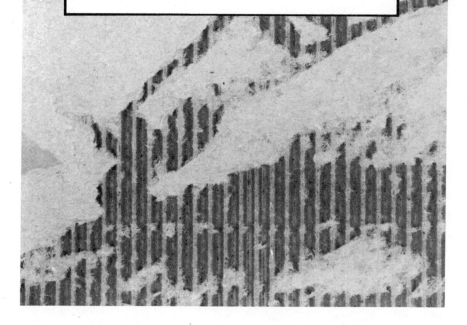

Kim's Game

M. D. Lake

"NORA, ARE YOU SURE YOU WOULDN'T LIKE TO PLAY KIM'S Game with us?" Miss Bowers called to her from over by the great stone fireplace.

"I'm sure, thank you," Nora replied politely, glancing up and then dropping her nose back into her book. Outside, she could hear the rain falling on the sloping roof of the lodge. It had rained steadily ever since they arrived at camp.

She was at the far end of the room, curled up on a sofa, her feet tucked under her, as far away from the other girls as she could get. It wasn't that she didn't like them exactly; it was just that, after being cooped up with them for three days, they didn't interest her very much. None of them liked to read, and they all seemed to have seen the same television shows and movies. As a result, she couldn't understand half of what they were talking about or, if she could, why they got so excited about it.

"Nora's not very good at Kim's Game," she heard one of the girls say, in a high, clear voice that was meant to carry.

"She beat us all yesterday," another one pointed out.

"Twice. The first two times. Beginner's luck. She lost the third game and then she quit."

Nora smiled to herself. She'd never played Kim's Game, never even heard of it, until she got to summer camp and the counselors were forced to come up with indoor activities because of the cold weather and rain. But after she'd won the first two games, she discovered it was too easy for her, and so she decided to have fun with the third game. She put down on her list things that weren't there—silly things, but the other girls didn't notice that— and left out obvious things that were—the teakettle, the butcher knife—and so, of course, she lost. Even then she didn't lose by much, because the other girls weren't very observant.

They didn't have to be, Nora supposed, in their lives. That thought went through her like a sharp knife and she realized she was suddenly close to tears. She straightened her back and put her feet firmly down on the floor and told herself she was glad she was so observant. It was a lot more important to notice things with your eyes than to cry with them.

She hadn't wanted to come to summer camp. She'd wanted to stay home, where she could keep an eye on her parents. She knew that something was wrong between them—worse than usual, a lot worse—and she thought that if she were there, she'd at least be able to figure out the meaning of all the little things she'd noticed and heard: her father's coming home late at night and going to work on the weekends, something he never used to do; his slurred, angry speech sometimes; the tears she'd seen in her mother's eyes; the abrupt changes of subject when she came into the room when her mother was entertaining friends; and the quarrels between her parents that got more and more frequent, when they thought she was in bed and asleep.

Usually they didn't insist that she do anything except home-work and chores, but this year they'd insisted that she go to camp. She wondered what she'd find when she returned home. She wondered if both of her parents would still be living in the house and, if not, which one of them would be gone.

The main door of the lodge opened and a wet figure in a raincoat and hat came in. It was Miss Schaefer.

She hung her coat and hat on a peg and stepped into the room, looked around, and saw the girls standing in a circle over by the fireplace. They were staring with great concentration at objects scattered on a blanket, with Cathy Bowers standing behind them, timing them with her watch.

Kim's Game! Lydia Schaefer had never liked it, thought it was stupid. She didn't have the kind of memory you need to be good at games like that, either.

She nodded to Cathy Bowers and crossed the room to the far corner, with its comfortable overstuffed chairs and a sofa and a coffee table littered with books and old magazines. She sat down in one of the chairs and picked up a magazine. She took her reading glasses out of a case and put the case back in her shirt pocket. As she did, she noticed a girl on the sofa opposite her, sitting up straight, her pointy nose buried in a book. She looked as though she'd been crying, or wanted to cry. Lydia Schaefer smiled and said, "I was always rotten at Kim's Game, too, when I was your age. Don't let it bother you."

Nora glanced up, as if surprised she was no longer alone. Her eyes met Miss Schaefer's without expression. She didn't like Miss Schaefer because she knew Miss Schaefer didn't like her—and not just her either: Miss Schaefer didn't like children period. Nora wondered why she was a camp counselor. Then she shrugged, decided it didn't matter. She had enough adults to try to figure out without adding another one to the list.

"What's your name?" Miss Schaefer persisted, somewhat uneasy under the child's stare. She also didn't like getting a shrug for a response. Hadn't she tried to console the child for being no good at a game?

"Nora." It wasn't just objects on a blanket Miss Schaefer wasn't able to remember.

"I'd probably be rotten at Kim's Game now, too," Miss Schaefer went on. "Oh, well, I'm sure you and I have inner lives that are much more interesting than theirs. Don't we?"

"I guess so," Nora said, wanting to get back to her book.

"It's probably why we wear glasses," Miss Schaefer went on, as if determined to make friends with Nora. "We don't need outer reality as much as other people, so our eyes—"

Before she could finish what Nora already knew was going to be a dumb sentence, a voice interrupted. "Could I see you in my office, Lydia?" Miss Schaefer turned quickly and looked over her shoulder, startled at the officious tone of voice. It was Ruth Terrill, the head counselor.

"Sure, Ruth," she said, trying to keep her voice normal. "Now?"

"Please," Ruth said.

Nora watched the two women disappear into the hallway. She'd known they hadn't liked each other for most of the three days she'd been at camp, but until that moment she hadn't known Miss Schaefer was afraid of Miss Terrill. She wondered why, then shrugged again. These adults, and the things going on between them, weren't her problem. Quickly she dipped her nose back into her book.

Over by the fireplace, the other girls were playing another round of Kim's Game. *You'd think they'd have just about every small object in the lodge memorized by now,* Nora thought.

She would have.

That night, when she first heard the voices, she thought she was at home and in her own bed, because they sounded the way her parents did when they thought she was asleep and wouldn't be able to hear them discussing whatever it was that was wrong between them that they were keeping from her. Then, seeing the log beams in the darkness above her and hearing the rain dripping from the eaves, she remembered where she was. She could hear the quiet sounds the girls around her made in their sleep and the sound of the wind in the forest outside. She hated the wind this summer, a sickly, menacing noise that never seemed to stop.

The voices were those of the camp counselors in the main room of the lodge. Just as she did at home when her parents' voices woke her up, she slipped out of bed and went to listen. She tiptoed down the row of sleeping girls, then down the dark hall to the door to the main room. It wasn't closed all the way, which was why she'd been able to hear the voices.

Lydia Schaefer was describing how, just a little while ago, she'd been hurrying up to the lodge from her cabin. She'd heard a sudden rustling in the forest next to the path, and then a man had grabbed her from behind. He had a knife, she said, and he threatened her with it, but she managed to tear herself away from him and run back to the lodge. She was still out of breath. Nora could hear that.

One of the other counselors asked Miss Schaefer why she hadn't shouted for help. She said she was too frightened at first and then, when she saw the lights of the lodge and knew the man wasn't going to catch up to her, she didn't want to scare the girls by making a lot of noise. The head counselor, Ruth Terrill, asked her if she could describe the man. It was so dark, Miss Schaefer answered, and it happened so fast that she didn't get a good look at him. But she thought he was tall—and he was wearing glasses, she was certain of that.

Miss Terrill said that she was going to call the sheriff, and they all agreed not to worry the girls with it.

That's what adults were always trying to do, Nora thought, as she tiptoed back down the hall to bed. *There's a rapist or even worse out in the forest, but they don't want to worry the girls with it! My mom and dad are breaking up, but they don't want me to know about it!*

Adults are a lot more childish than children in a lot of ways, she thought.

She was barely awake, trying to identify every creaking noise the old building made in the night, when she heard a car driving up the dirt road to the lodge. A car door shut quietly and, as she fell asleep, she could hear the voices again in the main room, a man's voice among them now. She dreamed of the forest and of a man waiting for her among the trees.

The next morning, Nora looked up from her book and saw, through the big front window, a police car pull up in front of the lodge and a large man in a brown uniform climb out. Miss

Terrill and Miss Schaefer must have been watching for him too, for they met him before he could come inside. They stood on the wide porch, out of the rain, talking in voices too low for Nora to hear.

She wondered if it was the same man who'd come when Miss Terrill called the police the night before. *The other girls probably wouldn't have paid any attention to him even if he'd come in,* Nora thought. *They were all sitting at the dining-room table, writing letters home, probably complaining about the lack of television and shopping malls and anything fun to do.* Nora wasn't going to give her parents the satisfaction of complaining about anything. Besides, she didn't know which of them would be there to read whatever she wrote.

The weather was clearing up and they were supposed to go horseback riding the next day. Maybe, on account of the man in the forest, they'd stay indoors. She hoped so.

After all the other girls were asleep that night, she lay in bed and thought about the man in the forest with the knife. She had a good imagination and could see the knife blade and the lenses of his glasses glittering in the moonlight as he watched the lodge from the darkness, watched and waited for somebody to come down the path alone. What would Miss Terrill do, she wondered, if he tried to come into the lodge, tried to kidnap one of the girls? Miss Terrill always slept in the lodge with them. The other counselors had small cabins of their own, two to a cabin except for Miss Schaefer, who had a cabin all to herself, farthest down the path. Apparently none of the other counselors wanted to share a cabin with Miss Schaefer, or else she didn't like any of them. Nora was glad she didn't have to sleep in one of those cabins, alone in the forest with the darkness and the sick wind in the pines that never stopped—and the man in the trees.

Then she heard a noise—it sounded like the start of a shout—coming from the lodge's main room, and then the sound of something falling. She sat up and strained to hear more, but there wasn't anything more—only the quiet breathing of the sleeping girls in the room with her, and the wind. She stared at the door to the main room, waited for it to open and for a tall man wearing glasses to come through, but nothing happened.

Maybe she'd been asleep and dreaming. Maybe it had been her imagination. But she couldn't stand it, here any more than at home. She had to know.

She slipped out of bed and crept silently down the dark hall on her bare feet. She opened the door a crack, very slowly, and peered into the room. At first she thought it was empty, except for the moonlight, but then she saw something on the floor by the fireplace, a huddled figure. She forgot the man in the forest with the knife. She forgot to be scared. She went across the room to see who it was.

It was Miss Terrill. She was lying on her back, staring up at the ceiling, the wooden handle of a knife protruding from her throat.

Nora stared for a long moment, seeing everything there was to see—Miss Terrill's brown leather bag on the floor by her hand and the things that had spilled from it, some of them in the slowly spreading blood and some where the blood didn't reach.

A sound, a flicker of movement, made her look up. Miss Schaefer was coming through the front door.

"What are you doing out of bed, child? You get— Ruth!" She rushed over to Miss Terrill and knelt by her, saw what Nora had seen, and scrambled back to her feet.

"Did you see what happened?" she asked.

"No. I just heard something, so I—"

"You can't stay here," Miss Schaefer said. "Come with me." She took Nora by the hand and, instead of taking her back to the dormitory, almost dragged her across the room and down the hall to the kitchen.

"What's your name again?"

"Nora."

"Oh, yes, Nora," Miss Schaefer said. "The little girl who likes to read. You stay here until I come back. You'll be all right.

Whoever did that to poor Ruth is gone now." She pushed Nora down onto a chair. "I'm going to call the police. Don't go back to the dorm—you might wake the other girls, and we don't want to scare them, do we? Promise?"

Nora promised and Miss Schaefer turned and went quickly down the hall.

Nora didn't like it in the kitchen. The clock on the wall made an ominous humming noise, like the wind outside. It was almost one A.M. There were knives on the drying board by the sink that the cook used to cut meat and vegetables, sharp and glittery in the moonlight pouring through the window, with handles like the one on the knife in Miss Terrill's throat. The man from the forest might have been here, might be here now, hiding in the pantry or the closet or in the darkness over by the stove.

A sudden noise behind her made her jump up and spin around, but nothing moved in the kitchen's shadows. It was probably a mouse. Nora didn't like that thought either, because she wasn't wearing shoes.

She didn't care what she'd promised Miss Schaefer. She ran back to the main room. She meant to cross the door to the fireplace, run to the room where the telephone was and Miss Schaefer, but when she got to Miss Terrill's body, she couldn't help it—she stopped to look again.

What she saw this time terrified her.

"I told you to stay in the kitchen," Miss Schaefer said, so close that Nora jumped and almost screamed. Her voice was soft and cold with anger—the worst kind—and she took Nora in her hard grip.

"I got scared," Nora said, trying not to tremble. They were alone with the body, the two of them, and the hallway door was closed. The other children slept soundly; the other counselors were far away.

"Scared? Of what?"

Then Nora blurted out, so suddenly it surprised her, "Of *him!*"

"Who?" In spite of herself, Miss Schaefer straightened up and looked quickly around the room.

"A man," Nora said. "He was looking at me through the kitchen window!"

"What did he look like?" Miss Schaefer sounded as surprised as Nora.

"He was big," Nora told her. "Tall—and he had dark hair. Miss Schaefer, what if he comes back?"

"I locked the door," Miss Schaefer said. "He can't get in now, nobody can." And then she asked, "How could you see him through the window, Nora? It's dark outside."

"Because," Nora said, and hesitated, trying desperately to think of an explanation, feeling Miss Schaefer's cold eyes on her and remembering the knives in the kitchen that glittered in the moonlight. "Because the *moon* was so bright, I could see it glittering in his glasses!"

Miss Schaefer thought about that for a moment and then she exhaled and relaxed her grip on Nora's arm. She almost smiled. "I called the police," she said. "They'll be here soon. I don't think you have anything to be afraid of now."

Nora didn't think so, either.

The police arrived, and the sheriff, the man she'd seen talking to Miss Terrill and Miss Schaefer that morning. The other counselors came too, staring down in horror at Ruth Terrill. One of them took Nora by the arm and led her over to the couch by the front windows, away from the body. She said that wasn't anything for a girl her age to see, but since she'd found the body, she'd have to talk to the policemen. Nora almost laughed at how dumb that sounded. She could see the heads of some of the other girls, crowded in the entryway to the dorm, their eyes big. A counselor was standing in front of them, to keep them from seeing too much.

Miss Schaefer explained to the other counselors that she'd been afraid to go outside and down the path to tell them what had happened—not with a killer on the loose—and of course she hadn't wanted to leave Nora and the rest of the children alone either. After all, he'd attacked her too, out there in the forest, but she'd been lucky—luckier than Ruth Terrill—she'd managed to get away from him.

The sheriff asked her why she'd come up to the lodge in the first place. She told him she'd left her book there, the one she wanted to read in bed before going to sleep. "I had my flashlight," she said, "and I ran all the way." Then she called over to Nora, as if anxious to turn attention away from herself. "Tell the sheriff about the man you saw at the window in the kitchen, Nora."

"I didn't see anybody," Nora answered. "But I saw something else—over by Miss Terrill's body."

"What did you see?" the sheriff asked. "Come over here and tell me."

"No. You go over by Miss Terrill's body."

"Go—" The sheriff hesitated, gave her a puzzled look, and then he did as she asked. Something in her voice made him do that.

"What's this all about?" Miss Schaefer wanted to know. "You told me, Nora—"

Nora didn't pay any attention to her, only looked to make sure one of the policemen was standing between her and Miss Schaefer. "You just tell me if I'm right about the things scattered around Miss Terrill," she called to the sheriff.

"Nora," Miss Schaefer said and tried hard to laugh, "we're not playing Kim's Game now."

"What's Kim's Game?" the sheriff asked.

"It's a game we play sometimes," Nora told him, "when we have to be indoors on account of the weather. Miss Bowers gives us about fifteen seconds to look at a lot of things she's put on a blanket on the floor and then we have to go to another part of the room and write down everything we remember. Whoever remembers the most things wins."

"Nora's just like me, sheriff," Miss Schaefer said. "She's not very good at it." Her laugh had the same sickly sound as the wind had in the forest, but the forest was quiet now.

Nora looked back at the sheriff and said, "There's a pen and a little tube of sun cream and a pocketknife with a red handle. There's a change purse too. It's brown."

"That's right," the sheriff said, glancing across the room at her. She was staring straight ahead, with her eyes wide open. The sheriff had a daughter too, but when she tried hard to remember things, she screwed her eyes tight shut.

"There're some keys on a ring," Nora went on, "in the middle of the blood, and there's a box of Band-Aids and a comb next to them. There's money too. Two quarters and some dimes—three dimes, I think."

"Is that all?" the sheriff asked.

"That's all there is *now*," Nora said. "But when I found Miss Terrill, there was a glasses case, and the glasses were still in it. It was blue and red—plaid—and part of it was in the blood. You can still see where it was, if you look—I could, anyway, when I came back in here, after Miss Schaefer took me to the kitchen and left me there alone. There's a kind of notch in the blood where the glasses case was. The blood must have run up against it and then had to go around."

The sheriff looked and said, "The notch is still there, Nora, in the blood. Do you know where the case is now?"

"No," she said.

"Do you know who has a glasses case like that?"

"Yes," she said, in a very small voice, but forcing herself to look at Miss Schaefer.

"You have a plaid glasses case, Lydia," Miss Bowers said to Miss Schaefer.

Miss Schaefer ran out of the lodge, but she didn't get far. Maybe she didn't try very hard; maybe she didn't want to be alone in the forest.

"I should have cut your little throat when I had the chance," she said to Nora when one of the policemen brought her back into the lodge. She was smiling when she said it, but it wasn't the nicest smile Nora had ever seen.

The glasses case had fallen out of Miss Schaefer's jacket pocket as she killed Miss Terrill. She didn't notice it was gone until she started down the path to her cabin, but when she came back to get it, Nora was there. After she took Nora to the kitchen, she went back and got the case, wiped off the blood, and then put it back in her pocket before she called the sheriff.

Why had she killed Miss Terrill? Nora never found out, and she didn't care anyway. It had to do with something that happened between the two women a long time ago—probably before Nora was even born—the kind of thing adults fight over, not really caring who gets hurt. It was the kind of thing kids aren't supposed to know about, so Nora only got bits and pieces of the story.

When they heard about the murder, some of the parents drove up the mountain and took their daughters home. For a while there was a regular parade of cars arriving and departing with little girls. Some of the cars had one parent in them, and some had both.

The sun was shining and Nora was getting ready to go horseback riding with the girls who were left when Miss Bowers came out and told her that her mother was on the phone and wanted to know if she wanted to go home.

Her horse had huge eyes, like brown marbles, with curiosity in them. Nora wondered what it would be like to ride a horse like that.

"Tell Mom I'm fine," she said to Miss Bowers, "and that I'm having a good time. Tell her to say hello to Dad for me too, and give him a big kiss if she can."

The man in charge of the horses showed the girls how to mount them, and when they were all ready, they rode into the forest together.

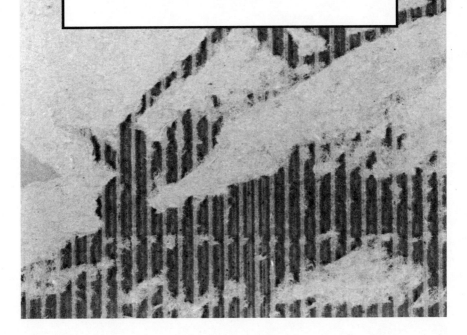

Darker than
Just Before
the Dawn

JOHN H. MaGOWAN

SEVENTY-FIVE CENTS FOR AN OUT-OF-TOWN NEWSPAPER WAS AN extravagance, one she would surely regret. She picked the top paper from the stack and reread the headline in the lower right corner of the first page: "SERIAL KILLER TERRORIZES NEW ENGLAND COMMUNITY." Unable to deny herself, she carried it to the cashier, partially compensated for her immoderation by substituting a pack of generic cigarettes for her regular brand, and hurried home. In the kitchen, she lit the burner under the teakettle and spread the newspaper out on the table.

"BETHLEHEM, New Hampshire, Dec. 10," she read. "Someone in this picturesque town, tucked snugly into a valley between the White and Green Mountains, has it in for optimists; cheerful optimism seems to be the only common thread among the victims of a puzzling series of grisly crimes that has plagued this community since early autumn."

She paused to open the cigarettes. Drawing one out of the pack she lit it, grimacing slightly at the unfamiliar flavor. "The first victim," she continued reading, "was lifelong resident Sarah Watrous, slain in early autumn. Her lifeless body was found, suspended from a brightly colored maple tree, by a New York family touring the fall foliage for which this area of the country is famed.

A neatly lettered sign pinned to her coat read: 'SHE'S HANGING IN THERE.' There was no apparent motive for the crime, and no suspects; the victim was retired, had no surviving relatives, and lived alone. Her modest estate was willed to several charities. 'Aunt Sal,' as she was known in the community, is remembered here as a cheerful woman who was a tireless dispenser of homespun New England wisdom."

When the teakettle's shrill whistle interrupted her reading, she dropped three used tea bags into a cup and covered them with boiling water. As they steeped, she remembered her conversation with Aunt Sal on the morning of the crime. "You youngsters wan't around in the Depression," Sal had said, "when times were really bad. We hung tough, we did. That's what you gotta do, girlie, hang in there."

One by one she squeezed out the tea bags, finding the three had combined to produce a barely acceptable cup of weak tea. Still, she pondered a moment before deciding to deposit them in the trash.

"Rev. Harold Mullens," she continued reading over the rim of the teacup, "a local clergyman, became the second victim a few weeks later. His badly mutilated corpse was found in a mixing vat at a local bakery. A sign taped to the vat read: 'HE IS A BATTER PERSON FOR THIS.' Again there seemed to be no motive; Rev. Mullens lived quietly with his widowed sister. A sometime author, his self-help book, *The Adversity Advantage*, appeared briefly on the *New York Times* (Nonfiction) Bestseller List last year. (See Community Terrorized, 7A, col. 6)," ended the page.

Before turning to find the continuation of the story, she snubbed out the cigarette she had left burning in the ashtray, sipped her tea, and remembered Reverend Mullens's visit on the evening before his death. He had been delighted to share his philosophy with her, telling her to be thankful for her difficulties. "Adversity," he had told her, "is your opportunity for personal growth. You'll be a better person for it."

Patting the side of the kettle, she decided the water was still hot, selected a fresh new tea bag and dropped it into her cup. After adding hot water she returned to the newspaper, turning the pages to find the continuation.

"The third link in this bizarre chain was a dual slaying at the local high school. Two teachers, believed to have been working late, were apparently bludgeoned into unconsciousness before having chloroform-soaked rags taped over their mouths and plastic bags tied over their heads. On the chalkboard, someone, most probably their assassin, left the message: 'THESE TWO SHALL PASS.'

"The theory that the slayer was seeking out optimists began to take shape. Physical education teacher Stanley Szenkow had been the school's basketball coach, and locally noted for his eternally cheery, wait-till-next-year optimism in the face of seventeen consecutive losing seasons, while English teacher Nancy Young was again directing the Drama Club's annual presentation of *It's A Wonderful Life*."

It was over coffee and doughnuts, after the last PTA meeting, that she had spoken with Stan and Nancy, supporting their weightless prattle, while amusing herself by wondering how long their grins would last if they knew a detective, hired by Stan's wife, had followed them on their last few trips to a small motel outside of Concord. The end of the conversation was still clear in her mind. "Remember," Nancy had offered happily as Stan nodded agreement, "this too shall pass."

"Outside Friendly Frank's Food Fair supermarket," continued the following paragraph, "a sign advertises, 'Friendly Faces—Friendly Phrases—Friendly Prices.' Inside, the walk-in freezer yielded the latest in this sequence of macabre crimes. Last Saturday the frozen-solid corpse of owner-manager Francis Caponetti was found grotesquely propped up in a corner with a note pinned to his apron: 'HE'S KEEPING A STIFF UPPER LIP.' "

Her thoughts turned to last week, when she had done the little shopping she could. It was a slow and careful process, trying to keep a running total in her mind as she matched coupons culled from the Sunday paper to boxes of macaroni, selected dried beans, peas, and lentils, and half-priced bread from the day-old shelf. Even then the total had been more than she had to spend. Frank himself had been working the register when she unloaded her cart, smiling patiently when she had to return a few items. "Keep a stiff upper lip" were his exact words as he loaded those few bags of groceries into the cart for the trip to the parking lot.

A rap on the door brought her back to the present. As she signed for the registered letter, she noted the return address of the mortgage company. She had been expecting it, but it was still one more drop in this endless deluge of disasters. The letter carrier had also seen the return address. He knew what it meant, and wanted to help. "You know what they say," he offered, "it's always darkest just before the dawn."

As he turned to go she glanced down and focused her eyes on the antique flatiron now used as a doorstop. *I'll bet,* she thought as she bent to pick it up, *it's even darker with a mail pouch jammed over your head.*

Late Developments

TERRY MULLINS

WHEN HE WAS EIGHTEEN, ROSSO PALLONE GRADUATED FROM parochial high school without distinction and started looking for a job. Neither his parents nor his teachers suggested that he consider going to college. He had hoped someone would. He had even sat beside the Villanova scout who looked over the high-school basketball players. He asked the scout what Villanova was like, but basketball scouts don't encourage short Italian kids from South Philly so Rosso got a job in a camera shop, lived at home, and saved his money.

He was alone in the shop one hot summer afternoon when Albert Brudzew was killed. Brudzew came in as Rosso's boss was leaving for lunch. He waited until the boss had left and then placed two rolls of film on the counter. As Rosso was writing up the order, Brudzew asked if his earlier film had come in. Rosso continued to write and said he would look it up. When he'd finished with the new film, he dug through the file of returned prints and found four packs. Brudzew paid for them but said there should have been six—he had turned them all in at the same time. As Rosso was going through the returned prints again, a large man with a red beard and dark glasses entered the store, drew a pistol, and shot Brudzew three times. Rosso dropped flat behind the counter, hitting the alarm button as he did. He heard the man walk over to Brudzew and he heard the rustle of paper. Then the man left quickly.

When the police came, there was a lot of confusion and Rosso was asked more questions than he could answer. He tried to describe the killer for them, but they didn't find his description very helpful. After he had said for the fifth time that the man was a tall Caucasian with dark glasses and a red beard, the officers gave up on him. At some time in the confusion, a detective had arrived. He talked with the officers, looked over their reports, gave some orders, and pretty much ignored Rosso until the body had been removed and the officers had left. By then, the owner of the camera shop had arrived. The detective, who said his name was Vance Furr, asked if he could talk with Rosso. They went into the office in the rear of the store.

He started slowly, having Rosso tell everything he could remember from the time Albert Brudzew came into the shop. He wanted the rolls of film Brudzew had brought in. He said they would develop and print them in the police lab—they could be important: "You see, Rosso, whoever the red-bearded man was, he took the four packs of finished pictures you gave Brudzew. That suggests that Brudzew's pictures were important. I want you to watch for the two rolls that hadn't come in. When they're returned, let me know right away. But don't say anything to anyone about it."

"Yes, sir."

"You said the man was tall. How tall?"

"Just tall—big and tall."

"Was he as tall as Brudzew?"

Rosso thought carefully. "No," he said, "almost, but he was a little shorter."

"Okay. Don't mention that to anyone, either. What kind of a gun did he use, an automatic or a revolver?"

"I'm sorry, I didn't see it that well. I didn't know he had a gun until he started shooting, then I dropped flat."

"Did he have the gun in his hand when he came in?"

"No."

"Then you must have seen him draw it."

"Yes—he reached inside his jacket and pulled it out real quick and started shooting."

"What kind of jacket?"

"One of those light summer suit jackets—light brown. It matched his pants."

"And his shoes?"

"They were brown, solid brown, with tan socks."

"Was he wearing a tie?"

"No, an open-collar shirt, a yellow shirt."

"What color hair?"

"I couldn't see. He wore a brown hat, like a Panama hat."

"You saw more than you thought you did, Rosso. Did either of them say anything?"

"No. I don't think Brudzew even saw him. He was watching me go through the photo file. Why don't you want me to tell anyone how tall the man was?"

"Because you witnessed a murder. The description you gave to the police at first that the reporter took down was vague—a tall man with dark glasses and a red beard. If the killer thinks that's all you saw, he'll feel safe, and you'll be safe. But if he finds out that you really saw a lot more, he may not feel safe, and you may not be safe."

So when Rosso got home, he just spoke about the tall man and the crowds who gathered around the camera shop until the police left. His mother burst out crying and said that he could have been killed. His father cursed the city for not protecting its citizens from criminals. And his two younger sisters said that he was a hero, presumably for not getting shot. Supper was long and animated, and though Rosso didn't say much the conversation began and ended with his adventure.

Brudzew's other two sets of prints arrived on Monday. Rosso found them first and put them aside. Then he called Vance Furr.

The detective came over at once. He asked if Rosso would come to headquarters during lunch. Rosso agreed eagerly. He had looked at the pictures.

He and Detective Furr ate hoagies in Furr's office while Furr went over the pictures. They were shots of two different groups of men on fishing trips. Brudzew was only in two pictures. The other forty-six showed one group of eight men boarding a fishing boat, catching different kinds of fish, and breaking up to go home, and another group of six men doing much the same thing.

"Brudzew was in this first group of eight," said Furr. "The question is why he took pictures of the second group."

"I think I know," said Rosso. "In three of the pictures there's a man I know—Renzo Cari. I know two others in that group, too, but the point is that Renzo Cari is supposed to be dead."

"I remember. He was out on the West Coast. There was a private-plane crash and an unidentifiable body was supposed to be his. How come you knew him? He's a member of the mob."

"He lived two blocks from us. My parents know his wife, Pomona. She's been trying to collect his insurance."

"What about the two others you know?"

"Giovan Crespino is in almost every picture and Piero Bene is in a lot of them."

"They're members of the mob, too, aren't they?"

"Well, they all work for Mike Agnolo. The newspapers say he's a mobster, but my folks seem to think he's a nice guy. You can't always believe the papers."

"Which of the men do your folks know best?"

"Cari and Agnolo are in our parish and Papa talks about them a lot. They're big shots in our neighborhood. We don't really know the others. There's one more thing about the pictures. The ones of Brudzew's party are a lot clearer than the others. I think the ones of the second group might have been taken with a telephoto lens."

"Good point. That would fit right in. I guess it's about time for you to get back to work, Rosso. You've been a big help. You ought to try out for the police academy."

Rosso slowed down his preparation for leaving. This was the first time anyone had ever said he should go to any kind of school. He gave Furr time to say something more, but the detective just stacked the pictures. Rosso said, "I'm too short for the police academy."

Furr seemed surprised that they were still talking about it. "No, you aren't," he said. "What are you—about five feet eight?"

"Yes."

"That's not short. I'm only five feet nine." He went to a file with the photographs and Rosso left.

But Furr called the next day and asked Rosso to come to his office again. He had enlargements of two of the pictures. One was the best shot of Renzo Cari. There was no doubt about it being him. The other was a man Rosso didn't know. "Could this be the man who shot Brudzew?" Furr asked him.

"I can't tell," Rosso replied.

Fur handed him a dark brown art pencil and a brick red one. "Draw dark glasses and a red beard on him," he said.

Rosso did. "It could be the man. I'm not sure, but it could be."

Furr nodded. "It probably is, then. He's Aretemo, the hit man for the mob. Stay away from him, he's dangerous. You say your folks know Agnolo, Cari, Crespino, and Bene?"

"Not as friends, but Agnolo and Cari are more or less neighbors and we see a lot of them. The other two show up in the neighborhood from time to time."

"If you hear anyone talking about Cari, listen carefully but don't let anyone know it. Just listen." Furr sounded serious.

From then on, Rosso stayed at the dinner table as long as anyone was talking. When one of his sisters commented on this new habit, he said that summer television was all reruns. He found the conversation boring, however. The family didn't seem to know anything that the rest of the neighborhood didn't. It was Thursday before anyone mentioned Cari. Then his mother said that Mrs. Cari had asked her about the murder in Rosso's store and they had spent a lot of time talking about it. So Rosso was prepared when Mrs. Cari visited them after supper and wanted him to tell her all about the murder.

Mrs. Cari was one of the most smartly dressed women in the neighborhood. She was about forty-five, and Rosso's parents often said that she must have been beautiful when she was young. Rosso doubted this. He tried to imagine her without her spectacular clothes and jewelry, with her hair done by the local hairdresser and driving a secondhand Buick instead of a new Audi, and the result wasn't beautiful.

On the other hand, it might have been more comfortable. The well-groomed woman who was quizzing him now made him uneasy. He tried to remember how he had answered the police and reporters just after it happened. A tall man with dark glasses and a red beard. That was the key. Don't think about anything else. And forget the late pictures. He was busy writing up the order. He hadn't seen much.

Mrs. Cari, however, seized on that. "He didn't just pick up four packs of prints, then? He brought some in?"

"Yes, he brought two rolls to be developed. The police took them and said they'd develop them in their lab."

"And did they?"

"They took them. I suppose they printed them." He had to keep reminding himself that he wasn't supposed to know that there was any connection between Brudzew and Cari. He had to think of Mrs. Cari as just another of Mama's nosy friends pestering him with pointless questions. It was a relief when she shifted from her naturally sharp questioning voice to her party voice and said she found his story thrilling but now she had to go.

When Detective Furr called on Friday, Rosso said he didn't think he should be hanging around headquarters anymore. Furr agreed. Rosso told him about Mrs Cari's visit.

"Now I *know* you'd better stay away from here," Furr said. "I called because I'd developed and printed those rolls of film and had copies lying on my desk. They were unimportant—just pictures of Brudzew and four different women on the beach—but they aren't here now. I don't know if they disappeared during the night or this morning—I've been busy—but someone took them."

As it turned out, the camera shop wasn't much safer than police headquarters. Friday night someone broke into the store and spilled packets of photographs all over the place. It was a mess—Rosso spent Saturday morning sorting the pictures out and putting them in new bags. Fortunately, the burglar didn't dump the pictures—he just tore the packets open to see what sort of pictures were there and then threw them aside. Nothing seemed to be missing.

Furr came over and examined the place. When they were alone in the back office, Rosso produced a half dozen packs of prints. "It's hard to open these with gloves on," he said. "And no matter how careful you are, it's hard not to leave fingerprints on photographs. These six packages of photographs all have fingerprints on them. Can you copy them without hurting the pictures?"

Yes, Furr could. "I'll make a point of getting these back to you this afternoon," he said. "Thanks, Rosso."

That afternoon when he brought the pictures back, Furr said, "This complicates things. I assumed that Cari's friends had burgled your place, but the fingerprints are of Brudzew's two brothers, Josef and Jan—two small-time hoods. The pictures accompanying their records looked familiar. They were two of those with Brudzew on the fishing trip. If they show up here asking for his pictures, let me know."

"Don't worry. If *anyone* shows up asking for those pictures I'll

let you know." Rosso hoped the detective would repeat his comment that he should apply for the police academy, but Furr
seemed to accept Rosso's assistance as a matter of fact now. Rosso
knew he couldn't simply decide to leave his job and apply, but
the thought was never far from his mind. There had to be some
word or a sign. Since words didn't seem easy to come by, he
decided to force a sign. He would ask for a raise. If he didn't get
the raise, he'd quit and seek admission to the police academy.

The next morning after the routine opening was finished, he
proposed a raise. The owner talked it over with him and not only
agreed to a raise but said they would call it a promotion—Rosso
would be assistant manager.

When he told his parents about the raise and the promotion,
his mother was proud and his father was astonished. Rosso steered
between the two attitudes.

"Being assistant manager sounds like more than it is," he pointed
out. "I'll be doing what I've always been doing. And there are
only four of us working there and two of them work part-time
and go to community college part-time. So the raise means more
than the title."

His parents might never have heard a word.

It rained on Sunday, and that afternoon Rosso drove his sisters to
church to attend a cousin's wedding. He let them out as close to the
door as he could and then joined a long line of cars double-parked. He
had a book to read while waiting for them to signal they were ready to
go home, but for now he just sat and watched the guests arrive.

Mrs. Cari's car drove up and she got out. Usually she drove
herself, but the heavy rain must have caused her not to. Rosso
looked to see who was driving for her. It was the man who
shot Brudzew.

Rosso averted his eyes quickly and sat very still, hoping the
man couldn't see him. Mrs. Cari went into the church and her
car drove off. Rosso found himself trembling. He opened the book
and pretended to read.

Naturally, his sisters were among the last to leave the church. Mrs. Cari had been one of the first, but she was still looking for her car. As Rosso's sisters jumped into the backseat, Mrs. Cari opened the front door and said, "Could I hitch a ride? My chauffeur seems to be lost and I don't want to wait here all day."

Of course Rosso said yes. She sat and talked about the wedding all the way home. There, her car was nowhere to be seen, and she looked worried as she entered her house.

Rosso dropped his sisters off and drove to a public telephone in another part of town. He called police headquarters, but Detective Furr was off duty. He called the home number and Furr answered. "I've just seen the man who shot Brudzew," Rosso told him. "He drove Mrs. Cari to a wedding today but he didn't come back for her. I had to drive her home."

"You're sure he's the killer?"

"Not completely, but I know he's the man you call Aretemo— the one in the picture I drew glasses and a beard on. He and her car are both gone and she didn't seem happy about it."

"OK. I know the car. I'll have— No, I'd better not. If we pick it up before she calls us, she'll know you were in touch with the police. Thanks, Ross. I can start a few things in motion, and be ready in case she calls."

The eleven o'clock news on Channel 10 covered the story of a stolen car found on a side road in Bucks County. The car was Mrs. Cari's. They also showed a body being carried to an ambulance in a plastic bag. An unidentified man had been found shot in the back of the head ten yards from the stolen car. Police were investigating.

Monday Mrs. Cari drove her car to early mass. Rosso's sisters waved at her but she didn't see them. After mass she was in serious conversation with Mr. and Mrs. Agnolo, so Rosso's family didn't try to speak with her. Rosso looked at the car carefully. It didn't seem damaged.

When he got home from work that day, his mother stopped

him at the door and said, "Mrs. Cari called and said she left her cigarette lighter in your car yesterday and would you bring it over. She'd come herself but Mr. Agnolo and some friends are at her place."

"Sure, right away," Rosso said. He went out and looked in the passenger seat of his car. There was the lighter, a lipstick, and a small bottle of perfume. He put them all in his pocket and walked to Mrs. Cari's house. As he walked up the steps to ring the door-bell, he noticed there were two cars parked across the street with men sitting in them reading newspapers. Thinking they might be police, Rosso said nothing when Crespino answered the door and told him Mrs. Cari was in the kitchen. He found her liquefying carrots in a blender. She thanked him and said she hadn't even missed the lipstick and perfume. As Rosso let himself out, he looked closer at the men in the car and recognized three of them as members of Brudzew's fishing party.

At the corner pizzeria, he stopped to use the public telephone to call Mrs. Cari. While at the phone, he could see her house. The two cars were still there.

Crespino answered the phone and Rosso said, "I think Mr. Agnolo should know that there are men in two cars across the street watching Mrs. Cari's house. Tell him, will you?"

"Sure."

When Rosso hung up, he decided to squander another quarter. He called Detective Furr. Waiting to be put through, he saw four men get out of the cars and walk across the street. When Furr answered, Rosso said, "Three of the men in the Brudzew pictures have been watching Mrs. Cari's house. They've just crossed the street and—no! Crespino opened the door and they shot him! Two of them are firing through the front window. Get some cars over here!"

Crespino lay dead on the steps. Inside, in the living room, Mrs. Cari was holding a dishrag to Agnolo's chest. The sofa was still smoldering with a dozen bullet holes, but Agnolo seemed the only person hit. Bene was there. Fishing keys out of Agnolo's pocket, he tossed them to Rosso. "Get his car started," he said. "I called Jefferson. They'll have Doc Wilson ready."

"Shouldn't we call an ambulance?"

"You want him to bleed to death?"

Bene and Mrs. Cari helped Agnolo up and Rosso kicked the doors open. Then he opened the car doors and got in front and started the motor. He had never driven a large, powerful car before and wasn't used to automatic transmission. He pressed the accelerator and the motor sounded like a transcontinental jet. He took his foot off the accelerator. Once Bene and Mrs. Cari were in back with Agnolo, he gingerly shifted into drive, holding his foot firmly on the brake. As the back door shut, he eased his foot off the brake. The car leaped forward like a greyhound out of the gate.

The doctor and an emergency crew were waiting with oxygen and intravenous equipment, but after a quick look at Agnolo the doctor waved them away and just put Agnolo on a stretcher and ordered him wheeled in. As the stretcher passed Rosso, Agnolo reached out and grabbed his arm. "Your call saved my life," he said. "Agnolo does not forget." He disappeared into the hospital, followed by Mrs. Cari and Bene.

Ten minutes later, Bene came out looking a bit less worried. "He got hit twice," he said, "but one was a flesh wound and the other missed his lung. He's going to be all right."

"Good," said Rosso. "Shall I wait for Mrs. Cari and drive us back?"

Bene looked wary. "No. No. I'll take the keys and park the boss's car. Pomona and I will stay until he says we should go. Thanks." And he got into the car and drove it slowly and sedately into the hospital parking lot.

Rosso walked back over the route he had so recently and frantically come. When he reached the Cari house, he saw police cars.

*   *   *

There was no sign of Crespino's body. Detective Furr met him and asked if he had witnessed the shooting. Rosso said, "Yes, sir. I was in the pizzeria on the corner."

Furr said, "Please come in and describe what happened."

They went into the Cari living room and sat down, avoiding the blood-soaked, bullet-riddled sofa. Furr said, "Crespino was dead. We found Renzo Cari hiding in a third-floor bedroom. He's wanted for embezzling and tried to disappear. Thanks to your call, we also caught the killers. They abandoned their cars at Vet Stadium, but we had them bottled in and they gave up without a fight. I hear you drove Agnolo to the hospital."

Rosso smiled away some of the tension. "He apparently wasn't badly hurt. What's this all about?"

"I think we have most of it figured out now. Renzo Cari was laundering money for the mob, using a small New Jersey bank in which he had bought controlling interest. He also embezzled five million dollars from the bank. Federal agents found out and were after him. So he went to the West Coast, and when there was a plane accident everyone tried to pretend he'd been killed. Actually, he came back here in disguise and has been living at home and keeping out of sight. From time to time he'd go fishing with his friends. It seemed safe enough.

"But Brudzew saw him and photographed him and then demanded money from Mrs. Cari. Aretemo shot Brudzew and stole the photographs he was holding as evidence that Cari was alive. I don't know if we can prove that Agnolo or the Caris ordered him to do it or paid him to do it. We'll try, but Cari is saying Aretemo acted on his own. It's Brudzew's brothers who killed Aretemo and tried to wipe out Agnolo and his friends. You were a great help, Ross. We probably would never have caught them if you hadn't called me when you did. Is there anything I can do for you?"

"Yes, Mr. Furr," said Rosso, "there is one thing."

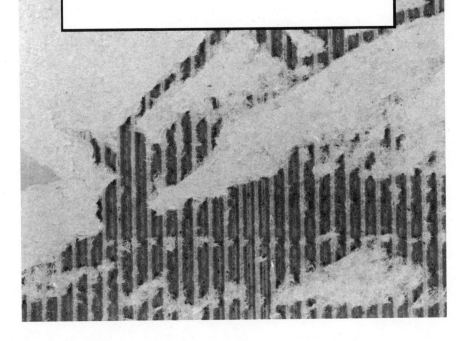

The Premonition

JOYCE CAROL OATES

CHRISTMAS WAS ON A WEDNESDAY THIS YEAR. ON THE PRECEDING Thursday, at dusk, as Whitney drove across the city to his brother Quinn's house, he had a premonition.

Not that Whitney was a superstitious man. He wasn't.

Nor was he one to interfere in others' domestic affairs, especially his elder brother's. It could be dangerous even offering Quinn unsolicited advice.

But Whitney had had a call from their youngest sister who'd had a call from another sister who'd had a call from an aunt who'd been visiting with their mother—Quinn had started drinking again, he'd threatened his wife, Ellen, and perhaps their daughters too; it was a familiar story, and depressing. For the past eleven months Quinn had been attending AA meetings, not regularly, and with an attitude of embarrassed disdain, but, yes, he'd attended meetings and had quit drinking, or, at any rate—and here opinions differed depending upon which family member you spoke with—he'd cut down substantially on his drinking. For a man of Quinn's wealth and local prominence, the eldest of the Paxton sons, it was far more difficult, everyone agreed, than it would be for an ordinary man, to join AA, to admit he had a drinking problem, to admit he had a problem with his temper.

Whitney had had a premonition the night before, and a feeling of unease through the day, that Quinn might lose control: might this time seriously injure Ellen, even his daughters. Quinn was a big man, in his late thirties, trained at the Wharton School, with an amateur expert's knowledge of corporate law, socially gregarious, good-natured, yet, as Whitney well knew from their boyhood, very much a physical person: he used his hands to express himself, and sometimes those hands hurt.

Several times that day Whitney had called his brother's house, but no one answered the telephone. A click, and the familiar husky tone of the answering tape, *Hello! This is the Paxton residence! We regret that we cannot come to the phone right now. But—* The voice was Quinn's, hearty and exuberant yet with an undercurrent of threat.

When Whitney called Quinn's office, Quinn's secretary said only that he wasn't available. Though Whitney identified himself each time as Quinn's brother, and though the secretary surely knew who he was, she refused to give out any more information. "Is Quinn at home? Is he out of town? Where *is* he?" Whitney had asked, trying not to sound upset. But Quinn's secretary, one of his faithful allies, said only, quietly, "I'm sure Mr. Paxton will be in touch with you over the holidays."

Christmas Day at the elder Paxtons' enormous house on Grandview Avenue, amid all the relatives!—in such a frenetic atmosphere, how could Whitney take Quinn aside to speak with him? By then, too, it might be too late.

So, though he wasn't the type to interfere in others' marriages, still less in his brother's private life, Whitney got in his car and drove across the city, out of the modestly affluent neighborhood of condominiums and single-family homes where he'd lived, for years, his unambitious bachelor's life, and into the semi-rural neighborhood of million-dollar homes where Quinn had moved his family a few years ago. The area was known as Whitewater Heights; all the houses were large, luxurious, and screened from the road by trees and hedges; none of the lots was smaller than three acres. Quinn's house was his own design: an eclectic mixture of neo-Georgian and contemporary, with an indoor pool, sauna, an enormous redwood deck at the rear. Whitney never drove his Volvo up the curving gravel drive, parked it in front of the three-car garage, approached the front door to ring the doorbell without feeling that he was trespassing, and he'd be made to pay, even when invited.

So he felt, now, distinctly uneasy. He rang the doorbell; he waited. The foyer was darkened, and so was the living room. He'd noticed that the garage door was shut and neither Quinn's nor Ellen's car was in the driveway. Was no one home? But did he hear music?—a radio? He was thinking that the girls had school the next day; the holiday recess wouldn't begin until Monday. It was a school night, then. Shouldn't they be home? And Ellen, too?

Waiting, he drew a deep breath of the cold night air. It was below freezing, yet no snow had yet fallen. Apart from the Christmas lights of a few houses he'd passed entering Whitewater Heights, he had no sense of an imminent holiday; he could see no Christmas decorations inside Quinn's and Ellen's house. Not even an evergreen wreath on the front door. . . . No Christmas tree? At the elder Paxtons' house on Grandview Avenue, an enormous fir tree would be erected in the foyer, and there was always quite a ceremony, trimming it. The annual ritual was still celebrated, though Whitney no longer attended. One of the privileges of adulthood, he thought, was keeping your distance from the font of discomfort and pain. He *was* thirty-four years old now.

Of course, he would spend Christmas Day with the family. Or part of the day. Impossible to avoid, so long as he continued to live in the city of his birth. Yes, and he'd deliver his share of expensively wrapped presents and receive his share; he'd be gracious as always with his mother and courteous with his father; he understood that he'd disappointed them by failing to grow into the kind of son Quinn had grown into, but, amid holiday festivities, so many people and so much cheerful noise, the hurt would be assuaged. Whitney had lived with it so long, perhaps it was no longer actual hurt but merely its memory.

He rang the doorbell again. He called out, cautiously, "Hello? Isn't anybody home?" He could see, through the foyer window, a light or lights burning toward the rear of the house; the music seemed to have stopped. In the shadowy foyer, at the foot of the stairs, were boxes—or suitcases? Small trunks?

Was the family going on a trip? At such a time, before Christmas?

Whitney recalled a rumor he'd heard a few weeks ago, that Quinn had spoken of traveling to some exorbitantly costly exotic place, the Seychelles, with one of his women friends. He'd discounted the rumor, believing that Quinn, for all his arrogance and his indifference to his wife's feelings, would never behave so defiantly; their father would be furious with him, for one thing. And Quinn was sensitive, too, of his local reputation, for he'd toyed with the idea, over the years, of one day running for public office. Their great-grandfather Lloyd Paxton had been a popular Republican congressman and the name Paxton was still a revered one in the state. . . . *The bastard wouldn't dare,* Whitney thought.

Still, he felt a tinge of fear. A further premonition. What if Quinn had done something to Ellen and the girls, in a fit of rage? An image flashed to Whitney's mind of Quinn in his blood-smeared chef's apron, barbecuing steaks on the sumptuous redwood deck at the rear of the house. Quinn, last Fourth of July. A double-pronged fork in one hand, his electric carving knife in the other. The whirring of the electric gadget, the deadly flash of the blades. Quinn, flush-faced, annoyed at his younger brother for having come late, had waved him up onto the deck with the strained ebullience of a man who is on the verge of drunkenness but determined not to lose control. How masterful Quinn had seemed, six feet three inches tall, two hundred pounds, his pale blue eyes prominent in his face, his voice ringing! Whitney had obeyed him, at once. Quinn in his comical apron tied tight around his spreading waist, the wicked-looking carving knife extended toward Whitney in a playful gesture: a mock-handshake.

Whitney shuddered, remembering. The other guests had laughed. Whitney himself had laughed. Only a joke, and it was funny. . . . If Ellen had seen, and shuddered too, Whitney had not noticed.

This image, Whitney tried to push out of his mind.

Thinking, though, that it isn't just desperate, impoverished men who kill their families; not just men with histories of mental illness. The other day Whitney had read an appalling news item about a middle-aged insurance executive who had shotgunned his estranged wife and their children. . . . But, no, better not think of that, now.

Whitney tried the doorbell another time. It *was* working: he could hear it. "Hello? Quinn? Ellen? It's me, Whitney—" How weak, how tremulous, his voice! He was convinced that something was wrong in his brother's household, yet, at the same time, how Quinn would scorn him, if Quinn were home, for interfering; how furious Quinn would be, in any case. The Paxtons were a large, gregarious, but close-knit clan, and little sympathy was felt for those who stirred up trouble, poked their noses where they weren't wanted. Whitney's relations with Quinn were cordial at the present time, but, two years ago, when Ellen had moved out of this house and begun short-lived divorce proceedings, Quinn had accused Whitney of conspiring with Ellen behind his back; he'd even accused Whitney of being one of the men with whom Ellen had been unfaithful. "Tell the truth, Whit! I can take it! I won't hurt her, or you! Just tell the truth, you cowardly son of a bitch!"—so Quinn had raged. Yet, even in his rage, there had seemed an air of pretense, for, of course, Quinn's suspicions were unfounded. Ellen had never loved anyone but Quinn; the man was her life.

Not long afterward Ellen had returned to Quinn, bringing their daughters with her. She'd dropped the divorce proceedings. Whitney had been both disappointed and relieved—disappointed, because Ellen's bid for freedom had seemed so necessary, and so right; relieved, because Quinn, his family restored to him, his authority confirmed, would be placated. He'd had no further reason to be angry with his younger brother, only, as always, mildly contemptuous.

"Of course I wasn't serious, suspecting *her* with *you*," Quinn had said, "—I must have been drunk out of my mind."

And he'd laughed, as if even that prospect had been unlikely.

Since then Whitney had kept a discreet distance from Quinn and Ellen. Except when they were thrown together, unavoidably, at Paxton family occasions, like Christmas Day.

Now Whitney was shivering, wondering if he should go around to the back of the house and try the door there, peer inside. But, if Quinn was home, and something *was* wrong, might not Quinn be—dangerous? The man owned several hunting rifles, a shotgun, even a revolver for which he had a permit. And, if he'd been drinking . . . Whitney recalled that policemen are most frequently shot when investigating domestic quarrels.

Then, vastly relieved, he saw Ellen approaching the door—*was* it Ellen? There appeared to be something wrong with her—this was Whitney's initial, though confused impression, which he would recall long afterward—for she was walking hesitantly, almost swaying, as if the floor were tilting beneath her; she was vigorously wringing her hands, or was she wiping them, on an apron; clearly she was anxious about the doorbell, whoever was waiting on the stoop. Whitney called out, "Ellen, it's just me, Whitney!" and saw her look of profound childlike relief.

Was she expecting Quinn? Whitney wondered.

It was flattering to Whitney, how quickly Ellen switched on the foyer lights, and how readily she opened the door to him.

Ellen exclaimed softly, "Whitney!"

Her eyes were wide and moist and the pupils appeared dilated; there was a look of fatigue in her face, yet something feverish, virtually festive, as well. She seemed astonished to see her brother-in-law, gripping his hand hard, swaying slightly. Whitney wondered if she'd been drinking. He had watched her now and then at parties, sipping slowly, even methodically, at a glass of wine, as if willing herself to become anesthetized. Never had he seen her intoxicated, nor even in such a peculiar state as she appeared to be in now.

Whitney said, apologetically, "Ellen, I'm sorry to disturb you, but—you haven't been answering your phone, and I was worried about you."

"Worried? About me?" Ellen blinked at him, smiling. The smile began as a quizzical smile, then widened, broadened. Her eyes were shining. "About *me?*"

"—and the girls."

"—the *girls?*"

Ellen laughed. It was a high-pitched, gay, melodic laugh of a kind Whitney had never heard from her before.

Swiftly, even zestfully, Ellen shut the door behind Whitney and bolted it. Leading him into the hall by the hand—her own hand was cool, damp, strong-boned, urgent—she switched off the foyer light again. She called out, "It's Uncle Whitney, girls!—It's Uncle Whitney!" Her tone suggested vast relief, and a curious hilarity beneath the relief.

Whitney gazed down upon his sister-in-law, perplexed. Ellen was wearing stained slacks, a smock, an apron; her fair brown hair was brushed back indifferently from her forehead, exposing her delicate ears; she wore no makeup, not even lipstick, thus looked younger, more vulnerable than Whitney had ever seen her. In public, as Quinn Paxton's wife, Ellen was unfailingly glamorous—a quiet, reserved, beautiful woman who took obsessive care with grooming and clothes, and whose very speech patterns seemed premeditated. Quinn liked women in high heels—good-looking women, at least—so Ellen rarely appeared in anything other than stylishly high heels, even at casual gatherings.

In flat-heeled shoes of the kind she was wearing this evening, she seemed smaller, more petite than Whitney would have guessed. Hardly taller than her elder daughter Molly.

As Ellen led Whitney through the house, to the kitchen at the rear—all the rooms were darkened, and in the dining room, as in the foyer, there were boxes and cartons on the floor—she spoke to him in that bright, high-pitched voice, as if she were speaking, and drawing him out, for others to hear. "You say you were worried, Whitney?—about me, and the girls? But why?"

"Well—because of Quinn."

"Because of Quinn! Really!" Ellen squeezed Whitney's hand, and laughed. "But why 'because of Quinn,' and why now?—tonight?"

"I'd been speaking to Laura, and she told me—he'd started drinking again. He'd been threatening you, again. And so I thought—"

"It's kind of you, and of Laura, to care about me and the girls," Ellen said, "—it's so unlike the Paxtons! But then you and Laura aren't really Paxtons yourselves, are you. You're . . ." She hesitated, as if the first word that came to mind had to be rejected, "on the periphery. You're . . ." And here her voice trailed off into silence.

Whitney asked the question most urgent to him, hoping he didn't betray the apprehension he felt, "Is—Quinn here?"

"Here? No."

"Is he in town?"

"He's gone."

"Gone?"

"On a business trip."

"Oh, I see." Whitney breathed more deeply. "And when is he coming back?"

"He's going to send for us, in Paris. Or maybe Rome. Wherever *we* are, when he finishes up his business, when he has time for us."

"Do you mean you're going away, too?"

"Yes. It's all very recent. I was running around all morning, getting the girls' passports validated. It will be their first time out of the country, except for Mexico; we're all very excited. Quinn wasn't enthusiastic at first, he had complicated business dealings in Tokyo, you know Quinn, always negotiating, always calculating, his brain never *stops*—" But here Ellen paused, laughing, as if startled. "Well—you know Quinn. You are his brother, you've lived in his shadow, how could you not know Quinn? No need to anatomize Quinn!"

And Ellen laughed again, squeezing Whitney's hand. She appeared to be leaning slightly against him, as if for balance.

Whitney had to admit, he was profoundly relieved. The thought that his brother was in no way close at hand, in no way an active threat to him—this restored Whitney's composure considerably.

"So. Quinn has flown off, and you and the girls are following him?"

"He has his business dealings, you see. Otherwise, we'd all have gone together. Quinn wanted us to go together." Ellen spoke more precisely now, as if repeating memorized words. "Quinn *wanted* us to go together, but—it wasn't practical, under the circumstances. After Tokyo he thought he might have to fly to—I think it's Hong Kong."

"So you're going to miss Christmas here? All of you?"

"I've done my Christmas shopping, though! I won't feel guilty about not participating. The girls and I just won't be at your parents' to watch our presents being opened," Ellen said cheerfully, with a peculiar emphasis, as if she were trying not to slur her words. "Of course, we're going to miss you all. Oh, terribly! Your dear father, your lovely mother, *all* Quinn's family—yes, we're going to miss you terribly. And so will Quinn."

Whitney asked, "When did you say Quinn left, Ellen?"

"Did I say?—he left last night. On the Concorde."

"And you and the girls are leaving—?"

"Tomorrow! Not on the Concorde, of course. Just regular coach. But we're tremendously excited, as you can imagine."

"Yes," Whitney said guardedly. "I can imagine."

Whitney deduced that Quinn *had* gone off with his latest

woman friend, to the Seychelles, or wherever; he'd managed to convince his credulous wife that he was on one of his "confidential" business trips, and she seemed satisfied by—grateful for?—the explanation.

How women crave being lied to—being deluded! Poor Ellen. Whitney thought, *I'm not the one to enlighten her.*

"How long did you say you're going to be gone, Ellen?"

"*Did* I say?—I don't remember, if I did!" Ellen laughed.

And she pushed gaily through the swinging doors into the kitchen, leading Whitney by the hand, as if in triumph.

"It's Uncle Whitney!" Molly cried.

"Uncle Whit-ney!" Trish cried, clapping her rubber-gloved hands.

The kitchen was so brightly lit, the atmosphere so charged, gay, frenetic, Whitney halfway thought he'd stepped into a celebration of some kind. This too he would remember, afterward.

Ellen helped him remove his overcoat as his pretty nieces beamed upon him, giggly and breathless. Whitney had not seen them in six months, and it seemed to him that each had grown. Molly, fourteen years old, was wearing a slovenly shirt, jeans, and an apron knotted around her thin waist; white plastic-framed sunglasses with amethyst lenses hid her eyes. (Was one of the eyes blackened?—shocked, Whitney tried not to stare.) Trish, eleven years old, was similarly dressed, but with a baseball cap reversed on her head; when Whitney entered the kitchen she'd been squatting, wiping something up off the floor with a sponge. She wore oversized yellow rubber gloves which made a sticky, sucking sound as she clapped her hands.

Whitney was fond, very fond, of his young nieces. Their girlish mock-rapturous delight in his visit made him blush, but he was flattered. "Great to see you, Uncle Whitney!" they cried in unison, and giggling, "Great to see *you*, Uncle Whitney!"

As if, Whitney thought, *they'd been expecting someone else?*

He frowned, wondering if perhaps Quinn had not gone, after all.

Ellen was hurriedly removing her stained apron. "It's ideal that you've dropped by tonight, Whit," she said warmly, "—you are the girls' favorite uncle by far. We were all thinking how sad it is, we wouldn't be seeing you on Christmas Day!"

"And I'll be sorry not to see *you*."

A distinctly female atmosphere in the room, Whitney thought, *with an undercurrent of hysteria.* A radio was tuned to a popular music station, and from it issued the simplistic, percussive, relentlessly shrill music young Americans loved, though Whitney could not see how Ellen tolerated it. All the overhead lights were on, glaring. Surfaces gleamed, as if newly scrubbed. The fan above the stove was turned up high, yet the kitchen still smelled—of something rich, damp, sour-sweet, cloying. The very air was overheated, as if steamy. Scattered about were empty cans of Diet Coke and crusts of pizza; on the counter near a stack of gift-wrapped packages was a bottle of California red wine. (So Ellen *had* been drinking!—Whitney saw that her eyes were glassy, her lips slack. And she too had a bruise, or bruises, just above her left eye.) What was remarkable was that most of the available space in the kitchen, including the large butcher block table at the center, was taken up with packages and Christmas wrapping paper, ribbons, address labels—Whitney was astonished to realize that, on the very eve of their ambitious trip abroad, his sister-in-law and nieces had given themselves up to a frenzy of Christmas preparations. How like women, to be thinking of others at such a time! No wonder their faces were so bright and feverish, their eyes glittering manic.

Ellen offered Whitney a drink, or would he prefer coffee?— "It's so cold out! And you'll have to go back out in it!" Ellen said, shivering. The girls shivered too, and laughed. *What* was so *funny?* Whitney wondered. He accepted the offer of a cup of coffee if it wasn't too much trouble, and Ellen said, quickly, "Of course not! Of course not! Nothing is too much trouble *now!*"

And again the three of them laughed, virtually in unison.

Do they know? Whitney wondered. *That Quinn has betrayed them?*

As if reading Whitney's thoughts, Trish said suddenly, "Daddy is going to the Seashell Islands. That's where he's going."

Molly said, with a little laugh, "No, silly—Daddy is going to Tokyo. Daddy is *in* Tokyo. On business."

"—Then he's going to meet us. On the Seashell Islands. 'A tropical paradise in the Indian Ocean.'" Trish ripped off her stained rubber gloves and tossed them onto a counter.

"The Seychelle Islands," Ellen said, "—but we're not going there, any of us." She spoke pointedly to Trish, voice slightly raised. She was making coffee with quick deft motions, scarcely paying attention to the movements of her hands. "*We're* going to Paris. Rome. London. Madrid."

"'Paris. Rome. London. Madrid.'" The girls toned in near-unison.

The fan whirred loudly above the stove. But the close, steamy air of the kitchen was very slowly dispelled.

Ellen chattered about the upcoming trip, and Whitney saw that the bruises on her forehead were purplish-yellow. If he were to ask her what had caused them, she would no doubt say she'd bumped her head in an accident. Molly's blackened eye—no doubt that was an accident too. Whitney recalled how, many years ago, at a family gathering on the lawn of the Paxtons' estate, Quinn had suddenly and seemingly without provocation slapped his young wife's head—it had happened so swiftly few of the guests had noticed. Red-faced, incensed, Quinn said loudly, for the benefit of witnesses, "Bees! Goddamn bees! Trying to sting poor Ellen!"

Eyes smarting with tears, Ellen recovered her poise, and, deeply embarrassed, hurried away into the house. Quinn did not follow. No one followed.

No one spoke of the incident to Quinn. Nor did they, so far as Whitney ever knew, speak of it to one another.

Whitney uneasily anticipated the comments that would be

made, on Christmas Day, when Quinn and his family were absent—willfully absent, it would seem. He wondered, but did not want to ask, if Ellen had spoken with his mother yet, to explain, and to apologize. Why hadn't they waited until January, to take a vacation? Quinn and his woman friend too?

No, better not ask. For it was none of Whitney Paxton's business.

Ellen gave Whitney his coffee, offered him cream and sugar, handed him a teaspoon, but the spoon slipped from her fingers and fell clattering to the damp, polished floor. Double-jointed Trish stooped to pick it up, tossed it high in the air behind her back and caught it over her shoulder. Ellen said crossly, "Trish!" and laughed. Molly, wiping her overheated face on her shirt, laughed too.

"Don't mind Trish, she's getting her period," Molly said wickedly.

"Molly—!" Ellen cried.

"Damn you—!" Trish cried, slapping at her sister.

Whitney, embarrassed, pretended not to hear. Was little Trish really of an age when she might menstruate? Was it possible?

He raised the coffee cup to his lips with just perceptibly shaking fingers, and sipped.

So many presents!—Ellen and the girls must have been working for hours. Whitney was touched, if a bit bemused, by their industry; for how like women it was, buying dozens of gifts which in most cases no one really wanted, and, in the case of the affluent Paxtons, certainly did not need; yet fussily, cheerfully, wrapping them in expensive, ornate wrapping paper, glittering green-and-red Christmas paper, tying big ornate bows, sprinkling tinsel, making out cards—"To Father Paxton," "To Aunt Vinia," "To Robert" were a few that caught Whitney's eye—with felt-tip pens. Whitney saw that most of the packages had been wrapped, and neatly stacked together; no more than a half-dozen remained to be wrapped, ranging in size from a small hatbox to an oblong container made of some lightweight metal measuring perhaps three feet by two. One unwrapped present appeared to be a gift box of expensive chocolates, in a gilt-gleaming cannister, metallic, too. Everywhere on the counters and the butcher block table were sheets and strips of wrapping paper, ribbon remnants, Scotch tape rolls, razor blades, scissors, even gardening shears. On a section of green plastic garbage bag on the floor, as if awaiting removal to the garage, or disposal, was a heterogenous assortment of tools—claw-headed hammer, pliers, another gardening shears, a butcher knife with a broken point, Quinn's electric carving knife.

"Uncle Whitney, don't peek!"

Molly and Trish tugged at Whitney's arms, greatly excited. Of course, Whitney realized, they didn't want him to discover his own Christmas present.

Yet he said, teasing, "Why don't I take my own present tonight, and save you the trouble of mailing it? If, that is, you have one for me."

"Of course we have one for you, Whit dear!" Ellen said reprovingly. "But we can't give it to you now."

"Why not?" He winked at the girls. "I promise not to open it till Christmas Day."

"Because—we just can't."

"Even if I promise, cross my heart and hope to die?"

Ellen and the girls exchanged glances, eyes shining. How like their mother the daughters were, Whitney was thinking, with a pang of love, and loss—these three attractive, sweet-faced women, like benign Fates, his brother Quinn's family and not, not ever, *his*. The girls had Ellen's fair, delicate skin and her large, somber, beautiful gray eyes; there was little of Quinn, or of the Paxtons, in them, only a twisty sort of curl to their hair, a pert upper lip.

They were all giggling. "Uncle Whitney," Molly said, "we just *can't.*"

The remainder of the visit passed quickly. They talked of neutral matters, of travel in general, of Whitney's undergraduate year in London; they did not speak of, or even allude to, Quinn. Whitney sensed that, for all their high spirits, and their obvious affection for him, they were eager to be alone again, to finish preparations. And Whitney was eager to be gone.

For this *was* Quinn's house, after all.

Like the kitchen, the guest bathroom had been freshly cleaned; the sink, the toilet bowl, the spotless white bathtub fairly sparkled, from a thorough scrubbing with kitchen cleanser. And the fan whirred energetically overhead, turned to high.

And there was that peculiar odor—a cloying, slightly rancid odor, as of blood. Washing his hands Whitney puzzled over it, uneasily, for it reminded him of something—but what?

Suddenly, then, the memory returned: many years ago, as a child at summer camp in Maine, Whitney had seen the cook cleaning chickens, whistling loudly as she worked—dunking the limp carcasses in steaming water, plucking feathers, chopping and tearing off wings, legs, feet, scooping out, by hand, moist slithery innards. Ugh! The sight and the smell had so nauseated Whitney, he had not been able to eat chicken for months.

With a thrill of repugnance, he wondered, now, if the blood-heavy odor had to do after all with menstruation.

His cheeks burned. He didn't want to know, really.

Some secrets are best kept by females, among females. Yes?

Then, as Whitney was about to leave, Ellen and the girls surprised him: they gave him his Christmas present, after all.

"Only if you promise not to open it before Christmas!"

"Only if you pro-mise!"

Ellen pressed it upon him, and, delighted, Whitney accepted it: a small, agreeably lightweight package, beautifully wrapped in red and gilt paper, of about the size of a box containing a man's shirt or sweater. *"To Uncle Whitney with love—Ellen, Molly, Trish."* Quite pointedly, Quinn's name had been omitted, and Whitney felt satisfaction that Ellen had taken revenge of sorts upon her selfish husband, however petty and inconsequential a revenge.

Ellen and the girls walked with Whitney to the front door, through the darkened house. He noticed slipcovers on the living room furniture, rolled-up carpets, and, again, in the shadowy foyer, a number of boxes, suitcases, and small trunks. These were preparations not for a brief vacation but for a very long trip; apparently Quinn had tricked Ellen into agreeing to some sort of wild plan, to his own advantage, as always. What this might be, Whitney could not guess, and was not about to inquire.

They said good-bye at the door. Ellen, Molly, and Trish kissed Whitney, and he kissed them in turn, and, breath steaming, feeling robust and relieved, Whitney climbed into his car, setting the present in the seat beside him. Girlish voices called after him, "Remember, you promised not to open it till Christmas! Remember, you promised!" and Whitney called back laughingly, "Of course—I promise." An easy promise to make, for he had virtually no interest in whatever they'd bought for him; there was the sentiment, of course, which he appreciated, but so little interest did he have in these annual rituals of gift giving, he arranged for his own presents to be sent out gift-wrapped from a department store, for all occasions requiring gifts; if items of clothing given him didn't fit, he rarely troubled to exchange them.

Driving back home across the city, Whitney felt pleased, however, with the way things had turned out. He'd been brave to go to Quinn's house—Ellen and the girls would always remember. *He* would always remember. He glanced at the present beside him, pleased too that they'd given it to him tonight, that they'd trusted him not to open it prematurely.

How characteristic of women, how sweet, that they trust us as they do, Whitney was thinking; *and that, at times at least, their trust is not misplaced.*

The Maltese Cat

SARA PARETSKY

I

HER VOICE ON THE PHONE HAD BEEN SOFT AND HUSKY, WITH just a whiff on the South laid across it like a rare perfume. "I'd rather come to your office; I don't want people in mine to know I've hired a detective."

I'd offered to see her at home in the evening—my spartan office doesn't invite client confidences. But she didn't want to wait until tonight, she wanted to come today, almost at once, and no, she wouldn't meet me in a restaurant. Far too hard to talk, and this was extremely personal.

"You know my specialty is financial crime, don't you?" I asked sharply.

"Yes, that's how I got your name. One o'clock, fourth floor of the Pulteney, right?" And she'd hung up without telling me who she was.

An errand at the County Building took me longer than I'd expected; it was close to one-thirty by the time I got back to the Pulteney. My caller's problem apparently was urgent: she was waiting outside my office door, tapping one high heel impatiently on the floor as I trudged down the hall in my running shoes.

"Ms. Warshawski! I thought you were standing me up."

"No such luck," I grunted, opening my office door for her.

In the dimly lit hall she'd just been a slender silhouette. Under the office lights the set of the shoulders and signature buttons told me her suit had come from the hands of someone at Chanel. Its blue enhanced the cobalt of her eyes. Soft makeup hid her natural skin tones—I couldn't tell if that dark red hair was natural or merely expertly painted.

She scanned the spare furnishings and picked the cleaner of my two visitor chairs. "My time is valuable, Ms. Warshawski. If I'd known you were going to keep me waiting without a place to sit I would have finished some phone calls before walking over here."

I'd dressed in jeans and a work shirt for a day at the Recorder of Deeds Office. Feeling dirty and outclassed made me grumpy. "You hung up without giving me your name or number, so there wasn't much I could do to let you know you'd have to stand around in your pointy little shoes. My time's valuable, too! Why don't you tell me where the fire is so I can start putting it out."

She flushed. When I turn red I look blotchy, but in her it only enhanced her makeup. "It's my sister." The whiff of Southern increased. "Corinne. She's run off to Ja— my ex-husband, and I need someone to tell her to come back."

I made a disgusted face. "I can't believe I raced back from the County Building to listen to this. It's not 1890, you know. She may be making a mistake but presumably she can sort it out for herself."

Her flush darkened. "I'm not being very clear. I'm sorry. I'm not used to having to ask for things. My sister—Corinne—she's only fourteen. She's my ward. I'm sixteen years older than she is. Our parents died three years ago and she's been living with me since then. It's not easy, not easy for either of us. Moving from Mobile to here was just the beginning. When she got here she wanted to run around, do all the things you can't do in Mobile."

She waved a hand to indicate what kinds of things those might be. "She thinks I'm a tough bitch and that I was too hard on my ex-husband. She's known him since she was three and he was a big hero. She couldn't see he'd changed. Or not changed, just not had the chance to be heroic anymore in public. So when she took off two days ago I assumed she went there. He's not answering his phone or the doorbell. I don't know if they've left town or he's just playing possum or what. I need someone who knows how to get people to open their doors and knows how to talk to people. At least if I could see Corinne I might—I don't know."

She broke off with a helpless gesture that didn't match her sophisticated looks. Nothing like responsibility for a minor to deflate even the most urbane.

I grimaced more ferociously. "Why don't we start with your name, and your husband's name and address, and then move on to her friends."

"Her friends?" The deep blue eyes widened. "I'd just as soon this didn't get around. People talk, and even though it's not 1890, it could be hard on her when she gets back to school."

I suppressed a howl. "You can't come around demanding my expertise and then tell me what or what not to do. What if she's not with your husband? What if I can't get in touch with you when I've found that out and she's in terrible trouble and her life depends on my turning up some new leads? If you can't bring yourself to divulge a few names—starting with your own—you'd better go find yourself a more pliant detective. I can recommend a couple who have waiting rooms."

She set her lips tightly: whatever she did, she was in command—people didn't talk to her that way and get away with it. For a few seconds it looked as though I might be free to get back to the Recorder of Deeds that afternoon, but then she shook her head and forced a smile to her lips.

227

"I was told not to mind your abrasiveness because you were the best. I'm Brigitte LeBlanc. My sister's name is Corinne, also LeBlanc. And my ex-husband is Charles Pierce." She scooted her chair to the desk so she could scribble his address on a sheet of paper torn from a memo pad in her bag. She scrawled busily for several minutes, then handed me a list that included Corinne's three closest school friends, along with Pierce's address.

"I'm late for a meeting. I'll call you tonight to see if you've made any progress." She got up.

"Not so fast," I said. "I get a retainer. You have to sign a contract. And I need a number where I can reach you."

"I really am late."

"And I'm really too busy to hunt for your sister. If you have a sister. You can't be that worried if your meeting is more important than she is."

Her scowl would have terrified me if I'd been alone with her in an alley after dark. "I do have a sister. And I spent two days trying to get into my ex-husband's place, and then in tracking down people who could recommend a private detective to me. I can't do anything else to help her except go earn the money to pay your fee."

I pulled a contract from my desk drawer and stuck it in the manual Olivetti that had belonged to my mother—a typewriter so old that I had to order special ribbons for it from Italy. A word processor would be cheaper and more impressive but the wrist action keeps my forearms strong. I got Ms. LeBlanc to give me her address, to sign on the dotted line for four hundred dollars a day plus expenses, to write in the name of a guaranteeing financial institution, and to hand over a check for two hundred.

When she'd left I wrestled with my office windows, hoping to let some air in to blow her pricey perfume away. Carbon flakes from the El would be better than the lingering scent, but the windows, painted over several hundred times, wouldn't budge. I turned on a desktop fan and frowned sourly at her bold black signature.

What was her ex-husband's real name? She'd bitten off "Ja—" Could be James or Jake, but it sure wasn't Charles. Did she really have a sister? Was this just a ploy to get back at a guy late on his alimony? Although Pierce's address on North Winthrop didn't sound like the place for a man who could afford alimony. Maybe everything went to keep her in Chanel suits while he lived on skid row.

She wasn't in the phone book, so I couldn't check her own address on Belden. The operator told me the number was unlisted. I called a friend at the Fort Dearborn Trust, the bank Brigitte had drawn her check on, and was assured that there was plenty more where that came from. My friend told me Brigitte had parlayed the proceeds of a high-priced modeling career into a successful media consulting firm.

"And if you ever read the fashion pages you'd know these things. Get your nose out of the sports section from time to time, Vic—it'll help with your career."

"Thanks, Eva." I hung up with a snap. At least my client wouldn't turn out to be named something else, always a good beginning to a tawdry case.

I looked in the little mirror perched over my filing cabinet. A dust smudge on my right cheek instead of peach blush wasn't the only distinction between me and Ms. LeBlanc. Since I was dressed appropriately for North Winthrop, I shut up my office and went to retrieve my car.

II

Charles Pierce lived in a dismal ten-flat built flush onto the Uptown sidewalk. Ragged sheets made haphazard curtains in those windows that weren't boarded over. Empty bottles lined the entryway, but the smell of stale Ripple couldn't begin to mask the stench of fresh urine. If Corinne LeBlanc had run away to this place, life with Brigitte must be unmitigated hell.

My client's ex-husband lived in 3E. I knew that because she'd told me. Those few mailboxes whose doors still shut wisely didn't trumpet their owners' identities. The filthy brass nameplate next to the doorbells was empty and the doorbells didn't work. Pushing open the rickety door to the hall, I wondered again about my client's truthfulness: she told me Ja— hadn't answered his phone or his bell.

A rheumy-eyed woman was sprawled across the bottom of the stairs, sucking at a half-pint. She stared at me malevolently when I asked her to move, but she didn't actively try to trip me when I stepped over her. It was only my foot catching in the folds of her overcoat.

The original building probably held two apartments per floor. At least, on the third floor only two doors at either end looked as though they went back to the massive, elegant construction of the building's beginnings. The other seven were flimsy newcomers that had been hastily added when an apartment was subdivided. Peering in the dark I found one labeled B and counted off three more to the right to get to E. After knocking on the peeling veneer several times, I noticed a button embedded in the grime on the jamb. When I pushed it I heard a buzz resonate inside. No one came to the door. With my ear against the filthy panel I could hear the faint hum of a television.

I held the buzzer down for five minutes. It's hard on the finger but harder on the ear. If someone was really in there he should have come boiling to the door by now.

I could go away and come back, but if Pierce was lying doggo to avoid Brigitte, that wouldn't buy me anything. She said she'd tried on and off for two days. The television might be running as a decoy, or—I pushed more lurid ideas from my mind and took out a collection of skeleton keys. The second worked easily in the insubstantial lock. In two minutes I was inside the apartment, looking at an illustration from *House Beautiful in Hell.*

It was a single room with a countertop kitchen on the left side. A tidy person could pull a corrugated screen to shield the room from signs of cooking, but Pierce wasn't tidy. Ten or fifteen stacked pots, festooned with rotting food and roaches, trembled precariously when I shut the door.

Dominating the place was a Murphy bed with a grotesquely fat man sprawled in it at an ominous angle. He'd been watching TV when he died. He was wearing frayed, shiny pants with the fly lying carelessly open and a lumberjack shirt that didn't quite cover his enormous belly.

His monstrous size and the horrible angle at which his bald head was tilted made me gag. I forced it down and walked through a pile of stale clothes to the bed. Lifting an arm the size of a tree trunk, I felt for a pulse. Nothing moved in the heavy arm, but the skin, while clammy, was firm. I couldn't bring myself to touch any more of him but stumbled around the perimeter to peer at him from several angles. I didn't see any obvious wounds. Let the medical examiner hunt out the obscure ones.

By the time I was back in the stairwell I was close to fainting. Only the thought of falling into someone else's urine or vomit kept me on my feet. On the way down I tripped in earnest over the rheumy-eyed woman's coat. Sprawled on the floor at the bottom, I couldn't keep from throwing up myself. It didn't make me feel any better.

I dug a water bottle out of the detritus in my trunk and sponged myself off before calling the police. They asked me to stay near the body. I thought the front seat of my car on Winthrop would be close enough.

While I waited for a meat wagon I wondered about my client. Could Brigitte have come here after leaving me, killed him, and taken off while I was phoning around checking up on her? If she had, the rheumy-eyed woman in the stairwell would have seen her. Would the bond forged by my tripping over her and vomiting in the hall be enough to get her to talk to me?

I got out of the car, but before I could get back to the entrance the police arrived. When we pushed open the rickety door my friend had evaporated. I didn't bother mentioning her to the boys—and girl—in blue: her description wouldn't stand out in Uptown, and even if they could find her she wouldn't be likely to say much.

We plodded up the stairs in silence. There were four of them. The woman and the youngest of the three men seemed in good shape. The two older men were running sadly to flab. I didn't think they'd be able to budge my client's ex-husband's right leg, let alone his mammoth redwood torso.

"I got a feeling about this," the oldest officer muttered, more to himself than the rest of us. "I got a feeling."

When we got to 3E and he looked across at the mass on the bed he shook his head a couple of times. "Yup. I kind of knew as soon as I heard the call."

"Knew what, Tom?" the woman demanded sharply.

"Jade Pierce," he said. "Knew he lived around here. Been a lot of complaints about him. Thought it might be him when I heard we was due to visit a real big guy."

The woman stopped her brisk march to the bed. The rest of us looked at the behemoth in shared sorrow. Jade. Not James or Jake but Jade. Once the most famous lineman the Bears had ever fielded. Now . . . I shuddered.

When he played for Alabama some reporter said his bald head was as smooth and cold as a piece of jade, and went on to spin some tiresome simile relating it to his play. When he signed with the Bears I was as happy as any other Chicago fan, even though his reputation for off-field violence was pretty unappetizing. No wonder Brigitte LeBlanc hadn't stayed with him, but why hadn't she wanted to tell me who he really was? I wrestled with that while Tom called for reinforcements over his lapel mike.

"So what were you doing here?" he asked me.

"His ex-wife hired me to check up on him." I don't usually tell the cops my clients' business, but I didn't feel like protecting Brigitte. "She wanted to talk to him and he wasn't answering his phone or his door."

"She wanted to check up on him?" the fit younger officer, a

man with high cheekbones and a well-tended mustache, echoed me derisively. "What I hear, that split-up was the biggest fight Jade was ever in. Only big fight he ever lost, too."

I smiled. "She's doing well, he isn't. Wasn't. Maybe her conscience pricked her. Or maybe she wanted to rub his nose in it hard. You'd have to ask her. All I can say is she asked me to try to get in, I did, and I called you guys."

While Tom mulled this over I pulled out a card and handed it to him. "You can find me at this number if you want to talk to me."

He called out after me but I went on down the hall, my footsteps echoing hollowly off the bare walls and ceiling.

III

Brigitte LeBlanc was with a client and couldn't be interrupted. The news that her ex-husband had died couldn't pry her loose. Not even the idea that the cops would be around before long could move her. After a combination of cajoling and heckling, the receptionist leaned across her blond desk and whispered at me confidentially: "The vice president of the United States had come in for some private media coaching." Brigitte had said no interruptions unless it was the president or the pope—two people I wouldn't even leave a dental appointment to see.

When they made me unwelcome on the forty-third floor I rode downstairs and hung around the lobby. At five-thirty a bevy of Secret Service agents swept me out to the street with the other loiterers. Fifteen minutes later the vice president came out, his boyish face set in purposeful lines. Even though this was a private visit, the vigilant television crews were waiting for him. He grinned and waved but didn't say anything before climbing into his limo. Brigitte must be really good if she'd persuaded him to shut up.

At seven I went back to the forty-third floor. The double glass doors were locked and the lights turned off. I found a key in my collection that worked the lock, but when I'd prowled through the miles of thick gray plush, explored the secured studios, looked in all the offices, I had to realize my client was smarter than me. She'd left by some back exit.

I gave a high-pitched snarl. I didn't lock the door behind me. Let someone come in and steal all the video equipment. I didn't care.

I swung by Brigitte's three-story brownstone on Belden. She wasn't in. The housekeeper didn't know when to expect her. She was eating out and had said not to wait up for her.

"How about Corinne?" I asked, sure that the woman would say "Corinne who?"

"She's not here, either."

I slipped inside before she could shut the door on me. "I'm V. I. Warshawski. Brigitte hired me to find her sister, said she'd run off to Jade. I went to his apartment. Corinne wasn't there and Jade was dead. I've been trying to talk to Brigitte ever since but she's been avoiding me. I want to know a few things, like if Corinne really exists, and did she really run away, and could either she or Brigitte have killed Jade."

The housekeeper stared at me for a few minutes, then made a sour face. "You got some ID?"

I showed her my PI license and the contract signed by Brigitte. Her sour look deepened but she gave me a few spare details. Corinne was a fat, unhappy teenager who didn't know how good she had it. Brigitte gave her everything, taught her how to dress, sent her to St. Scholastica, even tried to get her to special diet clinics, but she was never satisfied, always whining about her friends back home in Mobile, trashy friends to whom she shouldn't be giving the time of day. And yes, she had run away, three days ago now, and she, the housekeeper, said good riddance, but Brigitte felt responsible. And she was sorry that Jade was dead, but he was a violent man, Corinne had over-idealized him, she didn't realize what a monster he really was.

"They can't turn it off when they come off the field, you know. As for who killed him, he probably killed himself, drinking too much. I always said it would happen that way. Corinne couldn't have done it, she doesn't have enough oomph to her. And Brigitte doesn't have any call to—she already got him beat six ways from Sunday."

"Maybe she thought he'd molested her sister."

"She'd have taken him to court and enjoyed seeing him humiliated all over again."

What a lovely cast of characters; it filled me with satisfaction to think I'd allied myself to their fates. I persuaded the housekeeper to give me a picture of Corinne before going home. She was indeed an overweight, unhappy-looking child. It must be hard having a picture-perfect older sister trying to turn her into a junior deb. I also got the housekeeper to give me Brigitte's unlisted home phone number by telling her if she didn't, I'd be back every hour all night long ringing the bell.

I didn't turn on the radio going home. I didn't want to hear the ghoulish excitement lying behind the unctuousness the reporters would bring to discussing Jade Pierce's catastrophic fall from grace. A rehashing of his nine seasons with the Bears, from the glory years to the last two where nagging knee and back injuries grew too great even for the painkillers. And then to his harsh retirement, putting seventy or eighty pounds of fat over his playing weight of 310, the barroom fights, the guns fired at other drivers from the front seat of his Ferrari Daytona, then the sale of the Ferrari to pay his legal bills, and finally the three-ring circus that was his divorce. Ending on a Murphy bed in a squalid Uptown apartment.

I shut the Trans Am's door with a viciousness it didn't deserve and stomped up the three flights to my apartment. Fatigue mixed with bitterness dulled the sixth sense that usually warns me of danger. The man had me pinned against my front door with a gun at my throat before I knew he was there.

I held my shoulder bag out to him. "Be my guest. Then leave. I've had a long day and I don't want to spend too much of it with you."

He spat. "I don't want your stupid little wallet."

"You're not going to rape me, so you might as well take my stupid little wallet."

"I'm not interested in your body. Open your apartment. I want to search it."

"Go to hell." I kneed him in the stomach and swept my right arm up to knock his gun hand away. He gagged and bent over. I used my handbag as a clumsy bola and whacked him on the back of the head. He slumped to the floor, unconscious.

I grabbed the gun from his flaccid hand. Feeling gingerly inside his coat, I found a wallet. His driver's license identified him as Joel Sirop, living at a pricey address on Dearborn Parkway. He sported a high-end assortment of credit cards—Bonwit, Neiman-Marcus, an American Express platinum—and a card that said he was a member in good standing of the Feline Breeders Association of North America. I slid the papers back into his billfold and returned it to his breast pocket.

He groaned and opened his eyes. After a few diffuse seconds he focused on me in outrage. "My head. You've broken my head. I'll sue you."

"Go ahead. I'll hang on to your pistol for use as evidence at the trial. I've got your name and address, so if I see you near my place again I'll know where to send the cops. Now leave."

"Not until I've searched your apartment." He was unarmed and sickly but stubborn.

I leaned against my door, out of reach but poised to stomp on him if he got cute. "What are you looking for, Mr. Sirop?"

"It was on the news, how you found Jade. If the cat was there, you must have taken it."

"Rest your soul, there were no cats in that apartment when I got there. Had he stolen yours?"

He shut his eyes, apparently to commune with himself. When

he opened them again, he said he had no choice but to trust me.
I smiled brightly and told him he could always leave so I could
have dinner, but he insisted on confiding in me.

"Do you know cats, Ms. Warshawski?"

"Only in a manner of speaking. I have a dog and she knows
cats."

He scowled. "This is not a laughing matter. Have you heard
of the Maltese?"

"Cat? I guess I've heard of them. They're the ones without
tails, right?"

He shuddered. "No. You are thinking of the Manx. The Maltese—they are usually a bluish gray. Very rarely will you see one
that is almost blue. Brigitte LeBlanc has—or had—such a cat.
Lady Iva of Cairo."

"Great. I presume she got it to match her eyes."

He waved aside my comment as another frivolity. "Her motives
do not matter. What matters is that the cat has been very difficult
to breed. She has now come into season for only the third time
in her four-year life. Brigitte agreed to let me try to mate Lady
Iva with my sire, Casper of Valletta. It is imperative that she be
sent to stay with him, and soon. But she has disappeared."

It was my turn to look disgusted. "I took a step down from my
usual practice to look for a runaway teenager today. I'm damned
if I'm going to hunt a missing cat through the streets of Chicago.
Your sire will find her faster than I will. Matter of fact, that's my
advice. Drive around listening for the yowling of mighty sires and
eventually you'll find your Maltese."

"This runaway teenager, this Corinne, it is probable that she
took Lady Iva with her. The kittens, if they are born, if they are
purebred, could fetch a thousand or more each. She is not ignorant of that fact. But if Lady Iva is out on the streets and some
other sire finds her first, they would be half-breeds, not worth
the price of their veterinary care."

He spoke with the intense passion I usually reserve for discussing Cubs or Bears trades. Keeping myself turned toward him,

I unlocked my front door. He hurled himself at the opening with a ferocity that proved his long years with felines had rubbed off on him. I grabbed his jacket as he hurtled past me, but he tore himself free.

"I am not leaving until I have searched your premises," he panted.

I rubbed my head tiredly. "Go ahead, then."

I could have called the cops while he hunted around for Lady Iva. Instead, I poured myself a whiskey and watched him crawl on his hands and knees, making little whistling sounds—perhaps the mating call of the Maltese. He went through my cupboards, my stove, the refrigerator, even insisted, his eyes wide with fear, that I open the safe in my bedroom closet. I removed the Smith & Wesson I keep there before letting him look.

When he'd inspected the back landing he had to agree that no cats were on the premises. He tried to argue me into going downtown to check my office. At that point my patience ran out.

"I could have you arrested for attempted assault and criminal trespass. So get out now while the going's good. Take your guy down to my office. If she's in there and in heat, he'll start carrying on and you can call the cops. Just don't bother me." I hustled him out the front door, ignoring his protests.

I carefully did up all the locks. I didn't want some other deranged cat breeder sneaking up on me in the middle of the night.

IV

It was after midnight when I finally reached Brigitte. Yes, she'd gotten my message about Jade. She was terribly sorry, but since she couldn't do anything to help him now that he was dead, she hadn't bothered to try to reach me.

"We're about to part company, Brigitte. If you didn't know the guy was dead when you sent me up to Winthrop, you're going to have to prove it. Not to me, but to the cops. I'm talking to

Lieutenant Mallory at the Central District in the morning to tell
him the rigmarole you spun me. They'll also be able to figure out
if you were more interested in finding Corinne or your cat."

There was a long silence at the other end. When she finally
spoke, the hint of Southern was pronounced. "Can we talk in the
morning before you call the police? Maybe I haven't been as frank
as I should have. I'd like you to hear the whole story before you
do anything rash."

Just say no, just say no, I chanted to myself. "You be at the
Belmont Diner at eight, Brigitte. You can lay it out for me but
I'm not making any promises."

I got up at seven, ran the dog over to Belmont Harbor and
back and took a long shower. I figured even if I put a half hour
into grooming myself I wasn't going to look as good as Brigitte,
so I just scrambled into jeans and a cotton sweater.

It was almost ten minutes after eight when I got to the diner,
but Brigitte hadn't arrived yet. I picked up a *Herald-Star* from the
counter and took it over to a booth to read with a cup of coffee.
The headline shook me to the bottom of my stomach.

FOOTBALL HERO SURVIVES FATE WORSE THAN DEATH

Charles "Jade" Pierce, once the smoothest man on the
Bears' fearsome defense, eluded offensive blockers once
again. This time the stakes were higher than a touchdown, though: the offensive lineman was Death.

I thought Jeremy Logan was overdoing it by a wide margin but
I read the story to the end. The standard procedure with a body
is to take it to a hospital for a death certificate before it goes to
the morgue. The patrol team hauled Jade to Beth Israel for a
perfunctory exam. There the intern, noticing a slight sweat on
Jade's neck and hands, dug deeper for a pulse than I'd been willing
to go. She'd found faint but unmistakable signs of life buried deep

in the mountain of flesh and had brought him back to consciousness.

Jade, who's had substance abuse problems since leaving the Bears, had mainlined a potent mixture of ether and hydrochloric acid before drinking a quart of bourbon. When he came to his first words were characteristic: "Get the f—— out of my face."

Logan then concluded with the obligatory rundown on Jade's career and its demise, with a pious sniff about the use and abuse of sports heroes left to die in the gutter when they could no longer please the crowd. I read it through twice, including the fulsome last line, before Brigitte arrived.

"You see, Jade's still alive, so I couldn't have killed him," she announced, sweeping into the booth in a cloud of Chanel.

"Did you know he was in a coma when you came to see me yesterday?"

She raised plucked eyebrows in a hauteur. "Are you questioning my word?"

One of the waitresses chugged over to take our order. "You want your fruit and yogurt, right, Vic? And what else?"

"Green pepper and cheese omelet with rye toast. Thanks, Barbara. What'll yours be, Brigitte?" Dry toast and black coffee, no doubt.

"Is your fruit *really* fresh?" she demanded

Barbara rolled her eyes. "We don't allow no one to be fresh in here, honey, regardless of sex preference. You want some or not?"

Brigitte set her shoulder—covered today in green broadcloth with black piping—and got ready to do battle. I cut her off before the first "How dare you" rolled to its ugly conclusion.

"This isn't the kind of place where the maître d' wilts at your frown and races over to make sure madam is happy. They don't care if you come back or not. In fact, about now they'd be happier if you'd leave. You can check out my fruit when it comes and order some if it tastes right to you."

"I'll just have wheat toast and black coffee," she said icily. "And make sure they don't put any butter on it."

"Right," Barbara said. "Wheat toast, margarine instead of butter. Just kidding, hon," she added as Brigitte started to tear into her again. "You gotta learn to take it if you want to dish it out."

"Did you bring me here to be insulted?" Brigitte demanded when Barbara had left.

"I brought you here to talk. It didn't occur to me that you wouldn't know diner etiquette. We can fight if you want to. Or you can tell me about Jade and Corinne. And your cat. I had a visit from Joel Sirop last night."

She swallowed some coffee and made a face. "They should rinse the pots with vinegar."

"Well, keep it to yourself. They won't pay you a consulting fee for telling them about it. Joel tell you he'd come around hunting Lady Iva?"

She frowned at me over the rim of the coffee cup, then nodded fractionally.

"Why didn't you tell me about the damned cat when you were in my office yesterday?"

Her poise deserted her for a moment; she looked briefly ashamed. "I thought you'd look for Corinne. I didn't think I could persuade you to hunt down my cat. Anyway, Corinne must have taken Iva with her, so I thought if you found her you'd find the cat, too."

"Which one do you really want back?"

She started to bristle again, then suddenly laughed. It took ten years from her face. "You wouldn't ask that if you'd ever lived with a teenager. And Corinne's always been a stranger to me. She was eighteen months old when I left for college and I only saw her a week or two at a time on vacations. She used to worship me. When she moved in with me I thought it would be a piece of cake: I'd get her fixed up with the right crowd and the right school, she'd do her best to be like me, and the system would run itself. Instead, she put on a lot of weight, won't listen to me about her eating, slouches around with the kids in the neighborhood when my back is turned, the whole nine yards. Jade's influence. It creeps through every now and then when I'm not thinking."

She looked at my blueberries. I offered them to her and she helped herself to a generous spoonful.

"And that was the other thing. Jade. We got together when I was an Alabama cheerleader and he was the biggest hero in town. I thought I'd really caught me a prize, my yes, a big prize. But the first, last, and only thing in a marriage with a football player is football. And him, of course, how many sacks he made, how many yards he allowed, all that boring crap. And if he has to sit out a game, or he gives up a touchdown, or he doesn't get the glory, watch out. Jade was mean. He was mean on the field; he was mean off it. He broke my arm once."

Her voice was level but her hand shook a little as she lifted the coffee cup to her mouth. "I got me a gun and shot him in the leg the next time he came at me. They put it down as a hunting accident in the papers, but he never tried anything on me after that—not physical, I mean. Until his career ended. Then he got real, real ugly. The papers crucified me for abandoning him when his career was over. They never had to live with him."

She was panting with emotions by the time she finished. "And Corinne shared the papers' views?" I asked gently.

She nodded. "We had a bad fight on Sunday. She wanted to go to a sleepover at one of the girls' in the neighborhood. I don't like that girl and I said no. We had a gale-force battle after that. When I got home from work on Monday she'd taken off. First I figured she'd gone to this girl's place. They hadn't seen her, though, and she hadn't shown up at school. So I figured she'd run off to Jade. Now . . . I don't know. I would truly appreciate it if you'd keep looking, though."

Just say no, Vic, I chanted to myself. "I'll need a thousand up front. And more names and addresses of friends, including people in Mobile. I'll check in with Jade at the hospital. She might have gone to him, you know, and he sent her on someplace else."

"I stopped by there this morning. They said no visitors."

I grinned. "I've got friends in high places." I signaled Barbara for the check. "Speaking of which, how was the vice president?"

She looked as though she were going to give me one of her stiff rebuttals, but then she curled her lip and drawled, "Just like every other good old boy, honey, just like every other good old boy."

V

Lotty Herschel, an obstetrician associated with Beth Israel, arranged for me to see Jade Pierce. "They tell me he's been difficult. Don't stand next to the bed unless you're wearing a padded jacket."

"You want him, you can have him," the floor head told me. "He's going home tomorrow morning. Frankly, since he won't let anyone near him, they ought to release him right now."

My palms felt sweaty when I pushed open the door to Jade's room. He didn't throw anything when I came in, didn't even turn his head to stare through the restraining rails surrounding the bed. His mountain of flesh poured through them, ebbing away from a rounded summit in the middle. The back of his head, smooth and shiny as a piece of polished jade, reflected the ceiling light into my eyes.

"I don't need any goddamned ministering angels, so get the fuck out of here," he growled at the window.

"That's a relief. My angel act never really got going."

He turned his head at that. His black eyes were mean, narrow slits. If I were a quarterback I'd hand him the ball and head for the showers.

"What are you, the goddamned social worker?"

"Nope. I'm the goddamned detective who found you yesterday before you slipped off to the great huddle in the sky."

"Come on over then, so I can kiss your ass," he spat venomously.

I leaned against the wall and crossed my arms. "I didn't mean to save your life: I tried getting them to send you to the morgue. The meat wagon crew double-crossed me."

The mountain shook and rumbled. It took me a few seconds to realize he was laughing. "You're right, detective: you ain't no angel. So what do you want? True confessions on why I was such a bad boy? The name of the guy who got me the stuff?"

"As long as you're not hurting anyone but yourself I don't care what you do or where you get your shit. I'm here because Brigitte hired me to find Corinne."

His face set in ugly lines again. "Get out."

I didn't move.

"I said get out!" He raised his voice to a bellow.

"Just because I mentioned Brigitte's name?"

"Just because if you're pally with that broad, you're a snake by definition."

"I'm not pally with her. I met her yesterday. She's paying me to find her sister." It took an effort not to yell back at him.

"Corinne's better off without her," he growled, turning the back of his head to me again.

I didn't say anything, just stood there. Five minutes passed. Finally he jeered, without looking at me. "Did the sweet little martyr tell you I broke her arm?"

"She mentioned it, yes."

"She tell you how that happened?"

"Please don't tell me how badly she misunderstood you. I don't want to throw up my breakfast."

At that he swung his gigantic face around toward me again. "Com'ere."

When I didn't move, he sighed and patted the bedrail. "I'm not going to slug you, honest. If we're going to talk, you gotta get close enough for me to see your face."

I went over to the bed and straddled the chair, resting my arms on its back. Jade studied me in silence, then grunted as if to say I'd passed some minimal test.

"I won't tell you Brigitte didn't understand me. Broad had my number from day one. I didn't break her arm, though: that was B. B. Wilder. Old Gunshot. Thought he was my best friend on the club, but it turned out he was Brigitte's. And then, when I come home early from a hunting trip and found her in bed with him, we got all carried away. She loved the excitement of big men fighting. It's what made her a football groupie to begin with down in Alabama."

I tried to imagine ice-cold Brigitte flushed with excitement while the Bears' right tackle and defensive end fought over her. It didn't seem impossible.

"So B. B. broke her arm but I agreed to take the rap. Her little old modeling career was just getting off the ground and she didn't want her good name sullied. And besides that, she kept hoping for a reconciliation with her folks, at least with their wad, and they'd never fork it over if she got herself some ugly publicity committing violent adultery. And me, I was just the baddest boy the Bears ever fielded; one more mark didn't make that much difference to me." The jeering note returned to his voice.

"She told me it was when you retired that things deteriorated between you."

"Things deteriorated—what a way to put it. Look, detective what did you say your name was? V. I., that's a hell of a name for a girl. What did your mamma call you?"

"Victoria," I said grudgingly. "And no one calls me Vicki, so don't even think about it." I prefer not to be called a girl, either, much less a broad, but Jade didn't seem like the person to discuss that particular issue with.

"Victoria, huh? Things deteriorated, yeah, like they was a picnic starting out. I was born dumb and I didn't get smarter for making five hundred big ones a year. But I wouldn't hit a broad, even one like Brigitte who could get me going just looking at me. I broke a lot of furniture, though, and that got on her nerves."

I couldn't help laughing. "Yeah, I can see that. It'd bother me, too."

He gave a grudging smile. "See, the trouble is, I grew up poor. I mean, dirt poor. I used to go to the projects here with some of the black guys on the squad, you know, Christmas appearances, shit like that. Those kids live in squalor, but I didn't own a pair of shorts to cover my ass until the county social worker came round to see why I wasn't in school."

"So you broke furniture because you grew up without it and didn't know what else to do with it?"

"Don't be a wiseass, Victoria. I'm sure your mamma wouldn't like it."

I made a face—he was right about that.

"You know the LeBlancs, right? Oh, you're a Yankee. Yankees don't know shit if they haven't stepped in it themselves. LeBlanc Gas, they're one of the biggest names on the Gulf Coast. They're a long, *long* way from the Pierces of Florette.

"I muscled my way into college, played football for Old Bear Bryant, met Brigitte. She liked raw meat, and mine was just about the rawest in the South, so she latched on to me. When she decided to marry me she took me down to Mobile for Christmas. There I was, the Hulk, in Miz Effie's lace and crystal palace. They hated me, knew I was trash, told Brigitte they'd cut her out of everything if she married me. She figured she could sweet-talk her daddy into anything. We got married and it didn't work, not even when I was a national superstar. To them I was still the dirt I used to wipe my ass with."

"So she divorced you to get back in their will?"

He shrugged, a movement that set a tidal wave going down the mountain. "Oh, that had something to do with it, sure, it had something. But I was a wreck and I was hell to live with. Even if she'd been halfway normal to begin with, it would have gone bust, 'cause I didn't know how to live with losing football. I just didn't care about anyone or anything."

"Not even the Daytona," I couldn't help saying.

His black eyes disappeared into tiny dots. "Don't you go lecturing me just when we're starting to get on. I'm not asking you to cry over my sad jock story. I'm just trying to give you a little different look at sweet, beautiful Brigitte."

"Sorry. It's just . . . I'll never do anything to be able to afford a Ferrari Daytona. It pisses me to see someone throw one away."

He snorted. "If I'd known you five years ago I'd've given it to you. Too late now. Anyway, Brigitte waited too long to jump ship. She was still in negotiations with old man LeBlanc when he and Miz Effie dropped into the Gulf of Mexico with the remains of their little Cessna. Everything that wasn't tied down went to Corinne. Brigitte, being her guardian, gets a chunk for looking after her, but you ask me, if Corinne's gone missing it's the best thing she could do. I'll bet you . . . well, I don't have anything left to bet. I'll hack off my big toe and give it to you if Brigitte's after anything but the money."

He thought for a minute. "No. She probably likes Corinne some. Or would like her if she'd lose thirty pounds, dress like a Mobile debutante, and hang around with a crowd of snot-noses. I'd hack off my toe if the money ain't number one in her heart, that's all."

I eyed him steadily, wondering how much of his story to believe. It's why I stay away from domestic crime: everyone has a story, and it wears you out trying to match all the different pieces together. I could check the LeBlancs' will to see if they'd left their fortune the way Jade reported it. Or if they had a fortune at all. Maybe he was making it all up.

"Did Corinne talk to you before she took off on Monday?"

His black eyes darted around the room. "I haven't laid eyes on her in months. She used to come around, but Brigitte got a peace bond on me. I get arrested if I'm within thirty feet of Corinne."

"I believe you, Jade," I said steadily. "I believe you haven't seen her. But did she talk to you? Like on the phone, maybe."

The ugly look returned to his face, then the mountain shook again as he laughed. "You don't miss many signals, do you, Victoria?

You oughta run a training camp. Yeah, Corinne calls me Monday morning. 'Why don't you have your cute little ass in school?' I says. 'Even with all your family dough that's the only way to get ahead—they'll ream you six ways from Sunday if you don't get your education so you can check out what all your advisers are up to.'"

He shook his head broodingly. "I know what I'm talking about, believe me. The lawyers and agents and financial advisers, they all made out like hogs at feeding time when I was in the money, but come trouble, it wasn't them, it was me hung out like a slab of pork belly to dry on my own."

"So what did Corinne say to your good advice?" I prompted, trying not to sound impatient: I could well be the first sober person to listen to him in a decade.

"Oh, she's crying, she can't stand it, why can't she just run home to Mobile? And I tell her 'cause she's underage and rich, the cops will all be looking for her and just haul her butt back to Chicago. And when she keeps talking wilder and wilder I tell her they'll be bound to blame me if something happens to her and does she really need to run away so bad that I go to jail or something. So I thought that calmed her down. 'Think of it like rookie camp,' I told her. 'They put you through the worst shit but if you survive it you own them.' I thought she figured it out and was staying."

He shut his eyes. "I'm tired, detective. I can't tell you nothing else. You go away and detect."

"If she went back to Mobile who would she stay with?"

"Wouldn't nobody down there keep her without calling Brigitte. Too many of them owe their jobs to LeBlanc Gas." He didn't open his eyes.

"And up here?"

He shrugged, a movement like an earthquake that rattled the bedrails. "You might try the neighbors. Seems to me Corinne mentioned a Miz Hellman who had a bit of a soft spot for her."

He opened his eyes. "Maybe Corinne'll talk to you. You got a good ear."

"Thanks." I got up. "What about this famous Maltese cat?"

"What about it?"

"It went missing along with Corinne. Think she'd hurt it to get back at Brigitte?"

"How the hell should I know? Those LeBlancs would do anything to anyone. Even Corinne. Now get the fuck out so I can get my beauty rest." He shut his eyes again.

"Yeah, you're beautiful all right, Jade. Why don't you use some of your old connections and get yourself going at something? It's really pathetic seeing you like this."

"You wanna save me along with the Daytona?" The ugly jeer returned to his voice. "Don't go all do-gooder on me now, Victoria. My daddy died at forty from too much moonshine. They tell me I'm his spitting image. I know where I'm going."

"It's trite, Jade. Lots of people have done it. They'll make a movie about you and little kids will cry over your sad story. But if they make it honest they'll show that you're just plain selfish."

I wanted to slam the door but the hydraulic stop took the impact out of the gesture. "Goddamned motherfucking waste," I snapped as I stomped down the corridor.

The floor head heard me. "Jade Pierce? You're right about that."

VI

The Hellmans lived in an apartment above the TV repair shop they ran on Halsted. Mrs. Hellman greeted me with some relief.

"I promised Corinne I wouldn't tell her sister as long as she stayed here instead of trying to hitchhike back to Mobile. But I've been pretty worried. It's just that . . . to Brigitte LeBlanc I don't exist. My daughter Lily is trash that she doesn't want

Corinne associated with, so it never even occurred to her that Corinne might be here."

She took me through the back of the shop and up the stairs to the apartment. "It's only five rooms, but we're glad to have her as long as she wants to stay. I'm more worried about the cat: she doesn't like being cooped up in here. She got out Tuesday night and we had a terrible time hunting her down."

I grinned to myself: So much for the thoroughbred descendants pined for by Joel Sirop.

Mrs. Hellman took me into the living room where they had a sofabed that Corinne was using. "This here is a detective, Corinne. I think you'd better talk to her."

Corinne was hunched in front of the television, an outsize console model far too large for the tiny room. In her man's white shirt and tattered blue jeans she didn't look at all like her svelte sister. Her complexion was a muddy color that matched her lank, straight hair. She clutched Lady Iva of Cairo close in her arms. Both of them looked at me angrily.

"If you think you can make me go back to that cold-assed bitch, you'd better think again."

Mrs. Hellman tried to protest her language.

"It's OK," I said. "She learned it from Jade. But Jade lost every fight he ever was in with Brigitte, Corinne. Maybe you ought to try a different method."

"Brigitte hated Jade. She hates anyone who doesn't do stuff just the way she wants it. So if you're working for Brigitte you don't know shit about anything."

I responded to the first part of her comments. "Is that why you took the cat? So you could keep her from having purebred kittens like Brigitte wants her to?"

A ghost of a smile twitched around her unhappy mouth. All she said was "They wouldn't let me bring my dogs or my horse up north. Iva's kind of a snoot but she's better than nothing."

"Jade thinks Brigitte's jealous because you got the LeBlanc fortune and she didn't."

She made a disgusted noise. "Jade worries too much about all that shit. Yeah, Daddy left me a big fat wad. But the company went to daddy's cousin Miles. You can't inherit LeBlanc Gas if you're a girl and Brigitte knew that, same as me. I mean, they told both of us growing up so we wouldn't have our hearts set on it. The money they left me, Brigitte makes that amount every year in her business. She doesn't care about the money."

"And you? Does it bother you that the company went to your cousin?"

She gave a long ugly sniff—no doubt another of Jade's expressions. "Who wants a company that doesn't do anything but pollute the Gulf and ream the people who work for them?"

I considered that. At fourteen it was probably genuine bravado. "So what do you care about?"

She looked at me with sulky dark eyes. For a minute I thought she was going to tell me to mind my own goddamned business and go to hell, but she suddenly blurted, "It's my horse. They left the house to Miles along with my horse. They didn't think about it, just said the house and all the stuff that wasn't special to someone else went to him and they didn't even think to leave me my own horse."

The last sentence came out as a wail and her angry young face dissolved into sobs. I didn't think she'd welcome a friendly pat on the shoulder. I just let the tears run their course. She finally wiped her nose on a frayed cuff and shot me a fierce look to see if I cared.

"If I could persuade Brigitte to buy your horse from Miles and stable him up here, would you be willing to go back to her until you're of age?"

"You never would. Nobody ever could make that bitch change her mind."

"But if I could?"

Her lower lip was hanging out. "Maybe. If I could have my horse and go to school with Lily instead of fucking St. Scholastica."

"I'll do my best." I got to my feet. "In return maybe you could work on Jade to stop drugging himself to death. It isn't romantic, you know: it's horrible, painful, about the ugliest thing in the world."

She only glowered at me. It's hard work being an angel. No one takes at all kindly to it.

VII

Brigitte was furious. Her cheeks flamed with natural color and her cobalt eyes glittered. I couldn't help wondering if this was how she looked when Jade and B. B. Wilder were fighting over her.

"So he knew all along where she was! I ought to have him sent over for that. Can't I charge him with contributing to her delinquency?"

"Not if you're planning on using me as a witness you can't," I snapped.

She ignored me. "And her, too. Taking Lady Iva off like that. Mating her with some alley cat."

As if on cue, Casper of Valletta squawked loudly and started clawing the deep silver plush covering Brigitte's living-room floor. Joel Sirop picked up the tom and spoke soothingly to him.

"It's bad, Brigitte, very bad. Maybe you should let the girl go back to Mobile if she wants to so badly. After three days, you know, it's too late to give Lady Iva a shot. And Corinne is so wild, so uncontrollable—what would stop her the next time Lady Iva comes into season?"

Brigitte's nostrils flared. "I should send her to reform school. Show her what discipline is really like."

"Why in hell do you even want custody over Corinne if all you can think about is revenge?" I interrupted.

She stopped swirling around her living room and turned to frown at me. "Why, I love her, of course. She is my sister, you know."

"Concentrate on that. Keep saying it to yourself. She's not a cat that you can breed and mold to suit your fancy."

"I just want her to be happy when she's older. She won't be if she can't learn to control herself. Look at what happened when she started hanging around trash like that Lily Hellman. She would never have let Lady Iva breed with an alley cat if she hadn't made that kind of friend."

I ground my teeth. "Just because Lily lives in five rooms over a store doesn't make her trash. Look, Brigitte. You wanted to lead your own life. I expect your parents tried keeping you on a short leash. Hell, maybe they even threatened you with reform school. So you started fucking every hulk you could get your hands on. Are you so angry about that that you have to treat Corinne the same way?"

She gaped at me. Her jaw worked but she couldn't find any words. Finally she went over to a burled oak cabinet that concealed a bar. She pulled out a chilled bottle of Sancerre and poured herself a glass. When she'd gulped it down she sat at her desk.

"Is it that obvious? Why I went after Jade and B. B. and all those boys?"

I hunched a shoulder. "It was a guess, Brigitte. A guess based on what I've learned about you and your sister and Jade the last two days. He's not such an awful guy, you know, but he clearly was an awful guy for you. And Corinne's lonely and miserable and needs someone to love her. She figures her horse for the job."

"And me?" Her cobalt eyes glittered again. "What do I need? The embraces of my cat?"

"To shed some of those porcupine quills so someone can love you, too. You could've offered me a glass of wine, for example."

She started an ugly retort, then went over to the liquor cabinet and got out a glass for me. "So I bring Flitcraft up to Chicago and stable her. I put Corinne into the filthy public high school. And then we'll all live happily ever after."

"She might graduate." I swallowed some of the wine. It was

cold and crisp and eased some of the tension the LeBlancs and Pierces were putting into my throat. "And in another year she won't run away to Lily's, but she'll go off to Mobile or hit the streets. Now's your chance."

"Oh, all right," she snapped. "You're some kind of saint, I know, who never said a bad word to anyone. You can tell Corinne I'll cut a deal with her. But if it goes wrong you can be the one to stay up at night worrying about her."

I rubbed my head. "Send her back to Mobile, Brigitte. There must be a grandmother or aunt or nanny or someone who really cares about her. With your attitude, life with Corinne is just going to be a bomb waiting for the fuse to blow."

"You can say that again, detective." It was Jade, his bulk filling the double doors to the living room.

Behind him we could hear the housekeeper without being able to see her. "I tried to keep him out, Brigitte, but Corinne let him in. You want me to call the cops, get them to exercise that peace bond?"

"I have a right to ask whoever I want into my own house," came Corinne's muffled shriek.

Squawking and yowling, Casper broke from Joel Sirop's hold. He hurtled himself at the doorway and stuffed his body through the gap between Jade's feet. On the other side of the barricade we could hear Lady Iva's answering yodel and a scream from Corinne—presumably she'd been clawed.

"Why don't you move, Jade, so we can see the action?" I suggested.

He lumbered into the living room and perched his bulk on the edge of a pale gray sofa. Corinne stumbled in behind him and sat next to him. Her muddy skin and lank hair looked worse against the sleek modern lines of Brigitte's furniture than they had in Mrs. Hellman's crowded sitting room.

Brigitte watched the blood drip from Corinne's right hand to the rug and jerked her head at the housekeeper hovering in the doorway. "Can you clean that up for me, Grace?"

When the housekeeper left, she turned to her sister. "Next time you're that angry at me take it out on me, not the cat. Did you really have to let her breed in a back alley?"

"It's all one to Iva," Corinne muttered sulkily. "Just as long as she's getting some she don't care who's giving it to her. Just like you."

Brigitte marched to the couch. Jade caught her hand as she was preparing to smack Corinne.

"Now look here, Brigitte," he said. "You two girls don't belong together. You know that as well as I do. Maybe you think you owe it to your public image to be a mamma to Corinne, but you're not the mamma type. Never have been. Why should you try now?"

Brigitte glared at him. "And you're Mister Wonderful who can sit in judgment on everyone else?"

He shook his massive jade dome. "Nope. I won't claim that. But maybe Corinne here would like to come live with me." He held up a massive palm as Brigitte started to protest. "Not in Uptown. I can get me a place close to here. Corinne can have her horse and see you when you feel calm enough. And when your pure little old cat has her half-breed kittens they can come live with us."

"On Corinne's money," Brigitte spat.

Jade nodded. "She'd have to put up the stake. But I know some guys who'd back me to get started in somethin'. Commodities, somethin' like that."

"You'd be drunk or doped up all the time. And then you'd rape her—" She broke off as he did his ugly-black-slit number with his eyes.

"You'd better not say anything else, Brigitte LeBlanc. Damned well better not say anything. You want me to get up in the congregation and yell that I never touched a piece of ass that shoved itself in my nose, I ain't going to. But you know better'n anyone that I never in my life laid hands on a girl to hurt her. As for the rest . . ." His eyes returned to normal and he put a redwood branch around Corinne's shoulders. "First time I'm drunk or shooting somethin' Corinne comes right back here. We can try it for six months, Brigitte. Just a trial. Rookie camp, you know how it goes."

The football analogy brought her own mean look to Brigitte's face. Before she could say anything Joel bleated in the background, "It sounds like a good idea to me, Brigitte. Really. You ought to give it a try. Lady Iva's nerves will never be stable with the fighting that goes on around her when Corinne is here."

"No one asked you," Brigitte snapped.

"And no one asked me, either," Corinne said. "If you don't agree, I—I'm going to take Lady Iva and run away to New York. And send you pictures of her with litter after litter of alley cats."

The threat, uttered with all the venom she could muster, made me choke with laughter. I swallowed some Sancerre to try to control myself, but I couldn't stop laughing. Jade's mountain rumbled and shook as he joined in. Joel gasped in horror. Only the two LeBlanc women remained unmoved, glaring at each other.

"What I ought to do, I ought to send you to reform school, Corinne Alton LeBlanc."

"What you ought to do is cool out," I advised, putting my glass down on a chrome table. "It's a good offer. Take it. If you don't, she'll only run away."

Brigitte tightened her mouth in a narrow line. "I didn't hire you to have you turn on me, you know."

"Yeah, well, you hired me. You didn't buy me. My job is to help you resolve a difficult problem. And this looks like the best solution you're going to be offered."

"Oh, very well," she snapped pettishly, pouring herself another drink. "For six months. And if her grades start slipping, or I hear she's drinking or doping or anything like that, she comes back here."

I got up to go. Corinne followed me to the door.

"I'm sorry I was rude to you over at Lily's," she muttered shyly. "When the kittens are born you can have the one you like best."

I gulped and tried to smile. "That's very generous of you, Corinne. But I don't think my dog would take too well to a kitten."

"Don't you like cats?" The big brown eyes stared at me poignantly. "Really, cats and dogs get along very well unless their owners expect them not to."

"Like LeBlancs and Pierces, huh?"

She bit her lip and turned her head, then said in a startled voice, "You're teasing me, aren't you?"

"Just teasing you, Corinne. You take it easy. Things are going to work out for you. And if they don't, give me a call before you do anything too rash, OK?"

"And you will take a kitten?"

Just say no, Vic, just say no, I chanted to myself. "Let me think about it. I've got to run now." I fled the house before she could break my resolve any further.

The Werewolf Game

MAURICIO-JOSÉ SCHWARZ

I

IT WAS A NIGHT TO GO OUT AND PLAY.

Spice believes there's no point in talking. He says words garble feelings and make liars out of people, so we talk very little. It's only the two of us. We don't share this with anyone else, not even the rest of the group.

Unlike the real werewolves of movies, we go out any night, full moon or not, to roam after curfew. Of course there's no real curfew. Anyone can go out at any time, that's why this is a free country. But almost no one dares to be out in the streets after ten. Nine on Fridays and Saturdays. These free streets don't value life, oh no. There's too many people, so each one is worth less. That's why you have to take care of yourself and your own. No one else will.

I believe that these days the only real way to find your own place is by making it in the streets, where everything's dead serious. That's why I am with the group and that's why I play the game with Spice. But whenever I try to talk about it, Spice looks at me with a dark, dormant rage. I've heard it said that rage is a part of being on the street, but we don't listen. So I keep quiet. I have long given up on finding out why Spice plays the game.

We always meet on the corner by the old store, which peers at us through its glassless windows, its door-mouth silenced long ago by a rusty old chain held in place by a rusty old padlock. That's the beginning of the challenge, because that's exactly where our territory ends. Just cross the street and you're in their turf, their little country.

But we don't play the werewolf game against them, and never in their territory. We're not at war right now, although there's always the chance of meeting one of them during the night. But they shouldn't be on our streets at night. At night everyone is the same. I call it the great equalizer. Caucasian and mulatto, Latino and Asian. When the sun is down and you're in a dark street, it doesn't matter. Then there are only bodies moving, faceless, through the rancid air.

I would like to talk to Spice about these things, but it's useless. When he can't get silence outside, he builds it inside himself. He just stops listening to everything. Just as all of us close our eyes when we don't like something we see, Spice is able to close his ears, or maybe his mind. They say he once spent three weeks without saying a word. And without listening to any. He especially shut me out at first because I had an education. He doesn't like that, so I've tried to forget it, language and all. It's not easy to forget certain things, but I try hard and no one talks about it anymore. Just as if I had never left the town, the neighborhood, and the group to go to school.

We smoke a few cigarettes and look at the street emptying away. As it gets late, people walk faster. They want to get home; it shows.

Finally, Spice begins walking and the game is on.

At first we wander the big streets, the ones with lights. After a while when there's no one else around, we move away to the dark, narrow streets, the alleys, the vacant lots. There weren't as many lots when I was a kid, but now they're growing like liver spots in every street, surrounding the abandoned projects.

After a quick tour, we move out to the limits of our territory. We pick a starting point and begin wandering to the opposite side of our neighborhood. When we get there, we move back to where we started and the game is over. If anyone sees you, you lose, but you get to kill them.

In the movies, no one ever sees the werewolf and lives. There is never an eyewitness left who can say, "Yes, officer, it was this weird monster, like a man but pointy: with a pointy snout filled aplenty with pointy teeth, pointy ears, pointy nails. And covered with fur all over, yeah, like a big dog." When anyone sees the werewolf, he or she is the next victim. Right away, no questions asked, no way out. It's always that simple. And if anyone ever sees the monster and survives, it's usually the one who destroys it and gets the girl in the end. So it's bad business for the werewolf if someone gets away with his image. Just like in old tales: if they take your likeness, they steal your soul.

Eyesight kills. The eye meets the creature and then there is death.

That's the game.

We actually try to hide, to run the course all the way and back without being seen. But people who walk the streets at night have keen senses, honed just like those of all animals. They can see the slightest shadow in the dark. They can hear the sound of sneakers standing still. They feel when something shouldn't be there. They can sense when the city's night air is disturbed by the beating of your heart. So sometimes, unavoidably, they see us.

II

Spice's gaze seemed colder to me that night. When I arrived he was smoking his awful dark tobacco cigarettes. I didn't say a thing; I've said he prefers silence. So I was startled when he spoke.

"Tonight you start south. I'm going north."

"Why?"

"I'm bored."

We said nothing else, but I began to feel a cold fluid in my veins as I slowly understood the meaning of Spice's words. He wanted us to play the game against one another tonight. He wasn't getting high anymore when he won or when he had to hunt unsuspecting victims—and the last two had put up quite a fight. He wasn't enjoying the late-news accounts of the results of our game anymore. He needed something else.

I remembered that the last time we played I had seen a thread of blood trickling cruelly from his mouth, and I didn't for a second believe it was his own.

I could not run away, although I wanted to, mighty hard. The falling of the night was almost complete and so the game had begun, whether I liked it or not.

If I played I had a chance. If I didn't—

Spice offered me a cigarette. I hate dark tobacco, but I took it and savored it. I tried hard to re-create the way Spice might be thinking, to share his emotions or his lack of them. It could be very helpful if I ever wanted to go back home.

III

For the first time we parted and went opposite ways instead of running parallel, separated by maybe two or three blocks. He went to the northern limits of our turf. The big parking lot there used to double as a free motel for horny little couples in cars, but no more, since nowadays everything has its price, and using the parking lot might be the most expensive idea. I started toward the small bridge that was built over the creek and now crosses a storm drain. A couple of kids have drowned there. Or so they say.

I won't bore you with the description of my city. It's just like yours. Perhaps the potholes are in different places, or the air is thicker, or the hookers bunch all together in a street with a different name, or it's a bit bigger, or smaller. But it's basically the same. Just picture your own city.

What's important is the fact that I was scared.

Oh, I've been scared before. Like the time that guy spotted me in the middle of the game. It was raining and when he saw me he actually reached for a gun and half-crouched to shoot me. He was such a show-off, so scared that his only shot was off by a mile. But he fought like hell when I got to him. I still don't know why he didn't shoot again.

But this time I was *really* scared. Spice is good, and I only trusted that he would do his best not to be seen. If you don't give it all you've got, as they say, the game's worthless. It would just be like hunting, and anyone can do that. Sometimes Spice made it several days without being seen. Only problem: tonight it was werewolf hiding from werewolf, the best against the best, and I found myself hoping that I could actually become, just for once, the pointy and furry killing thing I had seen in so many movies.

The first twenty minutes of the game were almost bearable. I left the bridge and walked very carefully. I passed close to a tall woman without being seen. I was in top shape, sure. But a while later I got the twitches in my face and left hand, in my right shoulder and thigh. Spice was hiding just like me. We should be crossing paths soon. If we had the same ideas, if we chose the same alleys, if we acted like the same werewolf, one of us was not going to go home.

On the other hand, the neighborhood was large, and the time might pass without our even sensing each other's presence. We'd both win. That idea pushed itself to the forefront of my thoughts once and again, but I wasn't going to put my faith in it. I had spent a lot of time trying hard to be like Spice, and I couldn't imagine just how to be different all of a sudden. Finding each other could be frighteningly easy.

I thought of waiting in a dark corner until Spice had gone by, but he might think the same. Any detour I could plot, anything

I envisioned could very well be Spice's idea. We might be on a collision course, getting closer by the minute.

So I didn't try anything fancy. I went on almost in a straight line, watching my step and suffering the burden of a growing weight in my bladder. I almost pissed in my pants right in the middle of the trip, but I managed to reach the parking lot and relieve myself near a tree without hearing or seeing—or being heard or seen by—anyone. There were fewer people in the streets than usual. Maybe they could feel that this night was special and chose to hide in their homes where they could lie to themselves and believe they were safe.

IV

The way back was going to be a lot tougher. Any calculations of time were now very imprecise. There was no way of knowing if Spice had already reached the bridge or was delayed by someone who saw him. Or if, even as I thought, he was moving swiftly on his cat feet back toward me.

I hurried away from the tree and into the shadows of the nearest building. In the cold night I broke into a panicked, smelly sweat. For a moment I felt the stench was huge and unbearable, wafting through the whole neighborhood, invading the whole city, and ringing an alarm in everybody's nostrils: "The werewolf's here! Get him! He's right here!"

I sweated even more before getting a grip on myself. No one was going to win the game without a clear mind.

And one thing did work in our favor: we were both good at hiding, and unlike the others, the non-werewolves, were doing our best to remain unseen, to become a part of the night. We might be ensuring our mutual survival.

Then the high hit. And it was *really* something.

I felt it for a couple of seconds after my moment of panic. I had struck bottom and then soared joyously to feelings I hadn't

ever experienced. I was as alive as I ever was going to be. I was
here completely, definitely. The jolt was short and receded hastily,
but the aftertaste was enticing.

Once again I began walking, back to the bridge, thanking Spice
for the experience.

V

I didn't get far before I felt all the hair on my body stand at
attention.

A faint sound, sensed rather than heard, stopped me cold. I
didn't move for a couple of seconds. Then the sound came more
clearly from behind me. I turned slowly, trying to avoid even the
rustle of my jacket. A man was crossing the street. If he had
turned left he would have seen me. But he was hurrying rather
carelessly. That saved him.

The werewolf went on after a couple of beats. I slithered and
flowed, making the most of the darkness, trying to feel what a
shadow feels when it lays unmoving.

To think not like Spice, but like a real werewolf: that was the
illumination I had gained from those precious seconds in the parking lot. It felt just right. I ran silently along a building with barred
windows where people caged themselves for the night. I jumped
over crumpled beer cans and empty liquor bottles. I changed pace
and turned the corner, lithe as night, toward the street where
most of the neighborhood's stores are.

I wonder if someday I will be able to wake up without wondering why I stopped short behind a pile of black garbage bags that
were waiting patiently for the morning pickup. It was not to catch
my breath. Although I'd been running, I was not winded. I didn't
hear a thing. Nevertheless, I hunched there for a few seconds,
letting the smell of slightly fermented fruit surround me.

Then the man turned the corner across the street from where
I stood. He never saw me. But the man slowed down in the

middle of the street all the same and drew a sudden, fearful, wheezing breath.

He hadn't seen me. He had seen something else.

The other werewolf was very near. I didn't even peek out of my hideaway to know what was happening now. Spice would walk by as if he hadn't seen the man. Then he would find a place to hide and would wait until the man who had seen him felt safe and thankfully resumed his shivering walk. Suddenly, the werewolf would strike.

I wouldn't have looked when death had its moment, but the man screamed so shrilly, so loudly, that I had to see what Spice was doing. At first the figures were indistinct, but the glow of the city lights reflected off the low clouds, and I saw clearly for a moment what I had guessed some weeks before. Spice was savagely biting the man's neck. Then he threw back his head and howled in silence. I was able to see his eyes glistening with joy. Spice stood up and trotted to the far corner of the street, turning right with a fluid movement.

The path was open for me now. I had only to cross the street, go on for a couple of blocks moving opposite to Spice, and then turn right. The bridge would be easy to reach.

It began to rain and I moved more confidently. The splash of raindrops drowned out the sound of my footsteps. A few minutes later I reached the bridge. Walking to its center I again felt very much alive. The sensation was not as sharp as before, but now I was free to turn my head toward the sky, close my eyes, and howl.

I did, enjoying the sound moving up, toward the moon that lay hidden beyond the clouds.

Far, far away, another howling sounded. Maybe I imagined it, but I believed then it was Spice in the parking lot, answering me, winner to winner.

I began to howl again, but the sound was cut by a thought that hurt. I understood suddenly.

I saw Spice and he didn't see me.

But I have to kill him.

It's all part of the game.

Mother Always Loved You Best

BARBARA STEINER

THIS WAS THE FIRST TIME ABBY HAD BEEN IN BRENDA'S ROOM SINCE the accident. In their new house, their rooms had been built with an adjoining bathroom, but Abby had locked the door that opened to her sister's suite. Leaving it untouched after the memorial service, her mother had locked Brenda's door to the hall.

Abby wouldn't be here now if it weren't for Donnie, and she felt a bit guilty about him. How terrible could it be that she was dating Brenda's boyfriend? Donnie had first sought her out to talk about Brenda. One thing led to another, until suddenly, she found herself going out with him all the time.

She felt a lump in her throat that she hadn't expected as she entered the room and walked its length. Brenda wasn't a good sister. They weren't friends.

Her hand shook as she grasped the cold, ornate door pull and slid open the louvered panel on Brenda's closet. Immediately she was washed by a river of Cinnabar, Brenda's favorite scent.

"Would you do something for me, Abby?" Donnie had asked her last night. "Wear something of Brenda's tomorrow."

"You want me to look like her," Abby accused. "Is that why you're going out with me, Donnie? To pretend Brenda didn't die? Are you pretending I'm Brenda?" She heard the anger in her voice, but she didn't care. Why was *she* going with *him?* She had never liked Donnie Stover, even before. And now this idea.

"No, honest, Abby, I like you. I like you a lot better than I thought I would. It's just—just an experiment. Please. Wear Brenda's red silk blouse. I always liked that."

If she wanted to be honest, Abby would admit to herself why she didn't say no. Why she didn't tell Donnie to forget his crazy experiment.

She reached for the red silk blouse that had been a favorite of Brenda's. Brenda loved red, called it her power color. She wore it a lot. Abby liked pink better.

Pink. A faded shade of red. Abby. A faded image of Brenda. Laughing, relishing the coppery taste of bitterness, she jerked off her sweatshirt and pulled on the blouse. The silk slid through her fingers, caressed her skin, felt cool on her shoulders. Power, red for power.

Suddenly she was every bit as curious as Donnie. She kept on her jeans—Brenda usually wore the blouse with jeans. On her feet she wore black flats.

The carpet whispered as she hurried over to Brenda's dressing table, plopped down, stared at the sprinkle of spilled bronze eye shadow, the clutter of pencils and brushes, tubes of lipstick, gloss, Clearasil, Brenda's inhaler—she must have had another one with her when she died.

She reached for the small glass bottle of Cinnabar and dabbed it behind her ears and on her pulse points. The rich, smokey sweetness surrounded her. She smelled like Brenda.

Staring into the mirror, she could still see the obvious, of course. The plain twin stared back. There was more to do. Sliding drawers open until she found the curling iron, she reached over and plugged it in. She gripped the hard plastic handle of Brenda's brush, pulled it through her own hair until it crackled and shined. It was almost the same length.

While the iron heated, she smoothed lotion onto her face, then Revlon's Cream Beige. She highlighted her green eyes with bronze, underlined with soft brown, stroked her lashes with magic thickener. Close. Brenda was almost here.

It took more patience than she thought she had left to twist strands of honey-gold hair into the plastic teeth of the curling iron, until curls flipped up on one side and under on the other. Being Brenda took a lot of time. Was that why, in the past, Abby put up with people looking at her and shaking their heads? Why she listened to them say, "Poor Abby, even though they're twins, she doesn't have Brenda's beauty. At least she got her father's brains."?

Averting her eyes, she saw her father's face, missed him terribly. He was too young to have had a heart attack. She bit her lip and took a moment to think of him. She missed discussing a book they'd both read. Missed his helping her with a challenging algebra problem. He stared at her. *What are you doing, Abby?*

"I don't know, Dad. I don't know," she whispered, taking a deep breath, shoving his image away, staring at herself again. If Abby was so smart, why was she doing this? Why was she sitting here waiting for Donnie to ring the doorbell?

Donnie Stover had the IQ of a turkey, the muscles of a linebacker, the worshipful eyes of a puppy. He had followed Brenda around panting for almost a year, waiting for a bone or a pat on the head, whatever small favor Brenda chose to toss his way.

OK, I'm doing this because it's an experiment. She grinned at herself. Donnie's experiment.

And wouldn't her mother be surprised to see her? "Oh, I forgot to tell you, Mom. The duckling has become a swan. Do you love me now, Mother? Do you love me best now that you have no choice?" Brenda's wicked smile curled across Abby's mirrored lips.

Ding-dong, the witch is dead. She stuck a tissue and the tube of lip gloss into her pocket. *Ding-dong*, the power of red. Laughing, she thumped down the stairs and flung open the front door.

Donnie gasped, his finger in midair to ring the doorbell again. "Abby?"

"No, Brenda. You wanted Brenda, you got Brenda. Come on."

Donnie followed her to the car, breathing hard. He stared and waited until she pulled her feet in to slam the door.

Inside, he kept looking at her.

"So, where did you and Brenda like to go?" Abby asked.

"We—we drove around a lot." Donnie twisted the key and the engine hummed to life.

"So, drive around." Abby smiled. This was fun.

The fun lasted for about half an hour. The car reeked with the cloying scent of the perfume. No wonder Brenda had asthma. Abby felt smothered with Donnie's unsaid thoughts. He was never a great philosopher, but in the past they'd found a few things to talk about after he tired of talking about Brenda.

How could Brenda go with a guy who had no mystery about him, no surprises—ever? While Abby didn't date much, she knew several guys she liked to talk to a heck of a lot more than Donnie Stover. Guys who were more like her dad. Guys she knew her dad would have liked.

But Donnie had one surprise. The sky was a deep shade of slate blue when he stopped on the river bridge where Brenda's car had plunged over.

"I don't want to be here, Donnie," Abby protested. "Why are we stopping here?" She felt a wave of nausea start in her stomach and tighten her throat.

"Just for a minute, Abby. Please. I come here a lot."

Abby hadn't been on the bridge since the accident. She had seen the splintered guardrail, the dark, swollen river, heard the hiss of rushing water. She didn't need to see or hear it again.

But she found she couldn't sit in the car after Donnie left her. She clicked open the latch and slid out. The river, still in flood stage, roared below her. Was it her imagination, or did the boards under her feet wobble and bounce? She grabbed the rail where it was still intact and gripped it until her fingers ached.

"Oh, you look perfect," a familiar voice whispered behind her.

Abby swung around, pressing her back to the damp wood. "Brenda? Brenda! You're—you're—"

"I'm not dead, Abby, dear sister, Abby. Big surprise, isn't it?" Brenda's mouth stretched wide with glee as she stood, hands on her hips, staring at Abby.

"But why? Why—"

"That's a very logical question. You are always so logical, Abby. But look at you. You've been in my room."

"Donnie asked me—"

"I told him to. I wasn't sure you would. But once you got in there, I figured you'd be curious. You didn't want to look like me when I was alive, but you didn't have to be plain, Abby, to be different. We were always different."

Abby stuck to the same questions even though her mind was bombarded with dozens. "Why did you do this to Mother?"

"Mother, dear Mother. Has she grieved for me? Have you enjoyed watching her? That should have been sweet revenge, knowing she was stuck with you. She always loved me best, you know."

Abby did know. Brenda didn't have to remind her.

But Brenda kept talking, mimicking their mother's high voice. "You're the prettiest, Brenda. You're the smartest. That sometimes happens with twins. One of them gets everything, the other gets leftovers. Abby got leftovers. She used to say that to me every day, Abby. Until I believed it. I am the prettiest. I am the smartest."

"But—"

"Even with my makeup on, Abby, even with us both wearing red blouses and jeans, you aren't me. But close enough. No one will know the difference. Especially since I'm the one who's supposed to be dead. It's my body everyone is still looking for."

The first cramp of fear clutched Abby's chest. With a survivor's instinct, she reached back and felt the solid rail behind her, glanced up and down the road, hoping to see someone coming. "What do you mean, Brenda?"

Instead of answering, Brenda laughed, then she coughed and wheezed a little. "I don't think I can be you for long, though, Abby. I'll have to say I decided to fix myself up, like Brenda

always did. I'll borrow Brenda's makeup, since she isn't using it."
That idea made Brenda laugh even more. "Mums will have her
favorite. The one she loves best, and we'll live happily ever after.
I'll never have to share anything again."

"We've never had to share anything, Brenda," Abby said, talking
so she had some time to think. "Even, as you point out, Mother's
love. We always got two of everything, down to two rooms in
the new house. Course, we have to share the bathroom, but I just
wait till you get out."

"You're so kind and considerate, Abby. So sweet that it makes
me sick. It's better this way, believe me."

"Why this elaborate scheme, Brenda?" Abby glanced behind her
to see where Donnie had gone. He had walked some distance
away, but stared back at them. "Why not just push *me* over the
bridge in the car?"

"I tried, Abby, I tried. Remember how I kept begging you to
go someplace with Donnie and me? But you refused. You were
so happy stuck at home with your nose in a book. So we worked
out plan B."

"Where've you been hiding?" Abby wondered if she could out-
run Brenda. "Have you been living with Donnie?" The idea of
Brenda's being *with* Donnie while he was going out with her made
Abby's skin prickle. Shivers formed goose bumps on her arms.

Brenda laughed again. "Are you kidding? That dweeb? I was
only going with him because Mommy disapproved. You know,
rebelling, being independent, all that stuff we're supposed to do
as proper teenagers."

Brenda anticipated Abby's trying to get away from her. Grab-
bing Abby's arm, she swung her around to where there was no
rail on the bridge. As they struggled, Abby could hear the rush
of water, almost a roar, still swollen from all the rain they'd had.
The same rain that had slickened the bridge and caused Brenda's
"accident." She and Donnie must have pushed the car over.

Abby stumbled, lost her balance, but gripped Brenda's arm. If she went into the river, so did Brenda. The emptiness behind her felt hollow, a waiting, sucking void, eager to claim one of them, if not both.

With the other hand, she pounded Brenda, pushed her, slammed her into the bridge railing. The blows made Brenda start to cough. She loosened her hold on Abby enough so that Abby could step back even farther.

A crack like a lightning strike ripped the air. In the two or three seconds that followed, Abby had time only to see the surprised look on Brenda's face as the railing gave way, to grab for her, to catch her billowing sleeve. The material split and tore from Brenda's blouse.

"Abby—" Brenda's shriek trailed off as she fell down, down, down, tumbling like a rag doll.

Abby looked at the red scrap in her hand, shuddered, felt as if the tear were inside her chest. *Oh, Brenda, why? Why? You had everything. And I didn't mind taking leftovers—most of the time. I got used to it. It was just that way with us.*

The deep sadness she had fought since Brenda's accident renewed itself and filled her again. Carefully she stared over the open space until she felt dizzy. The rag doll had disappeared immediately into the spin of dark water. She let the sleeve slide from her fingers. It drifted down, dancing on the wind from the turbulent waters.

"Brenda, Brenda, are you all right?" Donnie ran toward her. "Is it over?"

He couldn't tell! Abby felt something surge within her, an energy, a quickening of her heart and psyche. She took a deep breath.

"Yes, Donnie, it's over. They'll find Abby's body now and think it's mine."

Donnie stared into the river. "I honestly liked her, Brenda. I didn't expect to like her."

"That's OK, Donnie. I don't mind."

---

*　　*　　*

When Donnie took her home, Abby saw that her mother had returned, but she was not prepared for her mother's words.

"We did it, Brenda. We did it, didn't we?" Her mother hugged her tight. "Now you really can have everything. I don't know why nature played that trick on me, giving me two when I wanted only one. But our plan has worked and we're alone."

Abby bit her lip, feeling as if Donnie had punched her in the stomach. She held back a wave of even blacker grief. Then she took a deep breath. "Say it, Mother. Let me hear you say it. You always loved me better."

"Oh, yes, you know that, Brenda. You were the prettiest, the smartest. I did. I always loved you best." Her mother hugged her again, so tight she felt smothered, breathless. "Now with your father and Abby out of the way, there are just the two of us. We won't ever have to share again, especially our delicious secrets."

They found the body five days later, bruised and tumbled, so that no one questioned how long it had been in the river. A proper funeral was held for Brenda. All her friends came. The cheerleading squad. The football team. Her teachers. Abby found that the tears she cried were genuine. Tears for Brenda, tears for her father, yes, tears for her mother, and then more for herself.

"You will have to dress like Abby for a short time, dear," her mother had said before the funeral. "And not wear makeup. But soon we'll say you had a makeover and you can be yourself again."

Abby nodded, unable to speak.

After six weeks and no suspicious questions, Abby's mother agreed that she could break up with Donnie.

"He was never good enough for you anyway. But let him down easy, love. He does know a lot."

Yes, he does, Abby thought. And she knew a way to make him feel better about losing her.

"Donnie, I can't go out with anyone for a while. I feel so

bad, and I'm terrible company. But you'll get over me. Nothing lasts forever."

"Brenda, I—"

"But I know one thing that can last forever, Donnie." Abby grinned up at him. Big puppy. Good dog, good boy. "You know what really happened when I had my accident. Keeping quiet should be worth something. I know Mother appreciates your silence. But I think she'd be willing to give you a little something each month to make sure you feel OK about keeping our secret."

"You mean—you mean money?" Donnie stared at her.

"Sure. You've earned it, and Mother has plenty. Don't be greedy and ask for too much. I'd say several hundred a month should be enough. And don't spend it too freely or someone will wonder how you got so rich. They'd come poking their noses into your business."

Donnie grinned, understanding. "You sure that will work, Brenda?"

"I'm sure. After all, with Abby gone, there's plenty to share. And Mommy just loves sharing."

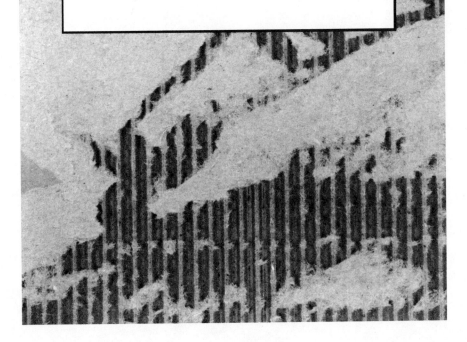

Just Lather,
That's All

HERNANDO TÉLLEZ

HE SAID NOTHING WHEN HE ENTERED. I WAS PASSING THE BEST of my razors back and forth on a strop. When I recognized him I started to tremble. But he didn't notice. Hoping to conceal my emotion, I continued sharpening the razor. I tested it on the meat of my thumb, and then held it up to the light.

At that moment he took off the bullet-studded belt that his gun holster dangled from. He hung it up on a wall hook and placed his military cap over it. Then he turned to me, loosening the knot of his tie, and said, "It's hot as hell. Give me a shave." He sat in the chair.

I estimated he had a four-day beard—the four days taken up by the latest expedition in search of our troops. His face seemed reddened, burned by the sun. Carefully, I began to prepare the soap. I cut off a few slices, dropped them into the cup, mixed in a bit of warm water, and began to stir with the brush. Immediately the foam began to rise. "The other boys in the group should have this much beard, too," he remarked. I continued stirring the lather.

"But we did all right, you know. We got the main ones. We brought back some dead, and we got some others still alive. But pretty soon they'll all be dead."

"How many did you catch?" I asked.

"Fourteen. We had to go pretty deep into the woods to find them. But we'll get even. Not one of them comes out of this alive, not one."

He leaned back in the chair when he saw me with the lather-covered brush in my hand. I still had to put the sheet on him. No doubt about it, I was upset. I took a sheet out of a drawer and knotted it around his neck. He wouldn't stop talking. He probably thought I was in sympathy with his party.

"The town must have learned a lesson from what we did," he said.

"Yes," I replied, securing the knot at the base of his dark, sweaty neck.

"That was a fine show, eh?"

"Very good," I answered, turning back for the brush.

The man closed his eyes with a gesture of fatigue and sat waiting for the cool caress of the soap. I had never had him so close to me. The day he ordered the whole town to file into the patio of the school to see the four rebels hanging there, I came face to face with him for an instant. But the sight of the mutilated bodies kept me from noticing the face of the man who had directed it all, the face I was now about to take into my hands.

It was not an unpleasant face, and the beard, which made him look a bit older than he was, didn't suit him badly at all. His name was Torres—Captain Torres. A man of imagination, because who else would have thought of hanging the naked rebels and then holding target practice on their bodies?

I began to apply the first layer of soap. With his eyes closed, he continued. "Without any effort I could go straight to sleep," he said, "but there's plenty to do this afternoon."

I stopped the lathering and asked with a feigned lack of interest, "A firing squad?"

"Something like that, but a little slower."

I got on with the job of lathering his beard. My hands started trembling again. The man could not possibly realize it, and this was in my favor. But I would have preferred that he hadn't come.

It was likely that many of our faction had seen him enter. And an enemy under one's roof imposes certain conditions.

I would be obliged to shave that beard like any other one, carefully, gently, like that of any customer, taking pains to see that no single pore emitted a drop of blood. Being careful to see that the little tufts of hair did not lead the blade astray. Seeing that his skin ended up clean, soft, and healthy, so that passing the back of my hand over it I couldn't feel a hair. Yes, I was secretly a rebel, but I was also a conscientious barber, and proud of the precision required of my profession.

I took the razor, opened up the two protective arms, exposed the blade, and began the job—from one of the sideburns downward. The razor responded beautifully. His beard was inflexible and hard, not too long, but thick. Bit by bit the skin emerged. The razor rasped along, making its customary sound as fluffs of lather, mixed with bits of hair, gathered along the blade.

I paused a moment to clean it, then took up the strop again to sharpen the razor, because I'm a barber who does things properly. The man, who had kept his eyes closed, opened them now, removed one of his hands from under the sheet, felt for the spot on his face where the soap had been cleared off, and said, "Come to the school today at six o'clock."

"The same thing as the other day?" I asked, horrified.

"It could be even better," he said.

"What do you plan to do?"

"I don't know yet. But we'll amuse ourselves." Once more he leaned back and closed his eyes. I approached with the razor poised.

"Do you plan to punish them all?" I ventured timidly.

"All."

The soap was drying on his face. I had to hurry. In the mirror I looked toward the street. It was the same as ever—the grocery store with two or three customers in it. Then I glanced at the clock—2:20 in the afternoon.

The razor continued on its downward stroke. Now from the

other sideburn down. A thick, blue beard. He should have let it grow like some poets or priests do. It would suit him well. A lot of people wouldn't recognize him. Much to his benefit, I thought, as I attempted to cover the neck area smoothly.

There, surely, the razor had to be handled masterfully, since the hair, although softer, grew into little swirls. A curly beard. One of the tiny pores could open up and issue forth its pearl of blood, but a good barber prides himself on never allowing this to happen to a customer.

How many of us had he ordered shot? How many of us had he ordered mutilated? It was better not to think about it. Torres did not know I was his enemy. He did not know it nor did the rest. It was a secret shared by very few, precisely so that I could inform the revolutionaries of what Torres was doing in the town and of what he was planning each time he undertook a rebel-hunting excursion.

So it was going to be very difficult to explain that I had him right in my hands and let him go peacefully—alive and shaved.

The beard was now almost completely gone. He seemed younger, less burdened by years than when he had arrived. I suppose this always happens with men who visit barbershops. Under the stroke of my razor Torres was being rejuvenated— rejuvenated because I am a good barber, the best in the town, if I may say so.

How hot it is getting! Torres must be sweating as much as I. But he is a calm man, who is not even thinking about what he is going to do with the prisoners this afternoon. On the other hand I, with this razor in my hands—I, stroking and restroking his skin—can't even think clearly.

Damn him for coming! I'm a revolutionary, not a murderer. And how easy it would be to kill him. And he deserves it. Does he? No! What the devil! No one deserves to have someone else make the sacrifice of becoming a murderer. What do you gain by it? Nothing. Others come along and still others, and the first ones kill the second ones, and they the next ones—and it goes on like this until everything is a sea of blood.

I could cut this throat just so—*zip, zip!* I wouldn't give him time to resist and since he has his eyes closed he wouldn't see the glistening blade or my glistening eyes. But I'm trembling like a real murderer. Out of his neck a gush of blood would spout onto the sheet, on the chair, on my hands, on the floor. I would have to close the door. And the blood would keep inching along the floor, warm, ineradicable, uncontainable, until it reached the street, like a little scarlet stream.

I'm sure that one stroke, one deep incision, would prevent any pain. He wouldn't suffer. But what would I do with the body? Where would I hide it? I would have to flee, leaving all I have behind, and take refuge far away. But they would follow until they found me. "Captain Torres's murderer. He slit his throat while he was shaving him—a coward."

And then on the other side. "The avenger of us all. A name to remember. He was the town barber. No one knew he was defending our cause."

Murderer or hero? My destiny depends on the edge of this blade. I can turn my hand a bit more, press a little harder on the razor, and sink it in. The skin would give way like silk, like rubber. There is nothing more tender than human skin and the blood is always there, ready to pour forth.

But I don't want to be a murderer. You came to me for a shave. And I perform my work honorably. . . . I don't want blood on my hands. Just lather, that's all. You are an executioner and I am only a barber. Each person has his own place in the scheme of things.

Now his chin had been stroked clean and smooth. The man sat up and looked into the mirror. He rubbed his hands over his skin and felt it fresh, like new.

"Thanks," he said. He went to the hanger for his belt, pistol, and cap. I must have been very pale; my shirt felt soaked. Torres finished adjusting the buckle, straightened his pistol in the holster, and after automatically smoothing down his hair, he put on the cap. From his pants pocket he took out several coins to pay me for my services and then headed for the door.

In the doorway he paused for a moment and said, "They told me that you'd kill me. I came to find out. But killing isn't easy. You can take my word for it." And he turned and walked away.

Translated by Donald A. Yates

The
Interrogation

ERIC WEINER

THE HEADMISTRESS OPENED HER OFFICE DOOR WIDE. SHE STARED out at the slump-shouldered girl who sat stranded on the wide leather sofa of the outer office, waiting for her. The headmistress smiled without warmth. "Come in," she said.

It wasn't an invitation, it was an order. The girl got up. She gathered the books she had piled beside her on the sofa and, cradling them against her chest as if for protection, filed past the headmistress into the room.

The headmistress's office at the Hadley School for Girls looked as if it had been designed specifically to wring confessions from students. Walnut wainscoting and a paneled wooden ceiling made the room dark and foreboding. Large oil portraits of former head-mistresses, all of whom seemed to stare down accusingly, hung on the walls. At the far end of the room loomed the headmistress's wide mahogany desk, dominating the entire space like a judge's platform. Across from the desk stood a high-backed wooden chair, floating alone in a sea of red Oriental carpet. This was the seat for students who must face the headmistress. This was the seat of the accused.

"Sit down," the headmistress said curtly.

The girl sat. She was fifteen and in her third year at Hadley, but she was a mousy sort of girl who made little impression. Miss Kendrick, the headmistress, only vaguely recognized her.

"I presume you know why you're here."

The girl shook her head no.

"Oh, come now," the headmistress scoffed. She leaned against her desk, arms folded. "You didn't hear about the trouble with Mr. Carr?"

The girl squirmed. "I haven't heard a thing," she said. Behind her glasses, she kept blinking.

Miss Kendrick stared at the girl.

"I haven't," the girl insisted. But even as she said it, her heart was pounding out the words *I have, I have, I have.* Every girl at Hadley already knew about the picture in Mr. Carr's classroom.

It showed Mr. Carr and the headmistress locked together in a wild position, which was probably physically impossible. Both figures were stark naked, and certain parts of their bodies had been drawn crudely out of proportion. And just in case the picture might seem to lack the old school spirit, the artist had added the Hadley school insignia as a tattoo on Mr. Carr's ———.

The girl lowered her gaze to the red carpet. Not only did she know about the picture, she thought the picture was very funny. But she wasn't about to say so.

Miss Kendrick sat down. Her chair was larger than the girl's, and a little higher. "Well then," she said, "I guess you're the last to know." She smiled briefly. "It seems that someone has painted an obscenity in Mr. Carr's classroom. Mr. Carr is understandably upset. And deeply hurt. As am I."

"I'm sorry to hear that," the girl said, shifting in her seat.

"Are you?"

"Yes, ma'am." The girl started biting her nails, then quickly put her hand back under her books in her lap.

"Well, let me tell you why I'm so concerned," the headmistress said. "You know about the term *in loco parentis?*"

The girl did. In fact, it seemed to her it was all they ever talked about at Hadley. *In loco parentis,* "in the place of a parent." What it meant was there was always someone at Hadley telling you what to do.

"While you are within these walls," the headmistress intoned in her deep voice, "we are responsible for you girls in every way. From the moment you wake up to the moment you go to bed, it's our job to see that you are educated physically, spiritually, mentally, and morally. To do that, it is imperative that we command your utmost respect. Understood?"

"Yes, ma'am."

The headmistress placed her hands on the glossy wood of her desktop and pushed herself slowly to her full, majestic height. She began pacing the room, circling around the girl. The girl could feel sweat beading on her upper lip. But she kept her hands under the books on her lap.

"Now. We know the picture was done during third period, because that's the only time Mr. Carr's classroom is idle. We've talked to almost every girl who has third period free. You're second to last."

The girl blinked nervously, gave a little smile. "I'm used to that," she said.

Miss Kendrick didn't smile back. "Are you?" she asked. She was by the window now. She turned her back on the girl. Outside, it was a dingy November afternoon and the girl could see one of her dormmates making her way through the quad, looking cold, forlorn, and depressed. Probably on an errand for some senior, the girl thought.

Miss Kendrick's next question sounded almost casual. "Did you do it?"

It took the girl a second to respond. "No!" Her voice was raspy with tension.

The headmistress sighed. "I didn't think so. It seems that nobody did." She chuckled dryly as she sat down again. "I guess that picture just painted itself."

The headmistress fixed the girl with her pale gray eyes. "Where were you third period?"

"I ... I ... I don't want to say."

"You don't want to say? What are you talking about?"

"I ... I just can't say, I'm sorry."

"You can't." Smiling, the headmistress glanced around the room as if she were sharing a joke with the paintings on the walls. "Good. So then you admit you painted the picture?"

"No!"

"Then where were you?"

The girl didn't answer.

The headmistress stared at the books on the girl's lap. "Put your books down," she ordered.

The girl's hands were shaking as she transferred the books to the carpet. She shoved her hands into the side pockets of her school uniform's plaid skirt.

The headmistress studied her for several moments, until the girl shivered. "All right," the headmistress said. "Let me see your hands."

"My what?"

"You heard me. Your hands. Let me see them."

At first the girl didn't move. Then she drew her hands out of her pockets. For a moment, she kept them in her lap palms down. Then slowly, reluctantly, the girl raised her hands.

"Closer!"

The girl stretched her hands out toward the desk. The headmistress leaned forward.

The girl's palms were spattered with black paint.

Miss Kendrick looked up slowly, her eyes boring into those of the girl. The girl looked down at her hands.

Then she started crying, large tears rolling down her cheeks. "OK, I admit it," she said softly, "I painted it. I painted it! OK? I painted the picture."

"You did."

"Y—yes."

"You're sure?"

"Yes! Yes!"

"You snuck in there and painted it?"

"Right."

"And that's why your hands are covered with black paint, is that correct?"

"Yes! Yes! That's what I'm saying! I painted that awful picture!" The girl's eyes were blurry with tears.

"Now why would someone do such a thing?" Miss Kendrick asked.

The girl snuffled loudly as she wiped her nose with the back of her hand. "I don't know. I guess I thought it would be funny."

"Funny? You call that filth funny?"

"Well, no, I don't, not anymore. I'm sorry. I really am." The girl waited, but the headmistress didn't say anything, so the girl said it again. "What else can I say? I'm really, really sorry."

"You are."

"Yes, ma'am."

The headmistress shook her head slowly, gravely. "OK, let's have it," she said. "What's going on?"

"What do you mean?"

"Why are you lying to me?"

"I don't know what—"

"Your hands are the wrong color."

"What? I don't under—"

"That little obscenity in Mr. Carr's classroom . . . it was painted in red."

The girl was about to speak, but she closed her mouth, swallowing the words.

"*All* red," the headmistress said.

The girl could feel her face flushing deeply. The headmistress's face reddened as well. They stared at one other. Then, abruptly, the girl started crying again. They were noisy sobs this time. "I'm . . . sorry," she struggled to say. "Oh, God. I'm sorry. I didn't mean . . . to lie."

"We'll deal with that later," the headmistress said. Her tone was almost gentle now. "Right now we just want to know who did it."

"But I . . . I can't!"

"Oh now, of course you can," said Miss Kendrick. The gentleness disappeared as abruptly as it had come. "I want the name. Now."

A last tear ran down into the corner of the girl's mouth. "If I tell, she won't get—suspended. Will she?"

"That's not your concern."

The girl looked down at her hands, studying her black stained fingers. "Laura did it," she said at last.

"Laura who?" the headmistress demanded, though there was only one Laura the girl could mean.

"Laura Templeton," the girl said. She covered her mouth, apparently horrified by what she had done. "Oh, God," she said, "I shouldn't have told, I—"

"Of course you should have," Miss Kendrick snapped. Her eyes were flashing. She was obviously stunned. "Well, come on," she said. "Let's have the rest of it."

"No, I can't, I—"

The headmistress snapped her fingers hard—twice—as if she were commanding a small animal. "Stop your whining," she ordered. The girl was silent. "Why did Laura Templeton paint that picture?"

"Well, she just did it for a gag, you know. She never thought Mr. Carr would get so mad. She really didn't—"

The girl gave the headmistress a pleading look, but Miss Kendrick's face offered her no hope.

"And?" Miss Kendrick asked.

"Well, when Mr. Carr got so furious, Laura got really scared. And she told me—" The girl hesitated.

"She told you what?"

"She told me that if I didn't take the blame for it, she'd fix it so"—a fresh sob escaped her—"so no girl ever talked to me again."

"I see."

Laura Templeton was a student Miss Kendrick knew and liked.

She was pretty, popular, athletic. This year, as a senior she'd been appointed proctor of Bingham Dorm. Proctors were in charge of checking that the other students observed all dorm rules. From everything that Miss Kendrick had heard, Laura was handling the job beautifully.

"I know, I know it doesn't seem like her," the girl said. "But . . ." She trailed off.

"But what? Listen, young lady, we're going to sit here until I've heard everything, so you can save yourself a lot of time and trouble by telling me exactly what is going on!"

The girl sighed. "It's like we're her slaves," she said quietly.

"Slaves? What kind of nonsense is this? She's only a proctor."

The girl nodded. "If she wants to, she can make your life a living . . . well . . . hell," the girl said.

"Go on," the headmistress ordered. "I want to hear it all."

The girl did as she was told. She told all, all the things the faculty didn't know about Laura. How Laura demanded total respect. And if you crossed her, she would get you. Laura and her friends would shortsheet your bed. Knock your books out of your arms when they passed you on the paths. Spill coffee on your homework. Reset your alarm clock so you'd be late for class. If Laura was really angry with someone, she'd get the whole dorm chanting that girl's name before assembly.

Hearing this last item, the headmistress reddened again. She had heard plenty of chanting this year at assembly, and she had never managed to stop it.

"A lot of it's just little stuff, you know?" the girl continued. "But it kind of adds up. And, and if you want to get back in her good graces? Well, it's like, you have to be Laura's maid. And you have to do all these favors for her. It doesn't matter what she asks you, you have to do it and—"

The girl stopped short as if she had just realized where her words had taken her.

"And that's what happened to you," the headmistress said.

The girl nodded, blinking back fresh tears.

"So now you had to do her *this* favor, confessing to a crime you didn't commit?"

She nodded again.

Miss Kendrick thought for several moments. "All right," she said at last. "You can go."

She walked the girl to the door. Before she opened the door, Miss Kendrick told her she should keep their discussion private for the time being. The girl promised that she would. Then the headmistress opened the door and said, "Laura, you may come in now."

Laura Templeton was sitting and waiting on the same sofa where the girl herself had waited. The girl stopped short when she saw her.

Laura stood, smiling brightly at Miss Kendrick.

As much as the girl hated Laura, the sight of her caused her a sharp stab of remorse.

Then the girl left. Her heart was pounding like crazy.

At one-thirty that night, long after all the other young residents in Bingham Dorm had gone to sleep, the girl was still wide awake. She slipped out of her room and went softly down the hall to the bathroom.

The bathroom was deserted. Still, the girl was taking no chances. She took off her robe and stepped into one of the two shower stalls, which had the privacy of a curtain. She turned the faucets on full blast.

That afternoon, the dorm head had searched Laura's room and found a red-stained paintbrush. Rumor had it that she was going to be expelled.

The girl carefully scrubbed her hands. The black paint ran down her legs and swirled down the little metal drain.

Then she went to work on the red stains underneath.

Undercover

ERIC WRIGHT

IN THE SECOND FORM OF GRAMMAR SCHOOL, WHEN WE WERE TWELVE years old, our favorite sport was making life miserable for substitute teachers. All the able-bodied teachers had gone off to fight in the war, so boys' schools were full of temporary replacements, like travel agents too old to be called up, whose jobs had disappeared because of the war. Some of them didn't last more than a few weeks; a few, even less.

One who did last was a substitute geography teacher, a refugee from Norway. He seemed to know everything. He used to ask us at the beginning of each class to pick a country and then he would talk about it. Any country. It became a game to try to find a country he knew nothing about, but we never did. Him we liked.

We liked Mr. Thomas, too, who came to teach us Physical Training and be our homeroom teacher. On the first day, when we started throwing paper darts and flicking paper pellets, he just laughed at us and told us to stop it, and we did, just like that. You can always tell when someone is really in charge.

Mr. Thomas wasn't like a lot of PT teachers; he didn't favor the athletes. And he wasn't a sadist like the one before him. He tried to get us all involved in the games; he didn't make fun of anyone, and he didn't make boys try things that frightened them, like vaulting a high horse. He just worked on getting us to enjoy ourselves. He even taught Kelly to swim. Kelly was a clumsy boy with thick glasses who had been terrified of the pool until Mr. Thomas came along, but Mr. Thomas just got in the shallow end with him and in a week Kelly could swim. Just a width, but enough to make Kelly worship him. Pretty soon, we all did.

Unlike our geography teacher, he didn't talk about his past, but we suspected that Mr. Thomas was a hero in real life, too. He had only one eye—he used to wear an eyepatch—and we soon guessed that he had lost the other in action against the enemy early in the war, and had been invalided out. When it was too wet to go outside, and another class was in the gym, he told us stories about the war. All the stories involved escapes from prison camps, and daring exploits at night involving rubber dinghies and wet suits, and we realized that he must have been a commando. We asked him, of course, but he just laughed and refused to talk about his past. "Never mind about me," he used to say. "My past is classified." So we knew.

Another substitute teacher who could keep order was Mr. Hattery. He came about a month after Mr. Thomas, but he was a different kind altogether. When he first arrived we wondered where he had come from, too, but he never told us, and before long we didn't care.

He kept control by frightening us. On the first day someone said something out of line and Mr. Hattery ran down between the rows, picked the boy up by the front of his jacket, and lifted him out of his seat, shouting at him. He didn't actually hit him, but we kept our heads down after that. The thing was, it ought to have been easy to make his life difficult because he couldn't teach. He didn't *know* anything except how to make things out of wood—he was supposed to be the shop teacher—and he couldn't explain how he did it. He used to tell us to watch while he made a toothbrush rack, say, then he'd finish with, "So that's how you make a toothbrush rack. Tomorrow I'll start on a breadboard." But after the first day, we didn't interfere. We just sat there waiting for the bell to ring.

Our school was right next to an army camp, a big one. There was a lot of activity around the camp that spring, and we knew for months that something special was going on. A large number of civilians worked at the army camp including the mothers of some of the boys at school, and these boys were always being warned never to repeat anything about the camp that they heard at home, especially to strangers. The slogan "Careless Talk Costs Lives" was posted everywhere. Roads were blocked off. We couldn't get near the beach for about a mile on either side of the town, and at the same time we were specifically warned against gossip.

Mr. Thomas talked to us one day about this. If we saw or heard of any unusual activity, or if anyone was approached by a stranger or even noticed a stranger around the school, we should report it immediately. We asked him who we should report it to, and he said that we should come to him and he would pass it on, so we knew he was part of the counterspy organization.

It was Lennie Glover who wondered about Mr. Hattery first. Lennie said he ought to be in the army, because he wasn't any older than our fathers, and there was nothing wrong with him that we could see. And then we began, Lennie and me, to try to follow him after school. It was just a game, at first, something to do, because we didn't like him. But right away we discovered that Mr. Hattery was a spy.

For three days in a row we followed him to the park in the next block (keeping out of sight, of course) where we watched him sit on a bench, pretend to read a newspaper, then get into conversation with another man, then, after a bit, hand him the newspaper and leave. Then the other man would pretend to read. We followed Mr. Hattery for another two blocks, but he just turned in to a pub and we had to go home to supper.

It was obvious to us that Mr. Hattery had been listening all day to us boys and had written down all the information he had picked up, hidden the document inside the newspaper, and passed it on in the park. We also wondered if there might be more to his spying: possibly he was receiving radio messages from a secret receiver behind the woodwork shop and was passing on orders.

Lennie was a member of the camera club, and he took a picture of the two men from across the park. We watched for two more days, and then we saw Mr. Hattery give his newspaper to a different man, in the same way as he did with the first. He was part of a network.

I wanted to leave then, because I was terrified of what Mr. Hattery would do to us if he caught us there, now that we knew about him. But Lennie said we had to take a picture of this second man, which he did, and then we ran.

After PT the next day we waited until everyone had left the changing room, and we told Mr. Thomas what we had seen.

He took us seriously, questioning us until he'd got all the details right, what the other men looked like, exactly how the handover was managed, everything. Lennie had developed the photos and he showed them to Mr. Thomas who looked at them for a long time and put them in his pocket. "Now boys," he said. "It's up to me. You're quite right. You've stumbled on something serious."

"Will you round them up?" Lennie asked.

"Probably. In the meantime, not a word, eh? Not a word." Then he questioned us some more until he was sure we hadn't said anything to anybody so far. "Right," he concluded. "I'll get someone to take over from you boys. You've done well. I'm very pleased with you." Then we all shook hands and Lennie and I went home to supper.

The next day there was an air raid, and we all walked quickly to the brick shelters in the school yard. Most homeroom teachers still tried to teach during the air raids, but with Mr. Thomas there was never any lesson and so we settled back and waited for him to arrive and tell a story instead. But he was delayed, and pretty soon we were making so much noise we wouldn't have heard a bomb drop. The headmaster put his head round the shelter door and asked where Mr. Thomas was. No one had seen him. Then Mr. Hattery appeared and the headmaster asked *him*, and suddenly Mr. Hattery turned and started to run across the yard to the gate.

Just then the school caretaker came in and said that there hadn't been a real air-raid alarm, but someone had set off the school alarm, and so we all went back into the school. All except Mr. Thomas and Mr. Hattery. They never came back.

Next day the headmaster said that both men had had to leave suddenly for personal reasons. This was the same thing they'd said about a couple of the teachers we'd driven barmy. Lennie said they ought to have called it "public reasons" in this case. Later on Simpson said he saw Mr. Hattery being driven around in an army staff car, and Kelly watched him come out of the police station one day. They said he wasn't handcuffed or anything, but they knew he couldn't get away.

A few weeks later Dawson, whose mum worked at the camp, was listening on the stairs when his mum started telling a friend about the whole thing. The way Dawson heard it, Mr. Hattery wasn't the spy. He was a government agent in MI5. It was Mr. Thomas who was the enemy agent. MI5 had found out about Mr. Thomas and set Mr. Hattery to watch him so they could get the whole network.

We thought Dawson had got it mixed up at first, but the clincher came when he told us his mum had told her friend that now that they knew Mr. Thomas had only one eye, they would get him soon.

"I bet they won't," Kelly said to me and Lennie, looking up at us through those thick glasses of his. "I went back to the changing room one day after everyone was gone, because I'd left my satchel there. Mr. Thomas was washing his face. He had both his eyes. He said he was working undercover and made me promise never to reveal his secret."

"Are you going to, then?" I asked.

Kelly looked over at Lennie who rubbed his chin. "It's a bit difficult, really," Lennie said. "Mr. Thomas could be on a solo mission no one knows about."

"If anyone could do it, Mr. Thomas could," Kelly said.

"But supposing we're wrong?" said Dawson. "Suppose Mr. Thomas is a spy?"

"Tell you what," Lennie said after a moment. "If they ask Kelly, if they actually *ask*, then he'll have to tell them."

Kelly nodded. But we all knew they wouldn't ask.

PERMISSIONS